THE VISITOR
LOVE. WITCHCRAFT. UNFINISHED BUSINESS

SARA SARTAGNE

Copyright © 2021 by Sara Sartagne

All rights reserved.

No part of this book may be reproduced in any form or by any electronic or mechanical means, including information storage and retrieval systems, without written permission from the author, except for the use of brief quotations in a book review.

This is a work of fiction. Names, characters, places and incidents are the product of the author's imagination. Any resemblance to actual persons living or dead, business establishments or events is entirely coincidental.

Amazon Print edition:

ISBN 9798718982237

If you'd like to keep up with Sara Sartagne's writing, why not sign up for her *no spam* newsletter and get news *first* of new releases and exclusive – free! – content.

Details can be found at the end of The Visitor.

ACKNOWLEDGMENTS

It might take a village to raise a child – but it takes several really good mates to help you write a book which has been 'brewing' since you were 21.

My gratitude goes to Jan Page who encouraged me through earlier versions of the manuscript and special thanks to Jilly Wood, who took me at my word when I asked for 'brutal' feedback. I think The Visitor is a better book because of her insightful comments.

And as always – thanks Fiona, you're my north star.

SARAH'S PROLOGUE: APRIL 1619

Sarah sat rigid as the images flew around her head.

The kettle on the open fireplace hissed and, startled out of the visions, she breathed in sharply. Her almanac slipped from her knee onto the stone flags, and the room swam back into focus. The cottage, lit by candlelight, seemed to soothe her rapid heartbeat and taking a cloth, she took the kettle off the fire and placed it on the hearth. She caught sight of her mother's Bible and pain stabbed her. Her father's tool belt still hung by the door, and grief crushed her chest.

She could hear Dorothy snoring in the other room and wearily, she made valerian root tea in the hope of easing her pain and getting to sleep before the sun came up. Sitting back in the chair, she felt her hair slip from under her cap and she pushed the strands away from her cheek.

Time passed, the tea cooled in her hands, and her eyes drifted reluctantly towards the fire. Gradually, the visions returned, and the future unfolded; the years, the intricate threads weaving together through time, connecting deeds and people. She saw the decisions she would have to take. The choices others would face and how chance would unfold, depending on the choices they made.

And finally, she glimpsed the features of a young woman, older than she was now. The woman had powerful skills, as strong as her own, but different. The woman would need her help, her guidance. Sarah drew a deep breath and it hooked in her throat, tears threatening as she glimpsed the enormity of the trial before her. To help this woman, and all the others, her sacrifice would need to be great.

A log shifted, sending out sparks and she blinked, the visions finally gone. The actors were like the planets circling the heavens, but they would slowly spin closer and closer until they aligned. She knew she would not see the visions again. But she had seen and could not unsee.

For those coming after her, she would need to screw her courage into an iron fist. Resolution bloomed. She would be ready.

CHAPTER ONE
STACIE

I put the key into the lock and opened the door. I winked at the misty Victorian lady in the light blue dress fluttering just out of my direct line of sight, as I usually did. She ignored me. The cat hadn't made an appearance today – no, I thought, dropping my bag – there it was, its ginger tail stroking round the doorjamb to the sitting room before vanishing. I grinned to myself. Mother and Dad would be back soon, and as it was Friday, we'd have fish. Perhaps that would explain the cat.

I shouted a greeting into the house, just in case. There was silence, and I headed to the sitting room. The cat was sitting on the window seat, licking its paws. It threw me a disinterested glance before slowly fading into the sunshine. When I blinked, it had completely disappeared.

I kicked off my shoes, sank into the overstuffed sofa, and sighed, closing my eyes. The end of term was always a trial, with over-excited kids, tears, tantrums and wet knickers. Still, I'd survived – just. Although I'd shed a couple of tears with Jo and Seb, and would genuinely regret leaving the children, it was time to be moving on. And moving up, I thought with satisfaction. And it was a personal victory. I'd avoided Neil for almost the entire week.

I struggled to my feet and walked to the kitchen, shaking my head to disperse memories of his thick lips.

I waited for the coffee to brew, resisting the urge to head into the garden which simmered in the July heat. I'd have some quiet time before Mother and Dad returned from the university. With Eleanor. My mouth twisted at the thought of my younger, brainier sister, a carbon copy of my parents. The coffee maker gurgled and spluttered and I gratefully poured myself a cup.

My eyes flicked to the child with the lace collar playing in the rose beds and idly, I watched him. Well, I assumed it was a 'him', I'd never really been able to tell, the blond curls were so long and feminine. Our house had been built in the 1970s, neither he nor the governess, as I called my Victorian lady, were connected to this address, despite my investigations. He faded into the greenery as I stared. I'd have half an hour in the garden, I decided, and I made my way upstairs to change.

As I pulled my dull shirt-waisted dress over my head, my phone pinged in my bag. Whatever it was, it could wait until I'd showered the ink off my hands and the dust out of my hair. I stood motionless under the spray as the stickiness and the giggles of the children I'd worked with for the last two and a half months washed away. It was a shame I couldn't wash away the groping hands of the head teacher as easily.

After ten minutes, I squeezed as much water out of my hair as I could and wrapped a bath sheet round me. Perching on the bed, I hunted out my phone. There was a long, rambling text from Seb, and I smiled, warmed by it. Seb rarely sent brief texts, unless he was watching the football when they bordered on the rude.

Seb was my secret crush; funny, sexy and rather better off than most teachers I knew, and often in the company of leggy models. I had too much sense to howl at the moon, so I packed away my yearning for my curly-haired colleague and we were mates. Another text pinged.

Good to see you escaped from Neil – he came looking for you. Fancy cinema/pizza/coffee/lunch/drink/walk/breakfast next week? (please tick preference). Love, Seb xx.

Seb and Jo had made life at Woodlands bearable, particularly after the staff Christmas party. Woodlands was too small a school, serving too small a locality for the news not to spread about the head teacher and the classroom assistant. Not to mention the slap, which everyone in the main hall apparently heard during a lull in the conversation.

After that, I put my nose up at the silence in the common room and filled in applications for new jobs as fast as I could. When I got the job at another school two miles away, we all got soundly pissed to celebrate and Woodlands sighed with relief.

I sighed. Jo – comfortable, plump Jo, with a vocabulary to put a fishwife to shame – was in Spain for the holidays. She'd kissed me as I flung my bag into my ancient car and whispered in my ear as we hugged.

"Don't spend the whole of the summer break doing fucking prep! You're more than good enough in class without it! Go and get yourself laid at least!"

Fat chance. Jo seemed to pick up men with enviable ease. Me, not so much.

Pushing away these depressing thoughts, my finger hovered over the 'reply' button to Seb. Pizza at some new retro place in the high street seemed a good idea, and by Wednesday I'd be looking for any excuse to get out of the house. I texted Seb. His response came barely twenty seconds later, a row of hearts and grins, suggesting seven o'clock.

I dried myself and dressed, pushing my feet into battered Crocs. The old, frayed shorts, faded almost white with washing, were perhaps too tight and actually, I reflected, with a grimace, too young for my advancing years. I pinned my hair up, feeling a moment of coolness on my neck before the heat settled on me again. My hair would soon dry while I worked in the garden.

In the mirror, the cat appeared behind me, making me

jump. I glared at it. It stared back, unconcerned. And then it rose from its position on the top of the chest of drawers, arched its back and gradually faded into the wallpaper. Tutting, I finally headed into the garden.

The sun was still hot, and I breathed in the shimmering greenery and the delicate scent of the roses before attacking the deadheading with a will. I'd made it around half the beds when I paused for breath. The child in the lace collar who had watched me solemnly, raised his head, and an expression chased across his face. A second later, he'd gone. I stepped out of the roses and meandered back towards the house, listening.

Five minutes later I heard the car pull up and from the sound of the gears, Ellie was driving.

"Such a fascinating lecture, it really impressed me..."

Ellie's voice reached me as I washed my hands. I looked at myself in the mirror, mentally stiffened my spine and went out to say hello to my family.

"How was your last day?" asked my father, smiling at me, his very blue eyes twinkling at me from behind his specs. My mother's lips pursed at the shorts and tee shirt, and I resisted the implication that I should get changed. I was bloody twenty-four, for God's sake.

"It was fine," I said. "I had a card and a cake at lunchtime."

"So sweet," said Ellie, swinging her foot as she perched on the arm of the sofa. I raised an eyebrow.

"So you begin at Grange Manor in September?" said my mother, mentioning my new school. I was impressed. I hadn't counted on her listening when I'd told them I had a new job. They'd been more interested in the teaching qualification, which was another reason I was moving schools, although the look of mild surprise on my mother's face still stung.

"I report for duty at the end of August for an inservice training day, and I begin the course in September," I volunteered unwillingly. The less the family knew about my job, the happier I was. Certainly, they were happier that way.

Mother nodded and, having shown sufficient interest in her

eldest daughter, disappeared into the kitchen to start dinner. I watched as my father fixed himself a gin and tonic and Eleanor stretched, much like the cat no one but me could see. I escaped back into the garden.

The evening was golden and still. As I crouched on the patio clipping lavender, snatches of conversation floated to me on the still air.

"Very impressive… has he moved to the UK permanently…?"

"…new book…"

I rolled my shoulders to loosen the muscles and lost myself in the task of tidying the borders and jumped when Ellie called me for dinner. As I sat at the table, the shorts dug into the soft flesh of my stomach and surreptitiously I undid a button.

As I helped myself to green beans, I dropped one onto the table and Mother suppressed a sigh, smiling weakly at my apologetic grin.

The cat jumped onto the window seat and fixed silver eyes on me. I slathered butter on my fish, imagining coriander and ginger, and ignoring the chorus of tutting from my mother and comments from Ellie about my eternal fight with my weight.

I zoned into the conversation, which was still about this new member of the academic staff. There was a thin tone of excitement in my sister's voice.

"He'll be a real asset," she said.

"Who's this?" I said.

"Nate Williams, our latest member of staff," said Dad. "He's got a stellar reputation as a scholar on European twentieth-century literature. There was even talk of a nomination for the Samuel Johnson prize for his last book on Ezra Pound."

My father's voice trailed off, his eyes unfocused at this potential accolade. Even I'd heard of this literary award, so I raised my eyebrows and looked impressed.

"So, a grand fromage, then?"

"Mmm, in the academic world, he's a rising star," Ellie said, sipping her wine.

"I think we're rather lucky to have attracted him. We felt sure he'd go to Harvard, and it was a surprise when he said yes," Dad said.

"The university has a worldwide reputation, darling," my mother rebuked gently.

"Well, he's certainly not coming for the money," Dad said under his breath.

"He's staying over the summer, isn't he?"

My mother's eyes swivelled to Ellie, and I knew why. Her voice sounded odd, a little strained. My father sipped his wine.

"If he can find suitable accommodation," he said doubtfully. "It'll take at least a month to find a house to rent long term, and that's an expensive hotel bill."

"We should invite him for dinner, introduce him to the area," said Ellie, a gentle flush on her cheeks. "We can show him around."

My eyes narrowed a fraction. Substituting 'I' for 'we' would be nearer the mark. I wondered what he looked like. My mother, oblivious to any agenda, frowned at the napkins and nodded absently.

"Yes, that's an excellent idea. Actually, now I consider it, should we offer him somewhere to stay for the summer, Henry? It would save the university a small fortune and Eustacia wouldn't bother him. And he can borrow my library room if he needs to."

I had shortened my name to Stacie as soon as I could, but Mother refused to recognise it, even telling callers by phone and in person, no one called by that name lived here.

"You're suggesting he stays here?" I said, frowning.

"Yes, why not?" said Mother. "There's plenty of room, and there'll be even more when your father and I go to Italy."

"You're going away?" Ellie said, almost choking as she swallowed.

"Yes, I told you last month, I'm sure I did," said Mother, sighing. "It's a promotional trip with your father's publishers. I wish you'd listen occasionally."

Mother had said nothing to me, nor Ellie from the look on her face. I frowned, troubled by the prospect of an unknown man in the house for the summer. The cat arched its back, and while one part of my brain registered that my ghostly pet was making a lot of appearances lately, the other was looking at the strange glint in Ellie's eyes.

"Hang on a second," I said, putting my knife and fork down. "Who is this bloke? I'm not sure I want a complete stranger in the house while I'm on my six-week break."

Mother looked at me, clearly astonished.

"But he's an academic colleague of your father's. What possible objections could you have?"

"How about the fact that I don't know him from Adam? That I have work of my own to do? That I may not have time to entertain him or show him around?"

"Don't be ridiculous, dear," said my mother. "You can hardly be so busy that you can't show him common courtesy. I'm surprised at you, Eustacia."

"And anyway, you'll have to concentrate on your preparation for your course, so it'll be me who'll show him around the area," said Ellie. "You know academic work is hardly your strong point."

I threw her a look of dislike. Dad put up his hand, stopping further bickering.

"Hopefully, an invitation to dinner will give you the opportunity to get to know him, Stacie. Shall we leave the final decision until then?"

"If Eustacia is vetting all our future guests, things will have come to a pretty pass!" tutted Mother, before clearing the plates, muttering about new napkins. I rose to help. The cat, still sitting on the sideboard, stared at me as I moved around the table. My father sipped his wine and smiled faintly at me when I returned from the kitchen.

"He's actually a charming man, Stacie. His father was a historian, I believe. American, handsome, cultured. I can't imagine you not liking him, he's delightful."

Let me be the judge of that, I thought. I forced a smile.

"Sounds quite a catch," I said, sinking back into my seat. "Is he single?"

He laughed.

"What's the line, 'a single man, possessed of good fortune must be in need of a wife'?"

"Something like that," I grinned. And then sobered. "But really, Dad, how long will he be staying? I wasn't joking when I said I had stuff to do to get ready for the course."

"I know," he said. "I know you'll want to focus. Just see how you get on with him. I daresay your mother and Eleanor are sorting out dates to invite him to dinner as we speak."

I was so irritated, the garden was the only place to go, despite the air turning heavy and oppressive. The ginger cat followed me as I tied back sunflowers, swaying drunkenly away from their stakes. I loved their huge and ostentatious flowers.

I cut roses to arrange in the hall.

"Storm coming," I said to no one in particular, as I passed through the living room. Mother gave a small cry of protest at my dirty sandals as I walked through and then turned back to marking her essays with a sigh as I grinned. I caught sight of Ellie, curled in an armchair, and the look on her face was unfocused, even dreamy. This was so unlike her, it made me pause.

She's definitely got the hots for this bloke, I sighed to myself. That would make for an interesting summer. Going away for a month seemed a great idea.

I trailed to my room to watch TV, but I could settle to nothing. I checked my bank balance, pleased at how my pot of savings was growing. I looked at a variety of houses to rent, but nothing caught my eye. In a month I should have the deposit. I hugged myself with anticipation.

The storm I had felt in the air didn't materialise. It was with something like relief that I climbed into bed, to be disturbed by vague shadows walking across my dreams, threatening and uneasy.

CHAPTER TWO
SARAH

Sarah's hands were chilly, despite the warm sunshine. The graves of her mother and father still seemed to stand out, obscenely new in the churchyard, the mounds of earth only slowly sinking. They seemed to nestle against the older graves of her brothers, as though seeking comfort. Alas, there was no comfort for her, and an icy hand closed around her heart.

As she bent to tidy the daisies on the grave, a lock of hair dropped from under her cap and she pushed the bright auburn strands beneath the stiff cotton again. The old parson had complained about her hair being 'unseemly' although she wasn't sure what she could do with it other than hide it. Glossy and shining, it slipped around like a live thing, including out of her cap. Some women in the village pursed their lips at its colour and she knew she ought to cut it off, but as her mother had so loved her hair, spending hours brushing it, she knew she wouldn't. And regardless, some stirrings of rebellion squashed the sensible side of her nature.

She heard the church clock toll the half hour and reluctantly stood and brushed her hands down her plain brown skirt. She ought to go, but she dreaded it. This would be the third burning this year, and she knew as well as she knew the sun would rise tomorrow, that Margaret Eames was no witch. She was just poor, and alone, with a limp and a temper which drew the ire of Mistress Whyte and her cronies. Reluctant, she walked slowly to the village square.

She saw Dorothy, her maid, standing by the door of the inn, her face slightly flushed with the excitement of it all. Sarah twisted her mouth in distaste. The crowd was large and silent. The faces of the watching village had hardened to stone, as she stood at the back of the crowd and looked carefully around her. Annie Whyte and Elizabeth Walters stood erect and unforgiving alongside their menfolk who had grave faces and tight lips.

Sarah forced herself to watch as Margaret Eames screamed, denying she had dealt with the Devil, despite the mark on her back found by the witch-finder. Small boys held lighted brush to the pile of wood and Sarah recalled Margaret had taught them their letters at one stage.

Margaret sobbed and pulled uselessly at the ropes around her wrists. If she had truly been a witch, she would have vanished by now, thought Sarah, her jaw clenching. The crowd moved restlessly, and she wondered if the sight of this thin, white woman who twisted and cried distressed her alone as the wood began to smoulder.

Drawing a deep breath, Sarah fixed her eyes on the screaming woman and willed her to find her in the crowd. She could not imagine Margaret's pain, but she could imagine her terror.

"Margaret, look at me," she muttered under her breath, and Annie Whyte glanced sharply at her. Sarah's heart beat rapidly and she determined to be silent. Mistress Whyte stared hard at her and then turned her face again towards the flickering flames in the marketplace.

Margaret, she called in her mind to the woman tied against the post. Margaret, look at me.

Margaret's pale blue eyes found hers and she stopped screaming, drawing breath and beginning to cough as the fire took hold beneath her.

Be calm. I will try to help you sleep, and it will all be over. But you must trust me. Sarah looked steadily at her, holding her breath and hoping that Margaret would not cry out against her. Margaret's eyes widened and again, she drew a breath.

Margaret, if you speak, I cannot help you at all! I cannot save you, but I can make it less painful. Stay silent, Margaret! Sarah warned. For a moment, Sarah wondered what would happen, but after a heartbeat, Margaret nodded her head in acknowledgement.

Good. You are very brave. Now, think of the harvest last year, and the beer we drank in the field. You sat with me and Ned Thompson, and the day was warm, and the air was still and drowsy with the sound of bees. You tried to stay awake but the sun was hot and you were tired, so tired. Think on that now… so tired.

Sarah focused, bringing all her concentration to make the memories bright and real in her head, and Margaret's eyelids drooped behind the smoke now rising thickly from the pyre beneath.

You had laboured so hard, remember; you lay on the soft, sweet hay and wanted to sleep. Do that now. Drift away like clouds in yonder blue sky.

She saw the flames flash around Margaret's legs and inhaled sharply. She curled her fingers into her palms and concentrated hard, frowning a little. Drift, Margaret. Sleep…

After several long minutes, Margaret's head lolled on her chest and a shudder passed through the thin body.

Sarah watched for a moment and seeing no further movement, relaxed a little. Margaret would burn but know no more. As soon as she dared, Sarah ducked her head and moved quietly away from the crowd which had begun to catcall, their faces ugly and their mouths wide.

She felt Mistress Whyte's eyes on her back as she walked

away and drew her cloak around her more closely. She would need to take care in the coming days. Unless she wished to share the same fate as Margaret Eames.

※

William Denning announced in church that Sunday that the new parson would arrive in a sennight and was coming from Launceston.

His florid face lit up with joy.

"Flock, your new shepherd comes!"

There was a buzz among the congregation which flapped like a group of startled crows. Sarah, at the back of the church, looked on, the corners of her mouth turning up. Parson Denning was fat and sweated much in the summer months, and she could smell him yards before she saw him. But he seemed to care sincerely for the souls in the village.

He had been kind when her parents had died, although the practical application of that kindness was only to offer to pray with her for their departed souls (outside the cottage, lest further infection remained) and to conduct the funerals. He had eaten his fill at the funeral feast and drunk the strong ale she had provided for the neighbours, as was customary. The tears pricked at the remembrance of her mother and she pushed them firmly away. They were in Heaven, it had been God's will, she had been told. She tried to believe it.

"Parson John Dillington is a learned man from Oxford," Pastor Denning continued in his booming voice, which echoed around the pews. Sarah pulled her cloak around her a little tighter. The May sunshine reached only to the door of the church and even though there was warmth outside, the church was chilled and the air stale. She glanced at the modest Bible in her hands, feeling the tooled leather against her fingertips and flipping open the frontispiece, she read her own name and the names of her two brothers written in the neat, lovely hand of her mother. The pain of her loss stabbed her afresh, and she gripped the book tightly.

She felt, rather than saw, Dorothy glance her way and she forced herself to relax. Her mother and father had spoken to Parson Denning about their hopes for Heaven, and there was a general view that her parents had been blessed – more so than many suffering from the fever who had fallen into delirium and not been able to make their peace with God before they died. Sarah pressed her lips together and wondered about the empty ache she carried now her parents had followed her brothers into the grave. She thought it likely that she was being punished for her ungodly thoughts, her ungodly talents. Even her work among the villagers, answering calls at all hours of the day and night, giving salve for bruises, potions for all kinds of ailments, failed to balance the scales of her redemption. Her thoughts skittered away from Margaret Eames, and she concentrated on Pastor Denning.

"What kind of man is Parson Dillington?" Goodman Whyte asked.

Parson Denning smiled so broadly Sarah wondered if his face might split.

"Devout and with a voice filled, they say, with the flame of the Holy Spirit!" he replied. "His sermons pierce the heart and shame the sinner. We should count ourselves blessed to have him in our parish."

He sobered slightly.

"He was promised to another parish, but his wife left this earthly life to join Our Heavenly Father but seven months ago, and he has requested a flock nearer his previous parish to be closer to her grave. He is consoled by a daughter who accompanies him. We must give thanks to God and pray for the departed soul of Mistress Dillington."

Sarah dropped to her knees with the rest of the congregation, but her thoughts were wayward and try as she might, she couldn't summon the energy to pray for strangers. Glancing up, the sharp, pale eyes of Mistress Whyte rested on her and

Sarah quickly looked down again. She gripped her Bible as if it would give her strength and stayed on her knees until long after the blessing. Dorothy put her hand under Sarah's elbow to help her rise, and Sarah gave her a smile.

"I'm not yet old, Dorothy, just a little weary."

"Aye, I heard you before dawn this morning."

Sarah was silent, remembering her tears and regretting that the maid had heard her grief. Tears were a luxury for her. Others believed she was resigned to the deaths of her parents and content to know they were in the arms of God. Her real thoughts she revealed to no one. She sighed. Aunt Hester might arrive soon, following news of her brother's and sister-in-law's deaths. That would lend her some respectability and with it, some protection.

"I am sorry I woke you," was all she said to the maid.

The congregation was shuffling towards the open doors and Sarah took her place and waited patiently. The sunshine made her squint, but she felt the slice of a hard gaze. Mistress Whyte's cold eyes fixed on her again. She straightened her spine and smiled sweetly at the portly woman. Mistress Whyte hid a sneer and came towards her.

"Mistress," Sarah dipped a curtsey, her eyes down to shield her thoughts.

"Sarah Bartlett, how do you do?"

"Well, I thank you."

Annie Whyte narrowed her eyes.

"You seemed much taken with the burning of that foul witch, Margaret Eames. I could swear your gaze never moved from her all the time she screamed like a pig. Even when she fell silent, your look never wavered." She paused, licking her thin lips. "I heard you whispering, did I not? Think you she was suffocated by the Devil? Seemed a simple death for one so steeped in sin."

Sarah raised her eyebrows in seeming surprise.

"Mistress Whyte, I was praying for her departing soul. Did you not?"

The thin lips pressed together, and Sarah saw Parson Denning bearing down on them with relief. She turned to him with a smile, a good reason to present her shoulder to the older woman.

"Good morrow, Sarah, what news?" he said heartily.

"None, sir," she replied, stepping away from the hovering Annie Whyte.

"What, no word from your aunt? It must be – what? – three weeks since your letter." A frown creasing his round, moonlike face, the parson fell in step with her. She hesitated before replying.

"Yes, sir. I trust she will arrive soon."

Parson Denning looked as though he would speak again, but one of the wealthier landowners in the area claimed his attention and Sarah could slip away, Dorothy grumbling behind her.

"'Twas no harm to stop and speak further to Parson Denning," she muttered, stepping over some filth in the path as they made their way back to the house.

Sarah kept silent, lifting her skirts to try to keep them clean. She could feel the silkiness of her hair escaping from the pins and hoped it would stay beneath her cap until she could close her front door.

Dorothy tried again.

"Mistress, why do you shun the kindness of our neighbours? Parson Denning was being charitable, asking after your kin, not interfering."

Sarah, who had a shrewd idea of the passion that lurked in Dorothy's thin, bony breast for the parson, threw her maid a glance. Her cheeks had high colour and Sarah saw a sheen of tears in her eyes.

She worries about not seeing him again with the arrival of the new parson, Sarah thought. The retort on her lips withered, and she said instead,

"Ah, Dorothy, his conversation pains me. I know he means well, but I would rather he cut me than constantly remind me I am alone now, asking how I do. Aunt Hester will arrive by and by and will help me decide my future."

"Will you marry Ned?"

Sarah pushed the door of the cottage open and the bands around her chest eased as she returned to familiar surroundings, away from eyes and malicious tongues. She drew a deep breath, comforted by the scent of her herbs hanging from the rafters. She should be more careful, especially around Annie Whyte.

"Well?" asked Dorothy. Sarah, who had hardly been listening, looked puzzled. "Will you marry Ned?" Dorothy asked again. Sarah stiffened.

"You are impertinent, Dorothy," Sarah replied coldly. "My parents dead but three months and your chattering about marriage simply adds to my headache. I will marry when I am ready. That time is not now. Be gone from my sight, woman, lest I beat you."

Dorothy sniffed and disappeared into the pantry.

Sarah's hair loosened, and she took off her cap and viciously dug the pins into her scalp to tame it. Tying on her cap again, she glanced out of the leaded window at the sunshine and defiantly grabbed her basket from the side of the hearth. Picking up her straw hat, she made for the door.

"Dorothy, I'm away to the woods to collect mushrooms. I will return betimes and then I need to visit Susan Braithewaite who suffers still from ague."

She heard Dorothy mutter something and then the door closed, and she was heading for relative freedom.

❧

The new parson arrived exactly a sennight later, as Parson Denning had predicted. Sarah was bartering with Thomas the blacksmith about a repair for her hoe for the garden when he walked into the village, leading a small, pale and sickly looking child on a horse. His hair was blond, almost white, and in his all-black attire, the parson looked spare and stern. The combination of his hair and clothes made him appear like an avenging angel, and Sarah remembered how angels are the reapers at the end of the world. She shivered.

She watched as villagers curtsied and bowed in silence, his demeanour seeming to suck the light and the laughter from the street. His face had a fierce beauty, and her pulse quickened as she beheld him, a strange yearning pulling at her chest. As he passed her, she too dropped a curtsey and raised her head to find him looking straight at her with the greenest eyes she had ever seen.

"Like a cat," came the thought into her head, and in a flash, the blacksmith's ginger cat slinked around her legs and hissed at the new arrival before darting back into the shed. She laughed softly and then stopped short as the green gaze seemed to slice right through her. She saw a muscle under his eye twitch slightly. After what seemed an age, he nodded his head abruptly and moved on, leaving her pink and hot. To her surprise, the child glared at her. Sarah frowned. Caring for her brothers had given her a way with children and most liked her on sight.

"Alas, not the parson's daughter," she thought, quirking an eyebrow at the girl who looked about ten or eleven. The girl's cheeks bloomed with fire, although Sarah saw this was not embarrassment – this was rage.

Parson Denning waddled out of the parsonage, puffing.

"Parson Dillington! We are surely blessed by your coming! Welcome, welcome!" he said formally, holding out his hand in greeting. Parson Dillington paused a moment before shaking hands and said something. Parson Denning made as if to slap the new parson on the back and then thought better of it, merely gesturing him into the house.

Sarah watched as the new clergyman carefully helped his daughter from the horse and watched as the girl gained her balance, almost as though her legs had gone to sleep. She was small and angular, with lank dun-coloured hair under her blue cap. Her face was pinched and drawn as if she had been suffering from illness.

Parson Dillington clasped an arm around her thin shoulders and Sarah's heart warmed slightly at the sign of affection; the child clasped his long, slender fingers, and they walked into the house.

The street seemed to breathe a collective sigh of relief as the tall, angular parson disappeared. After a moment, people began to speak again, but more quietly, more subdued. Sarah turned back to Thomas, who was looking at the closed door to the parsonage.

"Yon parson looks like the archangel Michael," he commented. "Come to overthrow Satan in our midst."

Thinking back to the burning of Margaret Eames, Sarah was troubled by his words, but strove to lighten the conversation, remembering her psalms.

"Indeed, he is fair enough to be an angel! Perhaps he is with us for a more gentle task, to keep us in all God's ways?" She smiled, grateful for her mother's care, which had taught her to read, uncaring of the prevailing views that girls should learn more domestic tasks.

Thomas smiled.

"I would it were so. We have seen enough of burning. Now, Mistress Sarah, is the hoe to your liking?"

Sarah put it to the ground and rested her weight on it to test the mended head. It didn't move.

She was about to leave with thanks when Thomas said,

"Abigail would speak with you. I will fetch her."

Sarah waited impatiently as the minutes passed. She had much to do, more than three pounds of wool to card and spin before midweek. Her eyes darted to the people walking, and her quick eyes noted the slight limp of a child who passed with a grin. She smiled and waved. Robert's leg was healing well, although he would always be lame, she feared.

"Sarah! Truly, you are a stranger!" Abigail's voice made her turn. The plump, sunny face of Abigail, one of her few friends, looked pleased indeed to see her. She found herself drawn to a soft, ample bosom and hugged. "Rebecca is crawling, and you absent these two weeks!"

Sarah disentangled herself with a laugh.

"I have had wool to spin, an orchard to tend, a servant to keep in luxury!"

"Aye, I see Dorothy in the market, giving herself airs. I know not how you keep your temper with that woman." Abigail, a merry girl, had no time for Dorothy, seeing only the thin lips and often humourless face. Sarah, who knew how gentle with pain Dorothy could be, and how good her heart, held her peace. They would never take to one another.

"Rebecca is crawling?" Sarah gently prodded her away from the subject of Dorothy. Abigail nodded eagerly.

"Marry, she's so quick! I think she's a prodigy. My sister's child ne'er walked till he was twenty months!" she said with the pride of one who knows her child is the best and ablest child in the world. "But will you sup with us?"

They agreed Sarah would visit the day after next, and Sarah left with a light step. But as she walked down the street, this faded and, without knowing why, she glanced back at the parsonage. She stopped dead, her stomach lurching.

Circling over the house was a flock of black crows, throwing their inky shadows over the sunny roof. As she watched, one detached from the flock and came towards her, casting a shadow over her face. She ran all the way home, knowing it had begun.

CHAPTER THREE
STACIE

I awoke to the sound of BBC Radio 4 playing in the kitchen and the smell of toast wafting up the stairs. I stretched, hearing my neck crack, and threw off the covers with an effort.

The shower washed away the sweat and griminess of my disturbed night, which had been heavy and too hot, but didn't wash away my weariness. I pinned up my hair, pulled on a favourite summer dress, and padded downstairs.

Mother was sipping coffee out of her favourite china cup, and I murmured a good morning.

"You're up early for a Sunday," she commented. I kissed her cheek.

"Hot last night."

"Mmm, Eleanor couldn't sleep either, she's gone to Holly's."

I went less often to Holly's stables now I had gained weight but still rode now and again. I should visit my favourite horse, Wellington. True to form, Ellie rode a horse called Napoleon.

The aroma of the rich roasted beans kicked my stomach into action. I reached for bread and the toaster after pouring a cup.

THE VISITOR

The Sunday supplement was on the table and I flipped through for the cartoons.

"Are you going to see your grandmother?" my mother asked. I nodded. "You spend more time there than you do here."

I didn't respond and buttered my toast, adding a dollop of jam. Yes, I spent more time with Gran than anyone else, but then again, she knew me better than anyone else in the family. Much, much better.

I peered out of the window. Cloudy, heavy, but no rain yet.

"Has Dad gone fishing?" I asked. Mother murmured something, and I took the response to be yes.

My parents had a clean, intellectual relationship, and as I wandered into the hall, I caught sight of an old photograph of Dad taken when he was a young student at Oxford. He had a roguish twinkle in his eye and looked fit and healthy in his rowing kit, almost virile. Marriage to my mother seemed to have washed him of all physicality. Faded him into chaste cheek kissing and proffered arms rather than a warm, clasping hand.

I headed to the garden to eat. The ginger cat was sitting on one of the garden chairs and, daring it, I went to sit on the same chair. Unperturbed, the cat evaporated, and I sat down with a bit of a bump, almost spilling my coffee.

I chomped through my toast, considering my day as I ate. Sunday meant driving to Gran's, a tussle with a demonic crossword, a trip to church and a visit to my grandfather's grave. Then we'd return here for lunch, where Mother and Gran would delicately snipe at one another. A bit of family tradition.

I saw the child with the lace collar in the flowerbeds and trying to work out if it was male or female, I studied it. To my surprise, it smiled, and I saw for certain that it was indeed a boy, despite the long curls. With a quick glance around to check no one was watching, I smiled back. His grin widened, and he skipped away, passing partway through the garden wall before turning and waving a hand in salute and fading into the milky mid-morning light.

I glanced at my watch and brushed crumbs away. Time to visit Gran.

※

She was frowning over an elusive clue in the crossword but looked up as I walked onto her small garden patio.

"Got it sussed?" I asked, bending to kiss her cheek.

"Hmm… Ah! Machiavelli!" she beamed, filling in the answer in ink. She looked at me. "I wasn't expecting you until later. You're up early."

I laughed. "Too hot to sleep."

Grandmother looked at me with dark brown eyes. "Will you take me to the church?"

"Of course. Are you going to the service?"

"No, I don't think so, so shall we go early? Cut me some flowers for the grave, and I'll make you a drink."

I collected the secateurs from the shed and walked around the garden. The sky had turned a sullen grey, and I felt the weather hang over me like a sentence.

God, I hope it breaks soon, I thought, moving towards the borders. For whatever reason, I never saw spirits at Gran's house, and I could relax there.

I caught my finger on a rose thorn. I put the rose gingerly on the lawn and sucked my bleeding finger.

"Heavy weather, isn't it?" said Gran, watching me from the patio.

"There'll be a storm this afternoon." I nodded, moving to less dangerous flowers to cut. When I had a fistful of flowers and greenery, I came back to the patio and wrapped the stems tenderly into the damp newspaper Gran had laid out.

I picked up my coffee, which, as normal, was just too weak for me. Gran thought too much coffee would turn my teeth brown. She turned once more to the crossword and with a bit of brain wracking and a sneaky visit to the internet on my phone, we completed it in about ten minutes. She told me about the family history project she'd started; she had traced our family back to the early 1800s with little effort. I wondered if she'd come across any other relatives that we didn't talk about in the family.

Gran sat back with a sigh of satisfaction, patting her dark brown curls. At seventy-four, any signs of silver in her shoulder-length hair were ruthlessly dyed. She spent a small fortune at the hairdressers, but I loved her spirit. With her glorious olive tinted skin, carefully protected from the sun over the years, she and my mother might almost pass for sisters. Not that I would ever say that to my mother.

"How was your last day?" she asked.

I shrugged.

"Nice. Cake, card, fond farewells. You know the sort of thing."

"What about Neil Hathersage?"

I looked up in surprise and my mouth flattened.

"What have you heard, Gran?"

"Well, my *interpretation* of what I heard was that he's a greasy little man with a failing marriage and no sense of personal space," she replied crisply. "I don't believe the gossip at bridge which suggested that your standards in men had dropped. But I'd like to understand why you've left Woodlands. You seemed very happy there, or at least you were until late last year."

I sighed and told the sorry story of the Christmas party and some seriously misunderstood signs.

"But why didn't you complain? I play bridge with half the board of governors!"

"My word against his? And I landed him one!"

She laughed and my ill humour vanished. "I decided he might make a complaint of assault against me, as he's such an arse, but that would screw up my chances of a new job elsewhere. So I decided to withdraw, once I'd got a decent reference from the deputy head."

Gran just looked at me. "Fair enough. Seems a shame you didn't complain, though. Anyway, shall we go?"

※

The graveyard was quiet and deserted. The bells hadn't yet sounded for morning service, and I was on high alert as I walked through the lychgate. Attending this church for my grandfather's funeral when I was twenty had been torturous not only for my grief but also for the worry of what I might see.

As it happened, I'd seen only one spectre, a fat, smiling priest who had looked on benignly during the whole funeral service. However, other visits here afterwards seemed like rush hour at King's Cross station, with figures appearing around every corner, every headstone, some rising out of the ground, some friendly looking, and others not.

This morning was not 'busy'. I saw a woman dressed in a white shift with a tiny baby who nodded, and there was an old lady who was too intent on the inscription of her headstone to notice me. There was also a spirit I hadn't seen before, a young girl in a white cap and brown cloak whose laughing eyes watched me carefully.

I nodded to them and followed Gran to the grave. As she knelt to re-arrange the flowers, I looked around. In the grey-green light, the churchyard seemed to be waiting for something and the hairs on the back of my neck prickled.

"Odd, isn't it?" Gran said.

"Yes, it's a bit portentous, something to do with the weather, I expect," I said. "As if they expected someone. Not great for a graveyard."

Gran changed the flowers, chuckling.

"I often wonder how it is for you. I know you've been seeing spirits for years, but I always wondered if coming here might be a trial."

"I think I'm used to it but I'm not sure I'd come here without you. I feel safer with you around."

She looked at the flowers, satisfied with their shape now.

"I wish I could see Gramps," I said wistfully, and she shook her head.

"I know. But he's here, Stacie, can't you tell? Even if you can't see him?"

I paused and a whiff of tobacco and Gramps' faint bergamot aftershave tickled my nose. I stared at Gran and she nodded.

"You've always been sensitive, Stacie," she said. "Your mother used to say you were abnormally sensitive, but then again, she's got the imagination of a duster."

"Mmm. I would have cost them a fortune in psychotherapy bills. Are you ready to go?"

I turned back to the car, to find the gaze of the young girl in the cap still on me, and it puzzled me. When I drew breath to mention her to Gran, she disappeared. Thoughtfully, I unlocked the car.

We entered the house to find my mother on her mobile.

"Yes, yes, I'll do that. Thank you for calling… no, of course not. Goodbye."

She looked worried, and kissed Gran, remarking that we were early. "But that's fortunate," she added, focusing as she became businesslike. "That was Mary Mills, from Holly's. Eleanor said she'd be back by half past nine and that was nearly two hours ago. There's no response from her mobile. Mary's quite worried."

"I know her normal route, I'll ride out and have a look," I said. She nodded.

"By the time you get there, she might have returned, but you might save her a drenching," Mother said, glancing out of the window at the threatening sky.

The electricity in the air made my hair crackle and the world seemed still and silent. As I climbed out of the car at the stables, I heard the first, faint rumble of thunder. Mary came out of the office to meet me.

"Stacie! Good to see you. Bit worried about that damned sister of yours. She left here in a dream on Napoleon." There was a frown on her brown face, her short grey hair ruffled where she'd run her hands through it. "I've rung her mobile every ten minutes for the last hour, no response."

Bloody Ellie. My mouth twisted.

"Do you have a horse for me to borrow? I can't take Wellington in this weather, he's too old."

"I saddled Flyer. Would ride out myself, but I'm expecting other riders back." I nodded and struggled into a waterproof jacket as we walked to the stables. Flyer was a magnificent animal, a glossy chestnut at least two hands taller than I normally rode. I looked at him doubtfully.

"Will I be able to hold him?"

"Just show him who's boss. You'll go on all right. Isn't a horse in these stables that you and Ellie couldn't ride. My best pupils."

She bent to give me a leg up. The chestnut sensed my uncertainty and pranced a little. I got him under control with a bit of difficulty, while Mary watched critically.

"Which way did she go?" I said at last when I could speak.

"Usual, I think; along the ridge, across the fields, down by the river and back by the bridle path," Mary said, as she adjusted a stirrup. I thanked her and set off towards the path, hoping to meet Ellie on the way back. The sky gave a low growl of thunder. The storm was getting closer, and the fields stretched before me, bleak and washed of colour in the dim light.

I took out my mobile and checked the calls. Nothing, and not much of a signal either. Perhaps that was the weather? I called Ellie.

"Ellie, it's Stacie. Where the hell are you? Everyone's frantic

THE VISITOR

and I'm now out looking for you. I'm taking your normal route, backwards – along the bridle path, then the river, across the fields." I looked around, scanning both sides of the path. Nothing, except a rapidly glooming sky. "If you get this, can you call me?"

I rode for another ten minutes, aware of the stillness that comes before a storm. The birds had disappeared.

"Heathcliff, Heathcliff," I muttered. Urging Flyer into a gentle gallop, I scanned the horizon again. There was no sign of my sister.

The thunder grew louder, and Flyer grew more nervous, sliding and skittering beneath me. I was finding it more difficult to hold him, best pupil of Mary or not.

As if to prove this point, Flyer took off, and it was all I could do to hang on, as the ground blurred beneath me at frightening speed. The ridge alongside the path, dropping steeply over boulders and scrub, seemed very close. Swearing, I was pulling him up when a streak of lightning ripped the sky apart, and Flyer reared. I hung on to the reins, gripping to the sweating horse with my knees as we headed towards the ridge and its drop.

From out of nowhere, a man appeared, the folds of his black cloak swirling around him in the wind. His arms were outstretched as if he was trying to catch the bolting horse. I caught sight of white hair and a white face. Flyer pulled up, away from the ridge, and swerved towards the fields. I screamed as he flung me from the saddle. I hit the ground, felt a sharp pain in my head, and everything disappeared.

CHAPTER FOUR
STACIE

The first thing I noticed was the throbbing in my head. Then my bruised muscles screamed at me. The next was a whispered conversation.

"But we should get a second opinion. You heard her. She was raving!" My mother sounded very unlike her cool and collected self.

"No, we should wait and see what happens when she comes round," came the voice of my grandmother, calm and quiet. "She's had a nasty bump on the head, and she was soaked to the skin. A mix of hypothermia and concussion is likely to make anyone say strange things."

I made a sound in my throat and the conversation stopped, and a cool hand took mine.

"Eustacia? Do you know where you are?" said Mother.

"Have some water," said Gran, and held a cup to my lips. I drank and eased open my eyelids. They stung with the bright light of the hospital room and I shut them again, but not before I glimpsed a man in a stovepipe hat standing by the window, beaming at me.

I could hear the rain against the window and taking a

breath, I opened my eyes again and looked at my mother's unusually white face.

"How do you feel?" she asked again.

"Bloody awful," I croaked. "I couldn't hold onto the horse." Memory flooded back, and I looked at Gran, who shook her head slightly. I stopped speaking.

"I'll get your father," said Mother, and slipped out of the room.

There was a silence before I said, "There was a man…"

"Yes, I know. You told us all about him when you were delirious," Gran said. Hot pincers seemed to grip my head. "Was he real?" she asked.

I paused and then shook my head slowly. "I don't know. But the horse reared when he appeared."

She said nothing for a moment. Then she patted my hand. "Yes, don't worry now, we'll talk when you're feeling better. Would you like a hot drink?"

I nodded. The man in the stovepipe hat walked about a bit and then went to stand by the window again. I closed my eyes and catalogued my aching body. When she returned with a pale green cup and saucer of some brown liquid masquerading as coffee, I said, "Has Ellie turned up yet?"

"She did indeed," said Gran in a dry voice. "She wandered back about half an hour after you'd left. Her mobile had run out of power and she just lost track of the time, she said. She found you."

"Typical. If I felt better, I'd bloody murder her," I said with my eyes closed, as the throbbing in my head increased.

"Speak of the devil," murmured Gran, as Ellie appeared, followed by Dad, his tall frame tiptoeing carefully into the room. I squinted at her. Ellie looked pale and worried. I managed a smile.

"Oh, thank God!" she exclaimed in a voice that rattled my skull. I winced. She lowered her voice. "Sorry. God, you had us all so worried!"

"Why? Did I look like a corpse?" A little to my surprise,

Ellie closed her eyes and shuddered slightly. So, I *had* looked like a corpse.

"How's Flyer?" I asked her.

"Oh, he's fine. He made his way back to the stables, to frighten the life out of Mary when she realised Flyer must have thrown you. All hell broke loose! We've had half the neighbourhood looking for you, Mother hysterical, Mary not much better, Dad out of mobile phone range…"

Her drawn face touched me and I smiled at her awkwardly. My mother walked in with the doctor. Now I looked at her properly, her eyes were a little pink, which surprised me somewhat.

The doctor firmly took away the coffee cup and shone a light into my eyes, asked me to repeat my name and address, touch my nose, and cross my eyes.

"Have you been sick? Are you nauseous?"

"No, neither."

"How's the rest of you?"

"Feeling like I've been run over by a truck." He smiled faintly and examined my ears.

"Hmm. We'll keep you in overnight. It was an enormous horse, I hear."

"It was," I agreed. He left, leaving me some evil-looking blue pills to wash down with the equally evil coffee.

"I'm surprised the horse threw you," remarked Dad. "You're normally such a fine rider." I considered for a moment before answering carefully.

"Well, I've never ridden Flyer before and he's huge. What with the storm and everything, I just panicked. You can't blame the horse for doing the same."

"You were delirious, you know, Eustacia. Father and I were very worried at one point. You kept saying something about a man in a black cloak." Mother watched me closely as I forced down the pills.

"I might have been watching too much *Game of Thrones*, Mother."

"Stacie ought to sleep now," said Gran diplomatically, and the man in the stovepipe hat nodded approvingly. "We'll call tomorrow and see when you can come home."

Dutifully, they filed out and, made drowsy by the tablets, I slept without dreaming.

The following morning, after soggy cereals and rock-hard toast, the doctor discharged me. After queuing for half an hour at the dispensary and seeing the man in the stovepipe hat and a few others in hospital gowns, I decided I would do without the drugs and waited for Gran to pick me up. By the time she arrived it was half past eleven and my headache, which had disappeared overnight, was again screwing at my temples.

She was in the full flow of an apology even before the automatic doors swooshed open.

"...couldn't get a parking spot, I'm absolutely *miles* away! I imagine you're bored silly waiting, aren't you?"

"It's fine," I lied, standing up. She looked at me keenly and then we stepped out into the muggy air. I glanced at the sky; we were in for another storm. Walking across the car park, Gran had stopped a little way behind me and surprised, I turned to see her standing beside a sleek, black, two-seater sports car. I frowned, looking for the estate car. She twinkled at me.

"Well, actually, I am late for a reason." She turned and looked fondly at the car. "I thought I was starting to be a bit... old. So I bought this. It arrived this morning, I almost forgot it was coming, what with the drama of yesterday."

Despite the headache, I laughed.

"It's only got two seats! And a sunroof! It's beautiful!"

She clicked the keys and there was a satisfying clunk as the doors unlocked. I lowered myself what seemed a long way into the leather seat and sat with my mouth slack as she gunned the powerful-sounding engine. As we moved off, I giggled.

"You'll be a real man-magnet with this! You'll be fighting them off!"

"No doubt. Although I do at the moment, you know, Stacie."

I sat in silent admiration as she manoeuvred out of the car park and I watched as a variety of heads turned to watch her. She tossed her head with satisfaction.

"Yes, I reckon I'll enjoy my new car," she said. As we got to the bypass, she glanced at me.

"How are you feeling? You look pale."

"I'm okay. I still have a thumping head and I'm aching, especially my back and shoulder. I fell off backwards, I think." I fell silent as the memory of the man in the black cloak filled my head.

The car purred past a lorry and it was a moment before my grandmother responded.

"What did you say about this strange man? The horse reared at the sight, you said. Have you seen anything like that before?"

"No. I'm beginning to wonder if it was someone off the set of a Bronte film. He might have been real. I'm grateful, anyway. We might have gone off the ridge if he hadn't stepped in front of the horse."

I closed my eyes and leaned back against the leather seats. The pain in my head was throbbing so hard I wondered if anyone could hear it.

When we reached Greenfields, Gran saw me into the house.

After asking how I was and whether I needed a drink, Mother wasn't sure what to do with me so I saved everyone the bother of nursing me and climbed the stairs to my room. As I lay on my bed, the ginger cat appeared and curled up by my feet. Strangely comforted by this, I fell asleep.

THE VISITOR

I awoke to a perfect summer's morning. The sunlight filtered through the gently swaying curtains, and my headache was just a dull pulse. I raised myself cautiously and groped for my alarm clock. Nearly eleven o'clock. I'd slept for hours.

I lay back on my pillows and listened to the silent house. I still ached, but my pain was less severe than before. The ginger cat stretched on the window seat and then faded to invisibility in the folds of the curtains.

I trailed to the bathroom and the solace of aspirin. My face stared back at me, pale with a purple and red bruise on the temple and shadowed eyes. I watched as the aspirin fizzed in the glass and when it was still, forced it down with a grimace. I caught sight of the governess who regarded me with sympathy.

I was sitting in the kitchen in my robe, blinking at the gleam of paintwork and the glare of aluminium when Ellie arrived with a lot of shopping.

"I thought you'd never wake up," she said, dumping the bags on the counter.

"Sorry, was I supposed to be up for something?"

"No, of course not! I was worrying a bit that you might still have concussion."

I moved slowly to refill my coffee, gesturing at the shopping.

"What's all this?"

"In all the trauma of you being in hospital, Mother forgot all about the shopping. And we have company on Friday."

"We do?"

"Nathaniel Williams is coming to dinner."

I wrinkled my brow and then remembered.

"Ah yes. The academic superman, right?"

She gave me a grin and nodded. "Oh, by the way, your phone was buzzing. I turned it off and put it on the dresser, but you might want to check it before you get a shower?"

Ellie was organising me. I took my coffee back to my room. I saw a few messages from Seb, and one from Jo with a photo of one of the best looking men I'd ever seen, all brooding eyes and stubble. Jo's text implied that as holiday romances go, this one was proving pretty satisfactory.

The first messages from Seb were a running commentary on a TV programme we both watched, but the last one said, 'Don't forget our dinner date on Wednesday. I practically killed someone to get the booking.'

Shit. I'd forgotten about dinner. Still, I glanced at the mirror, my bruise might have turned into something less technicolour by Wednesday.

In the end, I took a cab, rather than drive into the village. Even with someone else driving, Mother looked dubious.

"Are you sure you're well enough to go out, Eustacia? I was sure Sebastian would fetch you, rather than meet you there."

"I haven't told him I fell off a horse – he'd have laughed himself silly." I was looking in the mirror. I'd draped my hair over my face and pinned it as best I could. I'd tried to conceal the purple and blue-green bruise at my temple with a lot of make-up.

"Stop fussing, Julia. It will be good for Stacie to go out," said Dad, not looking up from the book on his lap. "She's seen nothing but these four walls for the past two days, and I for one think she's looking peaky."

At that moment, my phone buzzed to say that Stan, my driver, was waiting outside. I almost ran to the front door.

Mother's solicitude was unnerving, although she was probably still worried about me hallucinating. Mind you, Mother worrying about my mental state wasn't new. I'd been ten when I'd tried to tell her about my then ghostly companion, a lanky young man in a 60s suit. It hadn't gone well – she'd threatened to put me into a mental asylum. Thank God for Gran.

"Looks busy," commented the cab driver, jolting me out of my memories.

Diners already packed the pizza restaurant and I peered over the backcombed hairdos of the waitresses, looking for Seb's dark head. A soldier in a uniform appeared in front of me as I sidled through the tables and I stopped, rather than walk through him. He threw me a cheeky grin and evaporated. Seb, thankfully not noticing, grabbed me by the arms and kissed me firmly on both cheeks.

"God, it's heaving!" I said, sliding off my light jacket and sitting down carefully so as not to bump my bruised body. As I pulled the chair in, my hair fell away from my forehead and Seb's eyes zeroed in on my head.

"What's this?" he said, a scowl darkening his thin face. He lifted his hand, and I flinched a little as he eased my hair away from my face. He whistled. "Wow. What did the other guy look like?"

"I took a tumble off a horse I hadn't ridden before," I said, picking up the menu. His hand came out and pushed the menu back to the table.

"When was this?"

"Sunday."

"Have you had it looked at?"

"Yes, the doctor said I'd be fine."

"Have you been in hospital?"

"Yes, just overnight," I said reluctantly.

"And why don't I know this?" he demanded, his dark grey eyes flashing. My eyebrows rose. Seb looked cross.

"I was in and out before I knew it," I said, shrugging. "It was just a slight concussion. I came home on Monday lunchtime, took it easy today, and I'm much better now. What are you having?"

"Don't try to change the subject," Seb said. "What happened?"

I told him of Mary's frantic call, the ride out and the storm. During it, he waved away the waitress who was hovering. She scowled, and I mentally placed a bet she would not be back for our order for a good ten minutes.

"And where *was* your delightful sister during all this?" asked Seb, his eyes narrowed.

I shrugged. "Riding, phone dead, she lost track of the time…"

"So you went through all this bother…" He lifted my hair again to peer at the bruise, "…for someone not sufficiently organised to charge her phone?"

I smiled and picked up the menu again. Seb and Ellie didn't get on, and I was secretly rather pleased. I'd wondered if he would be yet another of Ellie's admirers when I'd first introduced them, but they were like oil and water. Seb took the piss out of my sister mercilessly, and Ellie, drilled in exquisite manners by Mother, barely knew how to respond.

"Well, anyway, what are you having?"

Seb looked as though he wanted to say a lot more but finally followed my lead.

When the waitress had taken our order, he leaned forward.

"So, how's the flat hunting going?"

"Oh, I'm still looking, but I should have the deposit in a month. The new job will help."

"I'm thrilled for your promotion, but I'll miss you – the prettiest girl on the staff, not to mention a fantastic teaching assistant." He twinkled at me and I laughed. Seb said this kind of thing a lot, and always with a smile. I looked at him critically. Unruly dark brown curls, wiry, and tall; over six foot, I estimated. Wearing a soft cotton shirt and expensive-looking chinos (although how he afforded them on a teacher's salary, I never knew) he looked relaxed, handsome. And completely out of my league.

"It's for the best," I said firmly.

"Is it? Not from where I'm sitting."

"I'm only up the road," I smiled, taking a sip of the wine. "It's not like I'm emigrating or anything! Although I'll miss you and Jo."

"Let's arrange something for the three of us when Jo gets back from shagging half of Spain." He paused while the waitress placed a pizza the size of a cartwheel in front of him. My pizza, one of those 'slimming' ones with a hole cut in the middle of the dough, filled with stringy rocket, also arrived. It lacked all the quality ingredients of a pizza like cheese oozing over the edge of the dough and pepperoni glistening with oil.

"I may be off on holiday myself to see my brother," he said casually. I looked up.

"What, to Australia? When?" Seb's family had always seemed quite glamorous, his brother abroad, his parents seemingly on holiday all the time after his father retired from the City early.

"Nothing sorted yet, but probably for three weeks in August. I want to do some touring."

"Isn't it the middle of winter there?" I said doubtfully, geography never having been one of my best subjects.

"Stuart's in Brisbane. The temperature's pretty warm all year round." Seb put a huge bit of pizza on his fork and looked at me. "Do you fancy coming along?"

"Me? I doubt I could afford it, Seb. I'm in touching distance of a deposit so I can get away from my bloody family."

He looked at me, chewing meditatively, and there was a pause.

"And anyway, surely you want to go away with one of your statuesque blondes?" I added.

"What statuesque blondes?"

I paused. Actually, that was a fair point, I had seen none of late.

"I'm sure you'll be looking for one on your travels," I amended. "And then I'd cramp your style."

He gave me a level look.

"Stacie, if we are on holiday together, there would be no blondes, statuesque or otherwise. There would be you and me, sweet pea."

I grinned at the endearment.

"I think it would be a stretch for me financially."

"I have friends in the industry for the fares and friends in Oz for us to stay with. You'd just need some pin money."

'Pin money'. How quaint. He would empty my savings account without even breaking a sweat. I smiled, took a bite of bitter rocket, and nodded.

"I'll think about it."

"Does that mean you'll think about it, or are you just trying to shut me up?" he asked, suspicious of my capitulation.

I smiled again, chewing greenery.

"I'll think about it," I repeated when my mouth was empty.

He filled up my glass again and blew me a kiss. My heart jumped at that, but I decided I was being stupid and shouldn't make too much of it.

CHAPTER FIVE
SARAH

The church was no more full than last Sunday, Sarah thought. But people looked more attentive, more expectant. As she looked carefully around the pews, she saw her neighbours somewhat neater than she remembered. A smile twitched at her lips, but this disappeared as she saw that others had filled her normal place at the back of the church.

Forced to take a seat on the aisle, far nearer the front than she would normally have chosen, she re-arranged her face to one of blank piety. Dorothy trailed after her and they sat down, causing a shuffle to spread along the pew as people made room.

Parson Dillington arrived almost unheard, taking his place at the front of the church and looking over his new congregation rather sternly. Everyone rose to their feet.

"I do know mine own wickedness and my sin is always against me," proclaimed the parson, and Sarah started in surprise. His voice was rich, deep, and generous, very unlike his wiry appearance. The tones of it rolled over her like warm spiced wine.

"Dearly beloved brethren, the Scripture moveth us in sundry places to acknowledge and confess our manifold sins and wickedness, and that we should not dissemble nor cloak them before the face of Almighty God Our Heavenly Father..." His green eyes flashed over the pews and Sarah noticed the congregation flinch.

After an almost imperceptible pause, he continued in a softened voice, "...but confess them with an humble, lowly, penitent and obedient heart, to the end that we may obtain forgiveness of the same by his infinite goodness and mercy." His face gentled and warmth spread through Sarah's limbs.

As the service continued, Sarah listened, not to the words, but to the lilt of the parson's voice, which seemed to her like music. For the first time in church, her attention was caught. She studied his face and the light and dark chasing over it, fascinated at the conflict she saw.

"A luxurious voice and an angel's face housed by a spare body," she thought. As soon as the thought surfaced in her mind, his eyes caught hers and she stared, terrified she might have said it out loud. His eyes bored into her and she quickly dipped her head, the sudden movement loosening the pins under her cap. For once, her prayer was real and heartfelt, even if it was only to keep her hair in place. After a moment, she glanced up to find he was looking elsewhere, and she slid a hand under her cap to push the pins in more firmly.

She rose automatically to receive communion, taking her place alongside Dorothy, and keeping her gaze down. She focused on the slender hands of the parson as he put the wafer on her tongue and gave her the cup to sip. Even though he didn't touch her, she felt the warmth from his skin. As she made her way back to her place, his eye was on her again and, unnerved, she missed her step. Only Dorothy's hand, grabbing her arm like a vice, saved her from falling.

"Careful, mistress," murmured Dorothy, and Sarah smiled gratefully at her. It was then she felt another stare on her.

The dark eyes of Parson Dillington's daughter glared at her

from a side pew. The malevolence Sarah saw lurking in the thin, pale face startled her, and once more Sarah lowered her gaze.

"O God, make clean our hearts within us," said the parson.

"And take not thy Holy Spirit from us," Sarah responded with the rest.

When the service was over, the parson stood at the church door, greeting his new parishioners. With him stood the girl, stiff, angular and awkward, her pale face set.

Sarah curtsied as Parson Denning made the introductions, his last duty before returning to his own village. She glanced at Dorothy, pink and upset, and hoped the maid would not cry as her favourite clergyman left them.

"This is Sarah Bartlett, a maid of some learning who helps the women of the village with herbal remedies and cures for their ailments," said Parson Denning, his gaze warm. "She is renowned for her care of others and she is a goodly child." Sarah, warmed by his words, dimpled at him.

"Pleased to meet you, Mistress Bartlett," said an unsmiling Parson Dillington in his glorious voice. Sarah nodded, straightening her face.

"Welcome to our village, sir."

His eyes held hers for a second too long, and the heat rose to her cheeks. She nodded again and turned away.

"What, is she a cunning woman, father? Mother said they were all witches."

Sarah steeled herself to walk away as though she hadn't heard the sharp voice of the girl. Mistress Whyte's eyes widened, and she muttered something about the mouths of babes, and Sarah walked steadily on, her heart beating fast.

As she turned the corner of the street, she looked back to see Parson Dillington still watching her.

She listened carefully. There was only the sound of the birds and the wind sighing softly through the leaves. Sarah's shoulders dropped in relief and she skipped along, lifting her face to the blue, blue sky. A smile tilted her lips.

Away from the village, she at last relaxed. Since Sunday service, a couple of neighbours had avoided her gaze. Mistress Whyte had been busy, no doubt, spreading gossip, and even Dorothy had warned her to have a care. So she'd shut her door, concentrated on her carding and spinning and ignored the sunshine, much as it called to her.

But not today. Her herb store was getting sparse, and she needed nettle leaves for tea. And when the sun peeked through the leaded lights, she'd been unable to resist its tempting. She'd crept out of the cottage before the church clock struck seven, pulling her hat low over her face, praying she would meet no one.

Now, however, she unpinned the hat from her head in the early morning light and the rays on her face, not yet warm, filled her closed eyelids with orange sparks.

Thrusting the hat into her basket, she left the path and walked through bracken and leaves to the bubbling stream which appeared briefly from underground. The water was icy and clear, and she cupped her hands to drink. Wiping her hands on her skirt, she sank to the ground and unearthed from her basket the bottle of small beer and the loaf with which she broke her fast.

As she ate, she thought of the past week and her brow creased. Mayhap she was imagining the slight coldness of her neighbours? She had, after all, not seen many of them, and even Ned had gone to another village to visit more distant family. She bit her lip. Ned was a good man, in his way, but she mistrusted his temper, which whilst held in check most of the time, had flared briefly when she had refused his offer of marriage. She sighed. He thought her contrary and wayward, she knew. But marriage was not in her future.

She had supped with Abigail and Thomas and made cooing

noises over Rebecca, who was crawling, as Abigail had said. But after this, she'd seen no one other than Dorothy, keeping her own company and as Dorothy said, 'staying out of trouble'.

But even the Warringtons, an elderly couple to whom she often gave spare vegetables and the odd morsel of butter, had not knocked at her door in the past seven days.

She'd attended church but made certain to arrive slightly later than everyone else, to keep from the notice of the new parson and his daughter. She puzzled over the girl who she now knew to be called Prudence. She knew not what had caused such enmity in one so young.

Her meal eaten, she brushed crumbs from her bodice and allowed herself to lie back in the fragrant long grass and stare at the sky and the hawks circling. She knew a moment of complete stillness before the thrush flew and perched on an overhanging branch. It warbled, its song sweet on the morning air. She smiled, understanding its tweeting, and tutted back at it. It put its head on one side and regarded her with a bright eye.

The dialogue continued a few moments longer and then the tone of the thrush's song changed and, flapping its wings a few times, it flew away.

Forewarned, Sarah scrambled to her feet and rammed her hat back on her head, snatching the bottle, thrusting it back into the basket as she strode from the clearing. Now she was alert, she caught the rustle of the footsteps in the grass to one side of her. They weren't far away. She stopped by a tree and re-tied the strings of her cap, before settling the hat more firmly. She took a deep breath and walked carefully away from the path once more.

When nothing had happened five minutes later, she set to searching for her herbs again, her senses sharpened. Another five minutes and her basket filled, her knife warm in her hand as she cut the tough stems. The rustle of a fox in the undergrowth was the first thing to startle her. The white head of the parson was the second. She let out a cry, not stifled quickly enough, and the parson, deep in thought, jumped and looked up at her.

"Mistress Bartlett." He nodded gravely. Sarah bobbed a curtsey. "You're abroad early this morning."

"Aye, sir."

"What do you do here?"

"I need more herbs, and nettles for tea, sir."

"Indeed. And you use these in your healing?"

"They can ease some pains, sir."

"I hear much of your skills."

Sarah noted the sour note in his voice and looked sharply at him.

"I do what I can for those who ask my help," she said carefully.

"But whence did those skills arise? Do you read?"

"Yes, sir. My mother taught me."

"And do you read your Bible?"

"I do, sir."

"Every day?"

Sarah didn't even hesitate.

"Yes, sir."

Those green eyes seemed to drill into her, the beautiful face still as stone.

"I do not think I believe you, Sarah Bartlett," was the dry response. "You arrive late to service as if to enter the house of God was an unwelcome duty."

Sarah thought for a second.

"I shall strive to do better, sir, but in truth, I hear well enough from the back of the church. There are many older than I who need to be nearer to you to receive the word of God."

He looked astonished for a moment, and then she saw a twinkle enter his eyes. He smiled slightly, and confusion swept through her as her heart beat faster. He straightened his mouth.

"You are a saucy girl. Mistress Whyte told me as much."

"Mistress Whyte should treat others as she would herself,"

said Sarah, before she could stop herself. "I speak ill of no one; I know not why anyone should speak ill of me."

There was silence.

"I bid you good day, sir," Sarah said, nodding her head stiffly.

"Good day, Mistress Bartlett. God bless you," was the murmured response as she turned on her heel.

❧

The sun was drifting lower in the sky and Sarah watched Dorothy stir the broth over the fire. The house was quiet, but Sarah was ill at ease. She glanced through the window and her breath caught at the shadow that fell across it. Then came the banging on the door.

"Save us!" Dorothy exclaimed as she dropped the spoon. Reluctantly, Sarah went to the door and opened it a crack.

Parson Dillington was outside, pacing.

"Mistress, pardon the intrusion, but my daughter is ill. Can you come?"

Sarah opened the door wider, and he pushed into the room, his tall figure reaching almost to the ceiling.

"What ails her?" Sarah asked.

"She complains of pain in her gut and writhes as if possessed."

She eyed him curiously. His pale face was flushed. He must be worried. She nodded and reached for her basket.

"What age is she?"

"Just past her thirteenth year." Parson Dillington looked at her as though she was mad.

Older than I guessed, Sarah thought. She simply nodded again and collected her herbs. Finally, she threw her cloak around her shoulders and said, "I am ready. Let us go."

The light was dim as they made their way up the street, Sarah running to keep up with the parson's long legs. He eventually recognised her struggles and slowed his pace.

"I am grateful," he said in a low voice as he pushed open the door to the parsonage. She nodded, looking around. There was a big fire burning in the fireplace, and two heavy oak chairs facing it. There was a cry from upstairs.

"Prudence, I have brought Mistress Bartlett to tend you," called the parson, shrugging off his cloak.

There was an ominous silence, and Sarah's heart sank. She climbed the stairs behind the parson, glancing at the paintings on the wall and comparing the surroundings with her cottage.

Prudence was lying pale and stiff on the bed, her eyes dark in her thin face. They flashed at Sarah before her eyelids fluttered closed.

Sarah sat on the stool by the bed, looking carefully at the flushed cheeks of the girl. A hand on Prudence's forehead showed no fever, however. As Sarah drew back the coverlet, the girl let out a squeal.

"Papa! She is hurting me!"

Sarah frowned and looked at the parson.

"Prudence, let Mistress Bartlett look," he said gently, and the beauty of his voice struck Sarah again. The girl hunched her shoulders on the sheet and lay still.

"Prudence, I am going to lay hands on your stomach," she said levelly. "Tell me if it hurts."

"You have already hurt me!" she whined.

She ran her fingers lightly over the girl's nightgown, noting the swell of the abdomen and also the slight breasts. She asked when the girl had last eaten.

"Midday."

"What did she eat?"

"Bread, and some cheese."

"Did you eat the same?"

"I did, and I have no ill effects."

"Has she sickened like this before now?"

"No."

"Could I speak to her alone?"

He stared at her. "Alone? Why would you need to?"

"Because I am talking to her of women's matters. You may stay if you wish, of course."

He flushed and left the room in haste, even despite his daughter's protests.

Sarah looked at the girl in the bed.

"When did the pains start?" she asked. Prudence turned her head away.

Sarah sighed.

"If you keep silent, I cannot help you."

Prudence glared at her.

Sarah waited.

"Yesterday... oh!" Prudence doubled over in sudden pain and then cried out as she saw the blood on her nightgown and the bed. "What ails me?" she cried.

"Only what ails all women," Sarah said calmly, rifling in her basket. "You have begun your monthly courses. If you eat well, they will come each month." She looked up. "Do you have a maid?"

Prudence nodded, sobbing.

Sarah called for the maid and when she arrived, she asked her to set water to boil and to find some clouts.

"And bring me a hot brick wrapped in flannel, too. Make haste!"

She shredded some betony and sage and after a moment's thought, added some yarrow leaves. The maid returned with the brick, wrapped as directed in flannel.

"Put this on your belly. I will make you some tea which should ease your pain," Sarah said, before hurrying downstairs. Prudence groaned but hugged the brick. She looked slightly less drawn when Sarah returned with the pewter mug.

"Drink this, it will help," she said. Prudence wrinkled her nose and hesitated. Sarah put her head on one side and regarded her.

"Shall I drink before you?" Sarah asked, sipping the brew. She had sweetened it with honey, and it was quite palatable as her potions went. She held out the mug and Prudence took it. She drank and made a face.

"How long will I feel like this?" she demanded. Sarah's eyebrows rose at her tone.

"I do not know, Mistress Prudence. All girls are different. You may never notice the courses again after this. Or you may suffer like this whenever they arrive," she replied.

"Can you not cure me?"

"What is there to cure? This is part of becoming a woman. The bleeding will be with you until you are with child." Prudence was silent, scowling. Sarah turned away and gathered her cloak and basket.

"Where are you going?"

"You have taken some tea. If you drink it all the pain in your belly will ease. I am no longer needed," Sarah said. "Change the clouts when you will. Loop them into your belt to hold them against you."

Prudence said nothing and Sarah, noting that there was no thanks from the girl, clamped down her own temper and left the room.

The parson was leaning against the mantel, staring into the fire. His hands and his visage had a remote beauty. He looked up.

"How does she?"

"If she drinks all the tea I gave to her, she will sleep and her pain will go, sir. It is as I thought and naught is seriously amiss." Sarah threw the cloak around her shoulders and paused as he straightened and moved towards her. He looked awkward, a pulse visible under his eye. She stood still, suddenly breathless. His green eyes searched her face.

"A young girl needs her mother," he said.

"Her maid will help, I'm sure."

He nodded. "I thank you. Will… will you not share some wine with me?" he gestured towards the chairs by the fire. She hesitated, greatly tempted, seeing the flames light up the hard planes of his face. She wondered if her feelings were writ large in her eyes, as he poured her a small goblet of ruby liquid. She tipped the cloak from her shoulders as she perched on one of the chairs by the fire.

She sipped carefully, for wine was not a drink that had passed her lips, and he observed her. He spoke gently about his previous living, how Prudence had been a sickly baby, how his wife had died from the fever. Carefully, she told him she was mourning her mother and father, and a kind of understanding passed between them. As it struck warmth into her heart, she came to her senses. She put the goblet on the hearth and gathered her cloak around her, while he offered more wine.

With a huge effort, she shook her head. It could not be, she reminded herself.

"No, sir, my supper awaits me," she said as lightly as she could. "But thank you," she added as an afterthought. A smile flitted across his face, softening his severe expression. He bowed his head.

She returned to her cottage. His face haunted her dreams all night.

CHAPTER SIX
STACIE

The level of activity from Ellie perplexed me. She had been in the kitchen all day. She strode purposefully around the house, walking through the cat and the governess who melted into the walls in response. I'd done my bit; tidied and flicked a duster around, picked flowers for the hall and living room and put out the best cutlery. I was too clumsy to touch the wine glasses, so I escaped back to the garden.

The overcast weather made the bright colours of the garden look sickly and I changed my mind almost immediately and sent a text to Seb, pleading with him to come for a walk.

I'd stared into space for half an hour or more when his response arrived, arranging to meet me at the edge of the woodland park in twenty minutes.

"God bless you, Seb!" I muttered and grabbed my denim jacket and made for the door.

"Where are you going?" asked Ellie from the kitchen door.

"Off out with Seb, why? Do you want anything from the supermarket?"

"No, but please don't be late. We have guests. It would be rude."

"Chill, sis. I won't be more than an hour, ninety minutes tops."

She shook her head, despairing, and returned to the kitchen.

I snatched the last space at the nature reserve, smiling sweetly at the man in the Volvo who glared at me as I deftly parked. Seb leisurely unfolded his long body from his car and ambled to meet me. He had two cappuccinos with him. I grinned guiltily. In my rush to leave the house, I'd forgotten any cash.

I kissed him on both cheeks.

"You're a star, Seb," I said, as he handed over the coffee. He grinned, his perfect teeth reminding me I ought to make an appointment to see the dentist soon.

"Why the escape plan?" Seb asked as we strolled down the footpath away from the car park.

"Oh, we're having some mega-professor to dinner and Ellie's doing her cordon bleu thing. I'm starting to feel I'm making the place untidy."

He laughed, well aware of my very basic cookery skills. A group of middle-aged women with dogs gave him the once over. His hair needed brushing, as usual.

"I have a nasty feeling that we might provide the good professor with bed and board for the summer while he finds somewhere else to live," I sighed, sipping my coffee and feeling a sense of peace among the green paths and dappled light. "I have an equally nasty feeling that Ellie fancies him and the idea of watching her seduce him makes me feel ill."

"I've already provided you with the perfect escape," he said, cocking an eyebrow. I laughed.

"Brisbane? It's a bit extreme, isn't it?"

"Sweet pea, all you need to do is say the word. As for money, if you're short, you can always pay me back in instalments." His grey eyes fixed on me rather intently, despite his smile. He stopped walking. I stopped too.

"Seb, it would take me ages to pay you back!"

"I know where you live. I quite fancy the idea of having you indebted to me."

"At your mercy?"

"Exactly. I could twiddle my moustache and take to wearing a cape."

I shook my head, smiling. To my surprise, he took my hand as we came to a stile and he helped me over. I got over without spilling my coffee.

"Stacie, playing host to a stuffy professor sounds like a dreadful way to spend your summer," he said earnestly. "Please, think about it? And you'll be doing me a favour, coming with me. I haven't seen my brother for two years and I could do with someone to deflect my brother's attention and help us over the initial bumps."

"And make excuses for you when you tell inappropriate jokes about Aussies?"

"See? You're already on my wavelength. I'm beginning to think that I couldn't possibly go without you." His hand was still holding mine, and it felt smooth and firm. "Think about it? Promise me you will."

I was quiet for a moment.

"Let me have an estimate. And then we can discuss it," I said, and he beamed at me.

Our discussion moved to more general things, how my head was, Jo's latest conquest, and a planned trip to the theatre.

The park soothed me, and the leaves glimmered in the hot sun. We wandered rather aimlessly, comfortable together. Glimpsing my watch, I was shocked at the time.

"Shit, I'll be late if I'm not careful. I'd better get off. Oops!" I said, swinging round and almost falling over my feet. Seb sighed and caught hold of my shoulders and held me steady for a moment.

"Before you go rushing off to the führer, remember how awful this summer might be, and how easy it would be just to come away with me."

I searched his face – for once, without its usual mockery. I nodded.

"I will."

To my surprise, his kiss fell on my mouth. I blinked and my heart did a somersault. He loped easily to his car while I scuttled to mine. He waved at me and then pulled smoothly out of the car park.

***

The smell from the kitchen was delicious, I thought as I let myself through the door. I could hear music playing and recognised it as the Waltz of the Hours from *Copélia*; Ellie, re-living dancing dreams from her teens, it seemed. The ginger cat sat on the stairs and considered me. I threw down my denim jacket.

"Hi, I'm back. Is everything okay?"

"Yes, everything is under control," said Ellie behind me, and I swung around. She wore her dressing gown, her hair in a towel.

"Right."

"Perhaps you could shower? Change?" Ellie looked me up and down rather doubtfully. I narrowed my eyes and gave in to the urge to be awkward.

"Actually, I need to do more in the garden."

She frowned, and I smiled before turning to climb the stairs to my room.

The ginger cat materialised on the windowsill as I was changing into my gardening scruffs. It washed, deliberately and slowly.

"I'm sorry, I'm not ready to primp yet!" I muttered under my breath, pulling on my shorts. I paused, feeling the waistband slightly looser than it had been. I then spent five minutes peering at myself in the mirror as I tried to work out where else I had lost weight. Finally, I pulled on an ancient Kings of Leon tee shirt and made my way to the garden shed. I could hear the music through the kitchen window and wondered idly if Ellie still had her ballet shoes.

The summerhouse gleamed in the overcast light, and I reminded myself that if I did nothing else this holiday, I must clear out the cobwebs and the remains of my potting-up. I pulled out a hoe and turned to see Ellie standing on the path with her hands on her hips, her hair still wet.

"I thought you were joking!" she said. "You're not *really* going to fart about in the garden, are you?"

"For God's sake, get a grip. It's barely five o'clock! I've got plenty of time to do some work and then get cleaned up."

She snorted.

"And sit at the table with bloody dirt under your nails? This is an important academic!"

I quietly lost my temper. "Important to you, maybe," I said, turning to pull out a trug. "I don't give a toss who he is."

"You're just doing this to be a pain," she said, her face astonished. "This is *so* childish, I can hardly believe it!"

Ellie swung away and marched back into the house. I breathed deeply, catching sight of the boy in the rose bushes.

I set to the hoeing with a vengeance.

"Stacie!" called Dad sometime later. I turned around, expecting an argument, but found my father there with a cup of coffee. "I thought you could do with a drink; it's awfully hot out here."

I clamped my teeth down on the comment I'd been going to make and nodded. A couple of seconds later, I managed a smile and thanked him. I drank the coffee thirstily.

"About ready to come in?" he said diffidently, and I smiled; a real one this time.

"Been sent to hustle me into the shower?" He nodded, twinkling.

"Before Ellie has a hissy fit."

I glanced at my watch. Six fifteen. I noticed he was wearing a new shirt, the creases still in the body, and one of his better pairs of cotton trousers.

THE VISITOR

"Okay, but I'm not wearing the tiara," I said, and he grinned.

"Fair enough," he said.

The shower felt wonderful, hot and sticky as I was. The overcast weather had turned even more threatening, and the air felt greasy with thunder. I threw a loose cotton shirt over my underwear and added palazzo pants. Sandals with something glittery on them, and I was dressed. The mirror told me I looked fine. The cat caught my eye in the reflection, and I sighed. I decided I would do. I heard the doorbell. The cat blinked, flicked its tail, and stalking off, slowly disappeared.

"Thanks for the vote of confidence," I said under my breath. It was almost seven.

He was certainly good looking, even with the brutal haircut, I thought, as I watched him arrive from the top of the stairs. The bannister dug into my belly as I craned over.

So blond, I wondered if his hair colour had come out of a bottle; his face, even from this distance and at this angle, looked striking. He was wearing monochrome clothes, a white tee shirt, black chinos, and a dark grey jacket. His face was handsome and serious.

"I'm delighted to be here," I heard him say in a resonating American voice. He glanced upward, as though aware of me, and I ducked out of sight. Everyone moved out of the hall and, feeling foolish for skulking upstairs, I went down.

They were in the garden.

"Actually, my daughter Eustacia does most of the work. She has very green fingers," Mother was saying. "She should be down soon. Oh, there you are. Nathaniel was just admiring the garden."

"Please, call me Nate."

I nodded. His eyes slid over me, and he nodded in return,

holding out his hand. His fingers were strong, the palms smooth and cool, even in the muggy heat.

"A typical English country garden," he added.

With typical English spirits and apparitions, I thought and just smiled. Although the boy in the lace collar was absent.

We sat on the assorted chairs and cushions and drank; gin and tonics for my family, sparkling water for our guest. Dad asked how he was settling into the English university system; fine, Nate said, although the administration was a nightmare. He was busy preparing notes for his next book, he added.

As they talked, I had time to study him. His face seemed drawn with straight lines: a strong aquiline nose, a square jawline underneath hazel eyes. His body was taut, almost military. I wondered if Hollywood was missing its Captain America.

I could also study Ellie, studying Nathaniel. She drank him in, smiling and laughing gently at anything remotely amusing. It was disturbing. I got to my feet, knocking over my glass and spilling ice and cucumber on the lawn.

"Shit! Sorry, I didn't see that there."

Mother sighed and rose gracefully to her feet and suggested Nathaniel – sorry, *Nate* – and Dad stay in the garden, while Ellie and I got dinner on the table.

"You're not letting me loose with *crockery*, are you, Mother?" I asked, and a smile flashed across Nate's face, transforming it. Ellie nudged me.

"Close your mouth," she said in a low voice.

My jaw snapped shut, and I followed them into the house.

※

Ellie had pulled out all the stops with scallops, tender stem broccoli and plaice in some winey sauce. I barely stopped myself wiping my finger around my plate.

Nate had eaten everything in front of him and, little by little, encouraged by my mother's spectacular social skills, he relaxed. He talked about his work and despite knowing little about twentieth-century literature, his passion impressed me. But something niggled at me about him. I wondered if it was his accent that grated on me, unfamiliar to my ears.

"T S Eliot and politics," said Dad thoughtfully, twisting the stem of his wineglass in his fingers. "And you say the publisher's already signed up?"

"Yeah. Although I'd be happy to self-publish if I had to and if I thought the finished product was good enough. I don't write for popularity."

"How fortunate you are," Dad murmured. I knew the struggles he'd had trying to get a new book deal and I sent him a sympathetic glance.

Mother began clearing the table.

"How's the house hunting going?" asked Ellie and for a moment, I thought she was asking me.

Nate shrugged.

"I've not made much headway, I'm afraid. The market is so crowded and so expensive, I wasn't really expecting this amount of hassle. I'm seeing another place tomorrow, but I took a cab and did a drive past and I'm already regretting making the appointment – it's a dump."

"You could do with someone who knows the area," said Mother. "Someone to tell you the places to avoid."

"Well, that sure would save a lot of time."

"We're happy to help, if you need some input," said Ellie, looking round the table. Dad and Mother smiled.

"That's real kind of you," Nate said, a glimmer of a smile on his face. His eyes rested on me and without realising it, I was shaking my head. "I don't want to impose, though."

"Stacie's going to be *terribly* busy preparing for her next term, but I'll be around if you want some thoughts on the best areas around here."

I felt Nate's gaze still on me, so I refrained from rolling my eyes at Ellie's gushing comment.

"I appreciate your offer, thank you," he said with a small

smile. He turned to me. "What do you do, Stacie, that's keeping you so busy? Ellie mentioned a term. Are you a teacher?"

"Oh, she's—"

"Perfectly capable of answering for herself," I interrupted Ellie, as my parents stared, surprised. "I'm a teaching assistant about to begin teacher training. I'm starting a new job in September."

"Do you enjoy it?" he asked. My mother shifted in her seat, anxious about the discussion of how I earned my living – my currently *tiny* living. Nate wasn't reading the vibes, I thought. It could be worse. I could be a dominatrix. I'd certainly earn more.

"I love everything about it – the kids, the work in class, the prep that's taking up all my time." I stared pointedly at Ellie. "I wouldn't do it if I didn't enjoy it."

As the conversation continued, I kept quiet. While Nate talked freely about his academic work, he was silent about anything personal. We learned nothing about his family or his early life. I glanced at his hand. No wedding ring.

To my horror, when I raised my eyes, I met his cool gaze. He curled his fingers and clasped his hands on the table. I felt myself flush.

"Coffee anyone?" I said when there was a pause.

"Perhaps you could put on a pot," said Dad. I nodded and escaped to the kitchen.

Nate left soon after coffee, pleading additional reading. He shook hands with Dad and kissed Mother and Ellie on the cheek. I thrust out my hand and his eyes locked with mine before he caught it in a firm grip. He didn't look back as he got into the cab.

"Well! What a charming man," said Mother as she closed the front door. "I think it would be a pleasure to have him over the summer, don't you, Henry?"

I stiffened.

"As we won't be here for much of it, I think it's irrelevant what we think," said Dad. He turned to me. "You were the one most concerned about having him in the house, Stacie. How do you feel now?"

I hesitated. Not good, I thought. I don't feel good about it at all, but for no reason I can identify.

"He's pleasant enough, sure, but he's still a stranger. I know nothing about him I couldn't get from an academic biography," I said finally. Mother frowned, shaking her head.

"But that won't matter, you'll barely see him," she said. "Really, Eustacia, I have no idea what's got into you."

"I *might* barely see him, but he'll still be *living* here!"

"I think he'll be a perfect guest; he's having such a bad time finding somewhere to live. I imagine he'll be good as gold," said Ellie.

"What? Like a toddler?" I said, barely able to believe my ears. Ellie went a little pink and tossed her head.

"I think you're being over-sensitive, Stacie," said Dad, patting my shoulder. "He's a nice chap, and I'd like to help him settle into his new role and get on with his new book, which will help the department no end."

More like you're angling for an introduction to his publisher, I thought, unexpectedly acid.

"Really, Eustacia, I do think you're being silly," Mother said. "He's got an impeccable academic reputation and I can't see how you could possibly object. I'm sorry you're uncomfortable, but in the guest suite, he won't even have to share a bathroom with the rest of the house. And if he wants to, he could work in the library, which you don't use, anyway."

"I'm not sure why you even asked if you're not going to take my views into consideration." I shrugged, walking away. Mother tutted.

I climbed the stairs and shut my bedroom door, seething. I picked up a book, spent five minutes looking at a page and not seeing anything, and eventually threw it aside.

Ten minutes later, there was a knock at the door and Dad poked his head in.

"Stacie, we've invited Nathaniel to stay while he finds a

house and he's accepted. Can you please make an effort to accept too? I'd hate for him to feel awkward."

"But it doesn't matter if *I* feel awkward?"

"I've rarely seen you like this, Stacie."

"Like what? Less *biddable*?"

Dad shook his head and sighed. He hated confrontation and, because I loved him, I forced a smile. I couldn't put into words what was wrong, but I knew something was off.

"Look, I'll do my best. But it's under protest, okay? This job means a lot to me and I don't want any distractions."

"How about I offer *my* office?"

"It'll help. Thanks."

He patted my hand and left.

CHAPTER SEVEN
SARAH

Sarah sighed as she stripped the dried leaves from the branches of bay. She had been an outcast before in the village and this seemed to be one of those times. Dusting off her hands, she rose and stirred the pot over the fire.

Dorothy bustled in with some wet laundry.

"You need to go out, mistress."

"I am busy with this."

"A lie, mistress. You know as well as I how the sunshine calls to you."

Sarah flicked her a glance.

"I never lie, Dorothy." The servant made a face and sniffed.

Sarah pressed her lips together. She did, in truth, long to get out of the house and into the woods, but she was uneasy for a reason she couldn't define.

"I need mushrooms, mistress. Your eyes are sharper than mine but if you will not venture outside, I needs must collect my own."

Sarah gave a snort.

"You would poison us both!"

"Then go. You should visit Abigail too. It's been a while since you went to supper."

Sarah knew. But with the sentiment of the village finely balanced, Sarah kept to herself. Although few would argue with Thomas, Abigail was a lively soul likely to talk herself into all kinds of trouble. Dorothy flung open the door, and the sunshine poured into the room. It hit Sarah's face, and she narrowed her eyes.

The late May afternoon was glorious; the washing Dorothy was hanging on the hedges would soon be dry. Sarah hesitated and then reached for her basket.

"I will not be long, but I will call on Abigail," she called. Dorothy said nothing but snorted in satisfaction.

Abigail beamed at her as Sarah stood in the door.

"I was afraid something ailed you!" she cried. "Welcome! We have Mistress Lawrence and Mistress Watson here! We were speaking of our parson and his plans for the school – surely a blessing for our village!"

Sarah tensed, testing the atmosphere, and then relaxed as the two women nodded. Not overly friendly, but not hostile. For the moment.

A wail came from the toddler by the hearth.

"What is it, sweeting?" crooned Abigail, swooping to pick up Rebecca, who wailed all the louder.

"Another tooth by the sound of it," said Mistress Lawrence, smiling at the red-faced Rebecca.

Sarah took in the swollen cheeks and the damp curls around the baby's forehead and frowned. She placed her basketful of mushrooms on the table and put her hand on Rebecca's hot forehead. Abigail caught her expression.

"Is aught amiss?"

"Could I hold her?"

Abigail put the toddler into Sarah's arms without a pause. The two other women who had been watching fell still.

Sarah pressed her fingertips against the breast of the squirming child, and the heartbeat was fast and frantic. She kept her voice calm and low with an effort.

"Has she eaten?"

"No, she has been off her food," said Abigail.

"When did she last feed?"

"Yesterday morning. I thought it strange but put it down to her teething."

Sarah sat on a stool and looked closely at Rebecca.

"She has a fever; that is the reason her cheeks are red and her face is hot. But it is not because she is teething…" Sarah was talking almost to herself.

"Lord save us!" said Mistress Lawrence and rose from her seat. "I'll take my leave. You will be busy with the little one."

Sarah barely noticed as the two women left Abigail's house with haste, concentrating as she was on Rebecca.

"I must fetch my herbs," she said, but Abigail, now pale and looking anxious, waved her to stay seated.

"I'll go. You stay with Rebecca."

"Tell Dorothy I need willow bark."

Abigail nodded and whirled out of the door. Sarah went to place the child in her crib, unlacing the dress to bare her heated skin. The door slammed shut and with her dearest friend gone, Sarah bit her lip. Little Rebecca had been a while coming for Thomas and Abigail. Although all children were precious, Rebecca was even more so to her parents.

She set a kettle to boil and dipped a cloth in the cold water that stood at the side of the hearth. As she bathed her, the child seemed to grow a little more comfortable, and the cries subsided a little. Sarah continued to dip the cloth, wring it out, and press the linen against the heated skin, now mottled and angry.

About a quarter of an hour later, the door flew open, and Thomas stood there.

"What ails her?"

"Shh! I'm trying to lower her fever."

"She has a fever?" Thomas said in a quieter voice.

"Yes. Abigail has gone for my herbs and will return anon."

Thomas strode over to the crib and frowned.

"Smile, Thomas, or you will frighten your daughter," Sarah advised, wringing out the cloth for the twentieth time. The face Thomas made was almost more frightening than his frowns and Sarah pushed him away, smiling with an effort.

"Go back to your forge. Here is Abigail with my basket, and you will be in the way."

Abigail was standing in the room, panting, her face rosy with running.

"Dorothy told me to tell you that the parson seeks you," she said, breathing hard and handing over the basket of herbs. Sarah was silent as her heart jumped, and then Rebecca gave a little cry and dragged her attention back. She shrugged.

"I am busy. I have boiled water and will make a weak tea to take the fever down. Then we need to watch her."

Abigail twisted her hands together.

"Will she be well?"

"I hope so. I have never treated fever in one so young before."

"And you lost your parents from fever," said Thomas unhelpfully. Abigail paled. Sarah took a deep breath.

"I was too late to treat them. I am here now for Rebecca."

"Pray God it be soon enough!" said Abigail, her eyes filling with tears.

"Amen to that," came the voice of Parson Dillington from the door. Sarah spun round. His pale hair gleamed white in the sunshine. "Your servant told me to find you here. But your child is sick?" he said, turning to Abigail.

Abigail curtsied.

"Aye, sir, she has a fever."

"Then we must pray for her." He bowed his head, and Abigail and Thomas did the same.

Sarah frowned as the kettle steamed on the fire. Time was passing. The parson raised his blond brows.

"May I make tea for her? I have willow bark which should bring down her fever."

The parson looked at her and pursed his lips, but after what seemed an endless pause, he nodded. Sarah leapt into action, took the kettle off the flame and took a pewter pot. The tea took only moments to make, and she set it on the table.

Then, mindful of the green eyes of the parson, she took a deep breath and bent her head.

"It should take a few moments to steep," she said.

"And so we can continue?" said the parson, his lips curling. Sarah flushed but folded her lips together. The parson prayed again and making the responses with Thomas and Abigail, Sarah kept her eyes fixed to the floor. After a little while, Rebecca started to cry again.

"You should administer your potion," said the parson, and Sarah smiled at him in gratitude. She saw the muscle tick under his eye and she hastened to the baby, breathless.

There was a knock at the door and Thomas answered it. Mistress Whyte's stout frame filled the door.

"What! Are you content to let this woman tend your child?" she said to Abigail, pointing at Sarah. Sarah was still a moment and then bent to pick up Rebecca, who was whimpering. With the baby in her arms, she turned to Abigail.

"Are you content, Abigail?"

Her best friend frowned. "I have known you these ten years and I know your skills. Continue."

Sarah needed no more bidding and, blowing on the tea to take the heat from it, spooned it into Rebecca's mouth.

Mistress Whyte gasped and turned to the parson.

"Not all skills are God given, Parson Dillington, mark my words."

The parson regarded her calmly.

"Aye, but I am also here, am I not? We have been praying

for the child this past quarter hour. But perhaps you do not consider me sufficient to guard against the Devil?"

Mistress Whyte cast a fulminating glare at the parson.

"Can I help you, mistress?" Thomas asked, taking charge. "Did you come to offer us aid?"

I doubt it, thought Sarah, holding Rebecca as she squirmed, the tea not quite to her taste.

"Do you have honey?" she said to Abigail in a low voice. "That might make it more palatable."

Abigail nodded, and with the increased bustle, Mistress Whyte was forgotten. Thomas firmly shepherded her to the door.

"Your charity in visiting does you credit," soothed the parson in his glorious voice as the matron stalked away. Sarah looked up to see an odd gleam in his eye and thought she heard irony in his tone. A glow ran through her. Mistress Whyte, more red than normal, finally left. Thomas sighed.

"Parson, may I offer you ale?" he said.

Parson Dillington shook his head.

"I am due elsewhere. Mistress Bartlett, may I speak with you when you have settled the child?"

Sarah's breath caught in her chest, and goosebumps rose on the skin of her arms.

"Is aught amiss?" she said, echoing Abigail's words from an hour before. Parson Dillington shook his head.

"No, mistress. But among many topics, I wanted to pass on thanks for your support to my daughter."

Caught unawares, Sarah smiled, thinking that Prudence must have hated the idea of gratitude. Again, the parson's muscle twitched.

"You are welcome, sir. It was naught."

The parson looked at her steadily and then turned to Thomas.

"I pray for your daughter a speedy recovery. Please let me know how she does. And Mistress Bartlett, I look forward to speaking with you anon."

THE VISITOR

After another two hours, Rebecca finally slept, her cheeks less red and her brow cooler. Sarah stretched her back and packed her basket.

"Mistress Whyte means you ill," commented Thomas out of Abigail's hearing.

Sarah nodded.

"I will take heed around her."

"Perhaps you should wed?"

Sarah rolled her eyes.

"Aye, you look so, but you are alone, and women alone are easy targets for gossip-mongers and those with acid tongues."

Sarah put the last bundle of herbs in her basket.

"I know. I will take more care."

"Mayhap the parson will take a shine to you." Thomas smiled. "He looks on you most intently."

Sarah flushed.

"Nay! He will have no joy of me!" she said before she could stop herself. Abigail raised her head.

"What's this?"

"'Tis naught, just Thomas teasing me," Sarah said, forcing a smile. She glanced out of the tiny window, mourning the loss of the sunlight which had dimmed hours ago.

"Remember, the parson wished to see you," Abigail said, staring at Rebecca as though the babe might disappear. Thomas caught Sarah's eye. She felt her cheeks blush, and then made her farewells, promising to return in the morning.

"But fetch me if the fever returns, no matter the time, and give her the tea every four hours."

She made her way slowly back to her cottage, watching the sun dip over the hill and the bats swoop through the trees. She hesitated at the fork in the road which would take her to the parson's house. A choice. She was tired. But she stood still in the road and then tensed.

"Were you coming to visit me?" said the deep voice of

Parson Dillington from the shadows. Sarah closed her eyes briefly and then turned to greet him.

"Yes, sir."

"How does the child?"

"Better, sir, I thank you. I hope the fever broke before I left, but the night may be long for her mother."

His pale hair gleamed in the fading light as he walked towards her. Sarah shivered, although the evening was mild, the warmth of the day still lingering. He loomed over her.

"Did you wish to speak to me?" she said, taking a step backwards. His mouth twisted.

"Will the child live?" he said, ignoring her question.

"I hope so."

"You were able to reach her early enough?"

She nodded.

"You have some skill, Mistress Bartlett."

There was a silence as Sarah searched for something safe to say. In the end, she nodded.

"I know my herbs. Anyone could do what I do, had they my knowledge and that which my mother passed to me."

His green eyes locked on to her face.

"Indeed. You are modest." He smiled slightly.

Sarah looked at the ground. He continued to look at her and her cheeks flamed. She moved her basket from one hand to the other.

"Allow me," he said, and to her surprise, took it from her. "I will walk you to your door."

"There's no need, sir!"

"No need, perhaps, but my wish."

They walked in silence. Sarah tried to make her stride longer to cover the distance more quickly, without appearing to hurry.

After what seemed like hours, they stood at the door to the cottage. She held out her hand for the basket. Their fingers brushed as she took it, and both of them jumped at the touch. She drew a deep breath.

"*Did* you wish to speak to me, sir?" she asked again as the scent of herbs drifted to her nose.

He smiled, the tic under his eye noticeable by the candle-light from the window.

"I did. And I have. Goodnight, mistress. I will see you at church 'ere long, I hope?"

Sarah's heart fluttered.

"Yes, sir." She curtsied. When she raised her head, he was staring at her face. She froze and whispered under her breath.

Parson Dillington made to lift his hand to her cheek, but at that moment, the bat swept down from the gathering gloom towards the cottage and he ducked, exclaiming. Sarah swiftly grasped the handle of the door and opened it. She heard Dorothy call out indoors.

"Take care, sir!" she said. The parson straightened, a frown on his face as he recovered his balance. "The bats are a pest. I should take a stick for the walk home."

She smiled and closed the door. But soon the smile dropped from her face and the trouble in her eyes never left them all night.

CHAPTER EIGHT
STACIE

I was up early, unsettled and cross. I'd settled in the garden under the sunshade with my books and some paperwork, but after an hour reading the same page, I gave it up in disgust.

Changed into my gardening scruffs five minutes later, I headed down to the summerhouse, determined to give it the cleaning of its life. It was therapeutic. I threw out old plastic pots, dead plants, half-filled bags of compost. I thumped the cushions of the old garden furniture and choked on dust and those irritating little whiteflies.

The governess flitted in and then out and seemed to approve of my housekeeping efforts, but other than that I was alone for at least two hours, sweeping, tidying and collecting rubbish. The windows were next.

I took out my phone. Seb had texted me.
You'll owe me £550 – all in.

I frowned. International travel was more Ellie's area, but even I knew that airfares alone to Australia cost more than that.

I texted back. *Are you planning on hijacking the plane?*

As I made my way back to the house, Ellie's voice floated

through the patio doors, high and a little unnatural. Our guest for the summer had arrived. I looked down at my grubby tee shirt and shorts and decided the social niceties could go hang.

Silence fell as I entered the kitchen with a bucket and cloth. I could see Ellie's mouth tighten, but Nate smiled and nodded at me. Once again, the sun was strong today, and the light ran through his short hair, turning it pale gold.

"How are you, Stacie?"

His quiet drawl fell into the silence. I ran water into the bucket.

"Fine, thanks."

"You look busy."

"I'm cleaning windows." I clamped my teeth together, so I didn't apologise for my dirt. The bucket slowly filled, and I hunted under the sink for detergent.

"On a house this size?"

"No, the summerhouse."

"Hence her appearance," added Ellie.

I sniffed and turned off the tap. I sloshed a little water on the kitchen tiles, and I left, ignoring Ellie's protests.

Washing more than six months of grime off the window panes soon turned the water black, but I smiled as the sun shone through the cleaned panes. The wooden floor, now swept and cleared, gleamed softly in the sunlight, and the cushions on the ancient sofa looked less grubby. The summerhouse had been one of Grandfather's favourite places. We had escaped here to play chess and for him to sneak the odd cigarette away from the tight-lipped gaze of my mother.

I would need fresh water otherwise I'd make the windows worse. And I was hungry. After throwing the water on a parched-looking shrub, I made my way back to the house.

I made a sandwich, grabbed a coffee, and sat in the garden to eat. Nate and Ellie were moving endless boxes and furniture into the guest suite, and my mouth twisted. How long was the man going to be living here, for God's sake?

The garden shimmered in the sun on this typical summer's

day, but something – not only Nathaniel Williams moving in – was wrong. I sat, trying to puzzle it out. Finally, shaking the sensation out of my head, I took my plate and mug back to the kitchen.

As I made my way out of the house, carrying the bowl of fresh water, it hit me. No ginger cat. No boy-girl in the rose beds or anywhere else. Apart from that brief appearance in the summerhouse hours ago, no governess. I concentrated on the bowl and tried to soothe the unease that tingled along my veins. My visions had been with me since childhood and to have them disappear – I hadn't realised how alone I would feel. I washed the remaining windows on automatic pilot, clamping down the panic that rose in me.

The house was silent when I came through the back door, and I paused, listening. Nothing. I called my grandmother.

"Hello, Stacie. Is everything all right?"

"Gran, all my spirits have disappeared!"

"Ah, is that what's happened? I guessed there was something. They've just gone?"

I looked around, searching for any of them but the world remained stubbornly normal.

"Just gone."

"Are you coming for a chat?"

"Yes please, let me get the dirt off me."

※

I was stepping out of the shower when I heard a crash.

"What the hell?" I muttered. Wrapping a towel around me, I pulled open the door. To my horror and his obvious embarrassment, Nate was on his haunches outside, picking up a pile of books from the floor.

"Oh!" I said as the heat spread to my cheeks. His eyes traced up my bare legs and along my wet arms and dropped abruptly back to the books.

"I'm real sorry to disturb you," he muttered, while I backed away. "I was carrying too many."

"No problem!" I said brightly. "Just checking everything's okay." I disappeared back into my room, shutting the door firmly behind me.

I pulled on clothes, dried my hair and was heading towards the door in record time when Ellie arrived with more groceries.

"Where are you going? I was hoping you could help us move some boxes," she said, eyeing my car keys.

"Can't. Off to Gran's. She wants a chat." Not a lie, I thought as Ellie protested.

I climbed into the car and drove away as fast as I could.

⁂

"You look flustered. Are you all right?" Gran asked as she closed her front door.

"I'm fine. I think. But it's weird that I feel so alone!"

She nodded. "I'm not surprised. You've been seeing them since you were, what? Twelve?"

"Ten. Remember? I came to you a week before my eleventh birthday, thinking I might be mad."

I stopped. Trying to tell my parents had gone so badly, for twelve months I'd simply kept my mouth shut, and tried to ignore the things that I saw. The wave of relief when I'd told my grandmother had been enormous. Since then, she'd been my rock, my sanity. My tribe.

Gran tutted, patted me on the shoulder and shepherded me into her cosy sitting room. There was a pot of tea, a pot of coffee and a plate of scones waiting by the sofa.

"Yes, I remember now. Your mother put the fear of God into you about your mental state, she's so hypersensitive about it. It still makes me cross."

She sat down and patted the seat next to her, and I sank into the cushions.

"So what's different about today?" she asked, pouring coffee.

"Well, our house guest arrived today."

"Oh?"

"Yes, Nathaniel Williams. Nate to his friends. A new lecturer at the university. He's staying over the summer."

"You're very grumpy about it."

"There's something about him that unnerves me, makes me uncomfortable. He seems nice enough, but... I don't know. It's irrational."

Gran smiled.

"Are you so rational, then? Is seeing ghosts particularly rational? It may be just your response to a stranger."

"Maybe. It doesn't help that I reckon Ellie fancies him."

"*Eleanor?*"

I grinned at her astonishment, drawn off topic for a moment. "Quite. At last, someone she might love more than herself! So, not only a stranger in my space but a new infatuation for my sister. Wonderful."

"*That's* why you're so grumpy!" Gran laughed. "You know, your ghosts will be around, but not showing themselves. I shouldn't jump to any conclusions, but look for other things that are different."

I finished my scone, deep in reflection. I was sure that my grumpiness was not about Ellie falling for the American lecturer and disturbing the precarious balance in our house. If the sightings didn't return, it would be strange to be without my ghosts. Not that they were *my* ghosts, they were their own ghosts.

"Perhaps I've grown out of them?" I mused. My grandmother snorted inelegantly.

"Your sight is not a feature of adolescence, Stacie! It's a lifelong gift and part of what makes you incredibly special. Together with your way with children."

I smiled at her. As the non-academic in an academic family, Mother and Dad acknowledged my skills but didn't value them. I'd grown a thick skin over the years, accelerated by being compared to Ellie, but Gran was my rock, my support, my cheerleader. She was looking exasperated again.

"Your mother has a rabid dislike of anything which she can't explain. God alone knows how she ever studied literature. She doesn't seem to realise that there are more things in heaven and earth," she muttered.

"Mmm," I agreed, sinking my teeth into a scone. "But you're right, she's very anxious about people's mental health, but I put that down to some ancient relative that no one talks about. Celine?"

"That's right. My great-great-great-grandmother. Her husband sent her to a lunatic asylum. Raving, he called her, according to my grandmother. She told me how accurate Celine was in her 'raving', the visions she'd had. Celine predicted the Titanic, you know."

I goggled.

"I didn't know *that!*"

"Oh yes. She even had the number of survivors correct. No one believed her, but after it happened, her husband's irritation changed to fear and he had her committed. He forbade the family ever to mention her again, which is why you've heard so little about her."

A cog seemed to slip into place in my head.

"Is that why Mother's so worried? She looked concerned in the hospital. Perhaps she assumed I was another loopy in the family."

Gran sighed and topped up her cup, tapping the tea strainer on the side before putting it back on its holder. She sat back in her seat.

"She's my daughter and I love her, but she can be remarkably narrow-minded. Not to mention that she's intolerant of anything that's not… quite perfect."

No kidding, I thought, reminded of all the damned-by-faint-praise conversations I'd had with her during my life.

"But you need to get rid of the idea that you're 'growing

out' of anything, Stacie," Gran said. "If your spirits have disappeared, it will be for a reason."

"Is there a reason why I don't see any spirits here?" I glanced around my grandmother's comfortable house.

"Perhaps my grandmother, who had her own kind of sight, has something to do with it? After all, this was her house."

This reminded me that the Haywards were, indeed, an interesting family – or at least some of them. I needed to get back to see what would happen next. I cleared the plates, now more convinced I was part of a special tradition in the family, rather than an outlier. A member of Team Witchy.

"I'll call you later, shall I?" I said.

"Not tonight, it's bridge. Tomorrow morning?"

I could hear my father's voice as I opened the front door. I closed the door softly and stood, not knowing what to do, or where to go. Common courtesy required me to make an appearance. I wanted – after appearing in front of our guest in a bath towel – to disappear into my room and not come out again.

Mother took the decision out of my hands when she bustled into the hall.

"Eustacia, are you in for dinner?"

My phone pinged, and looking for a negative answer, I took it out. "One sec."

My mother sighed and continued to the kitchen.

Seb's text appeared on my phone. A brilliant excuse for non-attendance.

Shall we discuss my maths over a steak tonight? I could explain, but it would be an even longer text than normal. Say yes.

I tried not to smile and responded.

"Sorry, Mother, I've got a date with a friend," I called. She came out of the kitchen with a bowl of olives.

"That's unfortunate. I was rather hoping we could all welcome our guest this evening."

"I'm sure Ellie can do my share," I muttered, turning to go up the stairs. "Sorry!"

Her tutting followed me as I ran up the stairs, two at a time.

I skulked upstairs for a while, having another shower, repainting my nails and changing my mind twice about what to wear. At last, I chose a cotton skirt and a gipsy-style top, I left my legs bare, thrusting my feet into sandals.

I looked for the ginger cat and saw no sign. It was often around when I dressed or put on make-up. This evening, my primping was cat-free.

I hesitated when I reached the hall. It would be rude not to say hello.

The conversation paused when I walked into the sitting room. Dad and Mother were sipping their customary G&Ts. Ellie lounged in the armchair, swinging her foot. Nate looked thoughtful as his eyes fell on me. He was wearing a blue shirt, rolled at the sleeves, and it gave a greenish hue to his hazel eyes. As I looked at him, I saw a tinge of red touch his cheeks.

Oh God, the bath towel, I remembered again, and my face grew warm.

"Well, I'm off now," I said rather too loudly. "I hope you have a nice evening. I'll see you later."

"You're not joining us?" said Nate.

I gave a tight smile.

"No, I'm out with an old colleague."

"Ah. The lovely Sebastian," said Ellie.

"Yes indeed," I said. "The lovely Seb. See you later."

I left.

CHAPTER NINE
STACIE

I cursed the bottle of ketchup and grasped the top more firmly. It didn't budge.

"Can I help?" came the American voice behind me, and I swung round, surprised.

"God, you made me jump!"

"Sorry. Can I help?" Nate asked again, holding his hand out. I gave him the bottle. It opened with a quiet pop.

"Thanks."

I took the bottle and carried on making my bacon sandwich. I had heard him at six, moving around the kitchen, opening cupboards and switching on the kettle. Then the front door clicked shut and I presumed he'd gone for a run. I muttered, turned over and reached for another hour's sleep.

He leaned against the wall, fresh from the shower. He didn't seem to wear any kind of cologne; it was just soap I could smell. I cut my sandwich in half with a sharp movement and put it on a plate, turning to go into the dining room. I normally ate breakfast in the kitchen, but I simply wanted to get away from him.

He breathed in as I passed him, and good manners prompted me to speak.

"There's plenty of bacon if you fancy a sandwich."

He shook his head.

"No, I need to get to uni."

Mother swept into the kitchen.

"Do you need a lift? Henry and I will be leaving in ten minutes."

Nate hesitated.

"Thank you. I'll get my stuff together."

I sat down at the dining table and took a healthy bite of my sandwich.

"God, Stacie, are you ever going to start that diet?" Ellie said, plaiting her hair as she walked in. I swallowed my mouthful and ignored her. She looked slender and elegant in her jeans and white shirt. I glanced down at my old tee shirt and denim skirt and shrugged.

Ellie's sniping wasn't the only irritant. None of the spirits I normally saw were around, and I missed them. I stared into the garden, barely noticing the farewells from my mother. Dad paused by the door.

"Are you okay, Stacie? Not unwell? You're very quiet."

I turned my head and smiled at him.

"No, I'm fine. Probably out too late last night with Seb."

He smiled at me and closed the door. I heard the car start and the crunch of gravel as they drove away. The silence of the house swept over me and I let out a sigh of relief.

My mind tiptoed over the past twenty-four hours. The evening with Seb had not been a success. The feeling of being a poor relation had intensified as Seb had talked about the Australian trip and I had disliked it intensely.

"We'll be staying with my brother most of the time; he's got a car we can borrow if we need it. I've found some cheap flights which I'll send over for you to look at. It means we have to fly at unsociable times, so we may not be speaking to one another very much," he said, smiling at me over a glass of wine the size of a goldfish bowl.

I frowned, doing sums in my head.

"Wasn't the plan to stay in Brisbane?"

"No, the Gold Coast isn't far and I thought we could tour even further."

"Where would we stay?"

"I'm sure we'll find somewhere with family."

"Seb, I don't know how many relatives you've got, but will they be willing to put up a complete stranger for weeks at a time?"

"Of course they will! You'll be with me! So all you'll need is a bit of spending money, and I'll sub you if you run out."

I hesitated. Seb sighed at my face.

"You've had a shit time recently, Stacie. You've got a new chapter opening for you with the job and the training, but you deserve this, you know you do."

I looked at him, considering, and trying to ignore my hopeful, misguided heart that wondered for a moment if Seb and I could be a couple.

"I've always been a girl who believes that if something looks too good to be true, it probably is. And this does. I looked up the flights and what you told me was half the cost on the website. And that's without anything else!"

Seb seemed to grit his teeth and picked up his wine glass again.

"What if I told you I wanted your company on holiday? That *as your friend* I considered that you needed a break? And that *as your friend* I could make it happen?"

'Friends'. My heart sank.

"I'd be hugely grateful," I said quietly.

"Then *be* fucking grateful and say yes! Jesus, what a performance. I'm not asking you to sleep with me"—

"I never dreamed you were!" But God, I was so *hoping* that he was!

"No? So what, exactly, is the problem?"

"I don't like to be beholden."

He looked at the ceiling.

"I'm sorry, that's how I feel," I stressed. "You know I'm trying to assert my independence and this goes counter to that, don't you understand?"

Seb carefully put his knife and fork together on his plate.

"Tell you what – why don't you mull it over for a few days?" he said, eventually. I nodded, and our miserable evening limped to a close.

I cradled my cooling coffee and looked at the shimmering sunshine outside, slowly turning the grass brown. We needed some rain soon.

My solitude continued for the next week. No contact from anyone dead or living, outside my home. I heard nothing from Seb.

I prepared lesson plans for my new job, ordered books for the course, but my heart wasn't in it. I found myself in the summerhouse for hours in the afternoon, with an unread book on my lap. Apart from a few words in the morning (never my most talkative time) and some desultory conversation in the evenings when everyone returned, I spoke to no one during the day.

Dad expressed his concern about my withdrawal, but I couldn't help it. Nate wasn't always with us in the evenings. Occasionally he worked late at the university, arriving back at the house to say he'd eaten out, to the obvious dismay of Ellie. He ran most mornings, and I lay in bed listening to his feet pad down the stairs.

On Friday afternoon, Gran arrived at the house and stood frowning at me when I opened the door.

"You look dreadful, Stacie."

"And it's lovely to see you too, Gran," I said, leaning in to kiss her cheek.

"You haven't called me for weeks. What's wrong?"

"Hardly weeks. I was at your place last Thursday. Tea?"

"Please, Earl Grey. And don't quibble. You seemed to disappear and here you are, moping around."

I switched on the kettle and sorted mugs and then changed one mug for a cup and saucer.

"I'm not moping. I'm working."

She snorted. "What's happened?"

"Well, Nate is here, being quietly charming. Ellie looks more besotted every day. Mother and Dad are oblivious."

"Yes, yes, but what about your spirit friends?"

I bit my lip. "Still nothing."

And I've had a row with my best friend. God, I would sound like a teenager. I stayed silent.

She pursed her lips as I made the tea. We sat in the kitchen and I tried to ignore her scrutiny.

"What have you tried?" she asked.

"What do you mean?"

"To find your sight again. Have you left this house at all this week?" I shook my head. She frowned again across her teacup and hmm-ed at me. "That's not like you, Stacie. Well, I'd like to try something," she said. "Will you come to the church with me?"

I stared. And then felt as though someone had put an electric charge through me. "Yes! Of course!"

She smiled at me and finished her tea. Five minutes later, we were climbing into Gran's little sports car.

I grew more nervous the nearer we got to the graveyard. Gran pulled up, and I was opening the door before she'd put on the handbrake. I ran towards the pretty church and unhooked the lychgate. Breathing hard, I walked among the graves and stood still.

The church clock struck four o'clock and my heart sank. All was still, and I drew a deep, unsteady breath.

I glimpsed a long skirt fluttering around a headstone and I could have shouted for joy. The young girl with the cap beamed at me and even waved from outside the church walls. Then I noticed the stern, thin lady with the babe in arms. Then the priest. Then a child in short trousers, and an elderly couple, their arms locked around each other's waists.

I sagged against a solid, craggy headstone and dropped my face into my hands, laughing.

"I take it your visions are still there, then?" Gran's voice interrupted my relief.

I nodded. "It's so bizarre how relieved I am!"

"So why can't you see spirits at home?"

I sobered. I knew the answer. Nate.

"Hmm. It's time I met your visitor," she said.

※

The front door opened as we got out of the car.

"Mother, what *is* that you're driving?" said my mother. "Are you having some kind of late-life crisis?"

Gran smartly clicked the keys to lock it.

"I can't tell you how much of a babe I've become since I bought it," she said sweetly. "I'm fighting them off at bridge." She swept past Mother into the hall. "I thought I'd come for dinner," she continued. "I haven't seen the family for a while."

Mother looked slightly put out and shot me an accusing glance. I shrugged and followed Gran into the house.

Muttering, Mother hunted out another piece of steak from the freezer while Gran sat in the lounge with a gin and tonic. When I returned downstairs, Gran was giving Ellie the third degree.

"But really, Ellie, what are you going to do after all this study? Or are you going to be yet another member of the family never to leave the security blanket of higher education?"

Ellie looked astonished at the attack.

"Well, I wouldn't call doing a PhD an easy option!"

"Really? Have you tried to earn a living?"

Dad came into the room and sniffed the air like a dog.

When he realised there was conflict, he backed out again to find something to do in the kitchen. Distantly, my mother's voice asked what the matter was.

Ellie's face turned a little pink.

"What? Like Stacie? Who can barely afford to pay Dad any rent? Really, some people might be proud of my achievements at university! They should certainly mean I earn more than the pittance Stacie does!"

"Leave me out of it," I said, throwing a cushion at her. "And anyway, I'm going to change that."

"Yes, I agree. You leapt to the assumption that I was comparing you with your sister and nothing could be further from the truth," Gran said. "All I asked was what you would do afterwards, and I didn't receive an answer. Do you know?"

Ellie looked down her nose.

"I may stay on, teaching is a possibility—"

"Oh yeah," I said. "*Lots* of money in teaching, as I can testify, earning as I do my pittance!"

"But I may join the United Nations," Ellie said, flushing pinker. "I'm still considering."

"Hmm. You need some exposure to the real world," Gran said.

"Thank you for your opinion," said Ellie. "I'll bear it in mind."

She flounced out.

"Play nice," I said to Gran. "You'll be banned from the house if you're not careful."

"Well, really!" she huffed. "I know you want a higher salary, Stacie, but at least you *are* making a contribution!"

I was about to answer when Nate walked in. Gran smiled and rose to her feet.

"You must be Nathaniel," she said, holding out her hand. "Stacie mentioned you were staying."

Nate glanced at me, and I sipped my drink.

"Nate, please. I'm lucky to have such generous friends," he said, shaking her hand.

"Yes, aren't you? Not everyone would give a stranger houseroom. You've started at the university already?" she said smoothly. Much as Ellie had done, Nate blinked, but then a smile twitched the corners of his mouth.

"I have, and when my semester finally ends, I'll be house hunting with a vengeance to make sure I don't outstay my welcome, ma'am. Say, is that your sports car outside?"

Momentarily diverted, Gran nodded.

"I'd sure appreciate a spin. I can exchange it for a turn on my motorbike, if you'd like? It's being delivered next week."

She beamed at him.

"How exciting! Yes, I'd like that very much!"

"You have a motorbike?" I said, concerned about the idea of my grandmother on two wheels.

"I signed the papers today. I didn't want to trespass on your parents' hospitality even further than I already have, and it'll be useful when I need to view properties." He turned back to Gran and unleashed the full wattage of his smile on her. It had the usual effect and her eyes widened.

"I'll look forward to it," she said thoughtfully.

Dinner was a mix of suspicion and affability. Suspicion from Ellie and my mother, and affability from Nate.

"How exciting to come to a new place, a new country, even!" said Gran to Nate, as she sipped sparkling water. "Or do you travel around regularly in your career?"

"Not much, ma'am," he said. "I was at Yale for seven years; I came because of this university's reputation."

"Did you grow up in the States?" Gran pursued.

He nodded and then grinned.

"But my dad told me I had English ancestors, so perhaps it was fate that I came here. My forefathers came to the US with the first settlers."

I felt an icy hand pass across my back, and I suppressed a shiver, not knowing why the words made me uneasy.

"And what do your parents think of you being so far away?" Gran asked, smiling back.

His face closed.

"My parents are dead."

My mouth dropped open, and Mother gasped.

"I'm truly sorry to hear that. You're so young!" said Gran, her face softening. "How did it happen?"

"They died in a road traffic accident when I was twenty."

"That's so awful!" Ellie breathed, reaching over to pat his hand. He moved it away.

"It was hard, obviously, but it's a long time ago, almost sixteen years. My mom was an author, and Dad was a historian. They were just driving to dinner when it happened, and they died instantly. It pushed me to do more with my life, recognising it might be so transient."

I looked at him, his hazel eyes like stone. A silence fell around the table and everyone, Dad especially, looked uncomfortable.

"That's a good philosophy. 'Death has a hundred hands and a thousand ways' – isn't that right?" I said, quoting one of the few lines of *Murder in the Cathedral* that I could remember. He looked at me, startled, and then smiled, breaking the tension.

"Absolutely."

"I'll get the pudding," I muttered and scurried off.

When I returned to the table with apple pie, Mother had moved the discussion onto more general topics, and Gran was looking thoughtful.

At the end of the meal, she dangled the car keys at Nate and said, "Well, would you like a spin now? It's still light. You can drive me home if you like."

"How would Nate get back, Catherine?" Dad asked.

"I could get a cab," Nate suggested.

"Or I could follow in the car and bring you back," Ellie said, scrambling to her feet.

"That's settled then," Gran said. "Shall we go?"

As she collected her bag and jacket, Gran held her thumb and little finger to her ear to indicate she would call me. I nodded.

"How was your ride home last night?" I asked.

"The man drives like a maniac," was Gran's grumpy response down the phone, and I grinned. "God alone knows how he'll be on a motorbike."

"What did you think of him?"

"Difficult to say. Charming, guarded. I think he was surprised to have said so much last night. Very intelligent, but not very aware, I would say. Eleanor was practically salivating when she arrived to take him home."

I pushed aside the papers I'd been working on and stared out of my bedroom window.

"Mmm. She's keen, isn't she?"

"Certainly looks like it. How are your visions?"

"Still absent. From here, anyway."

"Shall we give it a little more time to see if they return to the house?"

I sighed.

"Okay. I'll call if anything changes. I'll see you on Sunday as usual?"

"Yes, that would be lovely."

I spent the next fifteen minutes gazing blindly into the garden.

A week after this, Nate went away to Paris for a conference. The house seemed blissfully quiet, and Ellie moped about.

Seb hadn't called, nor had he responded to a cheery text I sent him about the soap opera we both watched. I missed him, and I composed a text to tell him just that and then deleted it. The more I thought about the holiday to Australia, the more tempted I felt. And the days of the summer break were ticking away.

Two days into Nate's absence, I awoke to see the ginger cat at the end of the bed. It stared at me.

"Well, now," I said. "Where did you get to?"

It simply flicked its tail and dwindled into the duvet cover. I got up and flung open the curtains, searching the garden. The boy in the lace collar was in the rose garden and I did a little dance. I reached for the phone and texted my grandmother.

Spirits returned! Cat and child in rose garden accounted for!

I headed for the shower, feeling cheered.

I bounced downstairs and Ellie glowered at me from the kitchen table.

"God, what's got into you? You're so noisy."

I said nothing, but smiled, got my coffee and wandered around the house, looking for the governess. I caught sight of her in the hall and nearly fist-pumped the air.

My phone buzzed and a message from Gran said: *What's changed?*

Nate away? I texted back.

I think we need to know a little more about Nate, texted Gran.

I'll see what I can find out when he gets back, I sent back.

CHAPTER TEN
SARAH

Sarah stiffened like a frightened deer as she stepped into church. Her timing had been perfect, she thought, just in time to take her seat unnoticed before Parson Dillington began the service. But no, she was wrong. Eyes turned to her. She could almost smell the change. Dorothy, behind, almost walked into her.

"Mistress! You need to take your seat!" she muttered, hustling Sarah into a corner of the church. Sarah dipped her head and sat down with as little noise as possible.

The parson strode to the front, and it seemed to her that his eyes sought her out. As he caught sight of her, he nodded; a tiny movement, but she saw it and her heart soared before it sank to the floor.

"Remember!" she thought savagely.

The service began, the parson's velvet voice dipping and swooping through the Litany.

"Spare us, good Lord," murmured the congregation.

"From all evil and mischief, from sin, from the crafts and assaults of the Devil, from thy wrath, and from everlasting damnation," said Parson Dillington. Sarah kept her eyes down but could almost sense the sideways stares from others in the congregation pricking her flesh.

"Good Lord, deliver us!" Was that Sarah's imagination, or did the voices seem louder? She almost missed the next response, as her heart beat faster.

"From fornication, and all other deadly sin and from all the deceits of the world, the flesh and the Devil!"

The tone of the parson's words seemed to pierce her ears and unwisely, she looked up. His cheeks were faintly flushed, and his eyes locked on her face. The heat burnt her own cheeks and she glanced down, clutching her Bible. Someone nudged their neighbour and her cheeks burnt even hotter.

The service continued.

Communion was the worst torture. She was the focus of all eyes as she walked to the altar. Her skin felt flayed, the air pressed down on her. She gripped the rail until her knuckles were white, praying not for the forgiveness of her sins, but that she wouldn't faint. The murmured words of blessing floated to her and the wafer and wine slipped down her throat unnoticed, but the tips of his fingers touched her lips. His breath hissed through his teeth. She swallowed, bent her head and forced her knees to lock as she stood up to walk what seemed like miles to her seat.

She caught sight of Abigail and Thomas, with a happy, healthy Rebecca. She smiled, glad of the friendly faces. While Abigail grinned, and waved Rebecca's plump arm in greeting, Thomas looked grave. Sarah knew what that meant. Thomas too – more experienced in the politics of the village – had noticed the chill when Sarah entered the church. In his forge, he may have heard the gossip from Mistress Whyte and her friends. Thomas had been right on one thing; as a single woman, she was unprotected.

She walked stiffly back to her place at the back of the church. Dorothy joined her a few moments later, her lips tight.

"Ill-favoured shrew!" Dorothy muttered of someone, possibly Mistress Whyte. Sarah hushed her and endured the rest of the service. However, to the surprise of the whole church, after the banns, there was an announcement.

"Brethren, the festival of St John approaches, and we need to give thanks to the saint who baptised our Lord Jesus," said Parson Dillington. "The ceremony of the Damask Rose will proceed as tradition requires." He nodded at the alehouse keeper, who would present the town councillor with a rose and his quit rent on the saint's day. The parson continued.

"The love of God prompts us to share what we have. I am happy to share what I have with my parishioners. Thus, after the ceremony on the twenty-fourth of this month, I invite all to break their day's fast and to join me for bread and wine and to give thanks for God's grace and endless bounty."

Sarah heard the intake of breath of the congregation as this news sank in – and also the implications. Parson Dillington must be wealthy indeed to invite the entire village to sup. Sarah put her head on one side and wondered if the good parson had a privileged background or well-born parents. And the devil in her wondered too about the likelihood of a rich man getting through the eye of a needle.

"I hear tell his wife came from wealthy merchant stock," whispered Dorothy.

Ah, thought Sarah. So that was it. The parson held up his hand and the muttering of the congregation stopped.

"I welcome individual household contributions to our feast, but none will be barred because they have little or nothing. It shall please me to see you all." His eyes glanced over Sarah at the back of the church, and quickly moved on, but not before she saw the tic under his eye.

She ducked her head. Dorothy looked at her curiously but said nothing. Sarah stood with the rest of the church as the front pews filed out, her gaze on the floor. As she stood, a lock of her hair loosened from her cap and she quickly put up her hands to stop it tumbling further, but too late. The razor-sharp eyes of Mistress Whyte had spotted the red-gold streak, and her breath hissed between yellowed teeth.

"Vain child! Your hair should be shorn for modesty!"

Sarah frantically tried to stuff her hair out of sight, but the thin fingers of Mistress Whyte curled tightly around her wrist, dragging her out of her seat and to the door.

"Is there no end to your wantonness? Parson, what say you to this girl whose hair offends female modesty?"

Parson Dillington looked coolly on as Sarah wrenched her wrist from the claws of Mistress Whyte.

"Why, Mistress Whyte, I would remember Corinthians, which says that 'if a woman has long hair, it is a glory to her, for her hair is given to her for a covering.'"

Sarah was torn, warmed by his defence of her, but recognising his words would only earn her more enemies. Mistress Whyte stared hard at him.

"I see," she said, a slight sneer on her lips. Sarah wondered if she did.

"You disagree with Scripture?" he said, eyebrows raised. "I am surprised."

At this, Mistress Whyte went pink and Sarah's sought to make waters smooth again.

"Sir, Mistress Whyte, I must apologise. My hair is a trial to me, I keep it long only in remembrance of my mother who told me she loved it. But she would be grieved indeed for it to cause offence, and I will—"

"You will continue to honour your mother," Parson Dillington said swiftly. "Mistress Whyte, a godly woman and a mother herself, would expect you to do so. Is that not right, Mistress Whyte?"

Annie Whyte pressed her lips together tightly. There was a second when she and the parson glared at one another, and then she nodded curtly and swished away, where Sarah saw her muttering to Elizabeth Walters.

"Mistress?" Dorothy's voice was uncertain.

"Yes, Dorothy, we must go home."

The parson shot out a hand to stay her. The heat of his hand branded her through her sleeve. "I trust I shall see you at the festival, Mistress Sarah?"

"Aye, sir."

"I understood that a relative was joining you after your parents died. Is that still the case?"

Sarah stared, unsure of what to say. There had been no word from Aunt Hester, and if truth be told, she expected none now. If her aunt had been of a mind to come, she would have arrived. It had been more than four months since she buried her parents, and she knew that her aunt had harboured no love towards her younger sister-in-law, with her strange practices and ways with herbs.

"I have no news, sir. She may be ill. Aunt Hester was always of a sickly constitution."

"Then she would be well advised to visit you," the parson said, smiling a little. Sarah shifted uneasily.

The parson pressed his lips together. "I grow concerned at your solitary state."

"I have Dorothy, sir." Sarah nodded at Dorothy, who was standing a little apart.

"I am sure she is an estimable woman, but she is a servant. You need family around you." Parson Dillington looked at the congregation in the churchyard, still speaking in small groups, casting covert glances at them.

Sarah wondered if he knew how hostile the villagers could be, and despite her yearning, looked to bring the conversation to an end. She spied Thomas and gave him a beseeching look. He walked slowly towards them.

"Mistress Sarah? My wife would have you look over the babe. Can you come?"

"Of course!" Sarah turned to the parson. "Sir, I shall bring cheese and bread, and perhaps some strawberries to the festival."

"God bless your offering," Parson Dillington said, his gaze like warm sunshine. She bobbed a curtsey and hurried away.

"Thank you," she muttered to Thomas.

"The parson seems smitten," he commented. Sarah brushed his words aside.

"Folly!"

"Nay, seems obvious to me, and all the other folk here." Sarah stopped short.

"Truly?"

"Why so distressed? He is a free, and wealthy, man, it seems. Would he suit you so ill?"

She shook her head, sick to her heart.

"Yes, Thomas. We should not suit at all. Where is Abigail?"

With a sigh, Thomas led the way into the cottage.

※

The councillor was sweating beneath his finery in the bright sunshine. Sarah watched as a glorious rose and four shiny pennies were presented to him by the alehouse keeper and his ruddy-cheeked wife. The 'rent' would be given to the poor as alms and would probably find its way back into the coffers of the inn before the day was out.

She stayed on the edge of the crowd, watching. So far, the villagers were sober. She hoped the feast promised by the parson would help line their stomachs before, one by one, the men would steal away to find ale and the wiser of the women would hustle their daughters indoors.

Sarah shifted the heavy basket to her other arm, the aroma of ripe cheese teasing her nose as it drifted up from the damp muslin. To add to her offering, she had picked four pounds of strawberries in the mid-morning sun and she hoped there would be at least a couple for her to sample when the feast began. She caught sight of Parson Dillington and his daughter, now looking, Sarah thought, more like a young lady than a child.

The parson was scanning the crowd, discreetly, but she saw his eyes flick over the heads of those laughing and applauding the alehouse keeper. She ducked her head slightly and Dorothy looked at her curiously.

"What is it, mistress?"

"Naught," said Sarah, putting the basket on the ground and making a show of resettling its contents. Dorothy tutted and then, as the crowd moved, she whispered.

"Rise, mistress! The parson approaches!"

Sarah closed her eyes briefly before slowly straightening up to meet the green gaze of Parson Dillington. She felt the heat in her cheeks and looked away.

"I trust I find you well, Mistress Bartlett? I did not see you in service."

"I was called unexpectedly to Mistress Meakin this morning. She was blessed with a son not two hours ago."

"Amen," said Parson Dillington. "God be praised. So now she is safely delivered, are you free to join the festivities?"

"I am," said Sarah, battling with warring instincts to run as far and as fast as she could, or to stay and be bathed in the glow of his awkward smile.

"Then let us go," he said, nodding to Dorothy. Sarah began to walk towards the vicarage, stopping abruptly when Prudence stepped in front of her. Sarah stared, taken aback by the fury in the girl's face.

"Father, may I take your arm?" Prudence said. The parson nodded, and Prudence took her place beside him, pushing Sarah out of the way. Sarah dropped back without a word.

"Gently, Prudence," said Parson Dillington. "Mistress Bartlett, walk on this side of me."

Reluctantly, Sarah did so, and they walked, three abreast, across the churchyard. Sarah tried not to notice the nods and nudges of the other villagers or the stony face of Mistress Whyte. As soon as they entered the hall, she darted off to hand the maid her cheese and strawberries and then to disappear as best she might into the background. As the hall filled with villagers and the afternoon wore on, she began to relax and when she found Abigail, she sat down and ate her share of the feast.

The councillor had slaughtered a pig and the smell of roasting pork from the spit in the garden drifted through the hall, making her mouth water. It tempted many of the villagers outside and hoisting Rebecca onto her hip, Sarah soon followed. Turning to say something to Abigail, she caught the tender glance between her friend and Thomas and reckoned there would be another child soon. She hugged Rebecca closer, who gurgled in her arms.

"How tightly you hold the baby!" said a voice behind her. Prudence's eyes gleamed. "You're old to be unmarried and childless, aren't you?" Sarah looked at her thoughtfully, gauging the malice and the rudeness in the comment.

"I have time enough, Mistress Prudence, and I am still in mourning for my parents," she replied.

"Alone with your potions," said Prudence. "I pity you."

"And how are you now, Prudence?" asked Sarah mildly. "Did my 'potions' as you call them help your pain?" The girl flushed and then shrugged.

"Well enough. The pains were going when you arrived."

"I shall tell your father he has no need of me the next time he calls."

"He *has* no need of you!" Prudence hissed, her face suddenly white. "He is content as he is!"

Oh, thought Sarah. So there's the nub of it.

Rebecca squirmed in her arms and so Sarah just nodded and returned to Abigail and Thomas.

"Mistress Dillington looks fierce," said Abigail.

"She's just a girl," said Sarah, tickling Rebecca under the chin.

"She glares at you so!" marvelled Thomas. "I would have a care. Young girls take strange passions."

Sarah nodded. She knew. She would need to be careful around Prudence Dillington.

THE VISITOR

The bonfire was lit just before the sun set, and despite the heat of the day that still lingered, Sarah shivered as she watched, remembering Margaret Eames. The children of the village were dancing around, begging for treats of sugared almonds and candied fruit. The child, Robert, recited the rhyme promising bad luck to her should she not respond, and Sarah gave him the last of her sweets. He smiled shyly at her and then scampered off. She noted that his leg, although limping, looked sturdy enough.

As the smoke and the haze from the fire grew, she gripped the handles of her basket more firmly, ready to slip away to cut her herbs. To cut them on this night would give them additional power, she knew. A movement on the edge of her vision alerted her to the parson, striding around the bonfire on long legs. His pale hair gleamed red-gold in the light of the flames.

She scurried quietly away, into the woods.

Sarah moved swiftly along the path, knowing she must make haste before the light fell. She knew what she wanted to gather: St John's Wort, more betony, and a divining rod, all best gathered on this night. Her heart beat faster than usual, she knew not why. The parson had not followed her, and by the time she returned to the cottage, all except the determined revellers would be at home.

She spotted the yellow stars of the St John's Wort and took out her knife to cut the upright stems, bending to reach into the thicket. An owl hooted in warning, and she froze before spinning around, just in time to avoid the thick-fingered grasp of a drunken stranger.

"A pox on you! C'mere!" He breathed heavily as he stumbled forward, and the ale on his breath was sour. She backed away.

"Nay, don't be afeared. I'm only being friendly." He lurched to one side, and she stepped to the other. He leered at her and she could see a stout, powerful body with a thick neck and a wide, frog-like mouth. She guessed he would be twice her weight and had no doubt that his intent was not to discuss her remedies.

"Sir, let me be." Sarah tried to sound calm, reasonable.

"But you are all alone and there is none to help," he sneered. She whistled under her breath.

"I am not so easily caught."

"We'll see." He leapt forward and although she was too quick for him to grab her arms, he caught her skirt. She whistled again, a little louder, while trying to wrench her skirts from his hands.

He chuckled and pulled on the cloth. And then, as Sarah was beginning to be dragged down to her knees, the owls came to her aid, swooping and diving around his head.

The man swore and tried to protect himself, but kept one fist in Sarah's skirts. She searched frantically for a log or stick to hit him, but there was none. The owls continued to plague him, and she finally tugged free. She whirled around and ran as fast as she could back to the path. His blaspheming and the thump of his feet followed her.

She glanced over her shoulder and saw him lumbering behind her. Panic gave her a spurt of speed – straight into Parson Dillington. The impact knocked her onto her backside and she sat in the road, panting. The stranger, seeing the parson, slowed with slightly more grace. The parson took in the scene with a chilly glance.

"Sarah? Are you hurt?" his voice rapped out as he bent to her.

"Not yet, sir."

"Explain yourself, sir." The glorious voice was frigid, and Sarah sagged with relief.

The stranger seemed to shrink and stuttered.

"I meant no harm, the lady seemed willing—"

Sarah hissed between her teeth as she scrambled to her feet and brushed down her skirt.

"I was looking for something to brain you with! I was very *un*willing! I had not laid eyes on you until this night and I wish never to do so again!"

"You—"

"Enough! Get you gone!" The parson put up his hand as the stranger lunged towards Sarah, who shrank back against the parson. Muttering, the stranger slouched away.

There was silence. Sarah finally looked up at the parson.

"Thank you, sir."

"You are like Eve, tempting a drunken, wanton man!" His voice was angry, and Sarah stepped away from him. "What draws you to the woods on such a night as this, when men have supped too much ale to be sensible?"

"I was collecting herbs—"

"You may wish to do so with your maid in the future, Mistress Bartlett! What foolhardy actions! What might have happened had I not been abroad?" Parson Dillington was working himself up to a fine fury.

"I am grateful."

"I do not want your gratitude!"

Sarah winced, his voice whipping through her words. The tic was under his eye again.

"You are like a child, spoiled and wilful. Your duty is to marry and get you a husband to give you guidance. And keep you safe."

Sarah hung her head, thinking it wiser to say nothing. The silence stretched on. The parson put his finger under her chin to lift her gaze to his bright green one. She shivered.

"You need a husband, Sarah. You are alone and unprotected."

She swallowed, drawn into those eyes and afraid as she had not been just five minutes earlier. Holding her gaze, he dropped his lips to her mouth and kissed her gently. She allowed herself the luxury of his touch for a second before she jumped back.

He drew a deep breath.

"I beg your pardon. But you *should* marry, Sarah."

She turned and ran to the cottage as though the devils of hell pursued her, tears in her eyes.

CHAPTER ELEVEN
STACIE

I surveyed my parents' bedroom with a sigh. Wardrobe doors hung ajar; clothes dripped out of all the drawers. My mother was sitting on the bed, hunting through her jewellery box.

"Eustacia, there you are! What do you think of this?"

She put aside the jewellery box and reached for a crepe de chine blouse in sunny yellow. I put my head on one side. The yellow was lovely but too strong for my mother's colouring. I wrinkled my nose.

"Hmm, that's what I thought," she said, and hung it back in the wardrobe. I looked at the pile of clothes on the bed and frowned.

"Mother, I don't want to interfere, but how many cashmere sweaters do you think you'll need in Florence in July? And this shawl?" I picked up a silk brocade wrap, glorious and stylish but too heavy for the heat of Italy.

"Yes, yes. I'm leaving that pile," she said, picking up her jewellery box again and rifling through its contents.

Dad was downstairs in his chair, reading the newspaper.

"Are you all sorted?"

He looked up at me over his spectacles. "I've never quite understood why your mother makes such a performance over packing," he commented. "I did mine in thirty minutes. She's been at it for about an hour and a half so far."

"She's concerned to dress her best," I said kindly. "All the dinners and things; she won't want to wear the same thing twice, not with the crowd you work with."

He laughed softly.

"Perhaps. It's rather a trial in some respects."

"How long will you be away?"

"After the conference, we'll head up to Fiesole and stay for a couple of weeks. We come back at the end of August. We're staying here."

He passed me the brochure, and I glanced through it, noting the asterisk alongside the rate for the twin, rather than the double room.

"Looks a wonderful hotel," I said. He nodded, looking pleased.

"It'll be hotter than I normally like, but at least Fiesole is up in the mountains, and we can visit around there. I'm thinking of a book proposal linking places of the Grand Tour to early nineteenth-century literature, and it'll give me a chance to make some notes."

"That sounds interesting. But I thought it was a holiday for you both, Dad?"

"I imagine your mother will amuse herself well enough at the expense of my credit card," he responded dryly.

I headed into the garden, feeling more alone than ever. With Dad and Mother out of the house, there was one less barrier between Ellie and our guest. I had sensed the tension in Ellie for a couple of days now, watching her blue-grey eyes darting this way and that, watching Nate as he moved around the house. I was endeavouring to find out more about him for Gran, and her proximity made it difficult. She took my casual questions as an attempt to compete for his interest. It was, I thought, rather tedious.

My phone vibrated and to my joy, there was a text from Seb. I hurried to the summerhouse to read it. I needed to be careful with the response, and this time, *not* piss him off. A cheery email from Jo saying she was in lust with a swimming pool attendant, had made me realise she wouldn't be back in England until she *had* to return or lose her job. So I was missing my friends badly.

Seb hadn't been in contact for nearly two weeks now, despite my texts and at least two calls. I flopped into one of the chairs in the summerhouse and studied my phone.

Sorry for radio silence, I've had a lot of thinking to do. I'm in Manchester right now, back next week. Shall we go to dinner and talk?

I frowned. No jokes, no emojis, just the message.

I texted carefully. *Of course! I've missed you. When are you back?*

Monday night. Want to meet up on Tuesday? I'll book somewhere.
Sounds great. Are you ok?
Yes, I'm good. I'll send dinner details by email.

And that was that. No further messages. No friendly 'x'. If we'd been dating, I would be expecting to be dumped. I chewed my lip.

I had earmarked my savings for something much less frivolous than three weeks in Australia, I mused. I needed to leave my parents' house. Charity from anyone, whether my parents and particularly from Seb, was unwelcome. But his offer tempted me. What had he said? '*As your friend*, I could make it happen.' I wouldn't be human if, considering the year I'd had, I didn't want to just get away from it all. But this absence felt a little like blackmail, and I didn't respond well to that. But given how things were at home…

I'd think about it, I told myself, looking again at my phone. I'd seriously consider it.

My parents left the house on Wednesday morning with the minimum amount of fuss. There was toast and cereal, tea, cool kisses from Mother and a warm hug from Dad. And then they were gone in a cab to take them to Stansted Airport.

Ellie had already left the house for a run, and I presumed Nate had left early for the university on his new motorbike. The house was silent, still, and even unfriendly as I cleared the remains of breakfast. I reached for the radio and the smooth, calm tones of Radio 4 filled the kitchen.

I half listened as a politician repeated some well-worn phrases about 'the will of the British people' and the interviewer repeated his questions, hoping vainly for an answer. The world was on rewind, caught in some space-time continuum where we were condemned to say the same things, do the same actions, over and over until the sun blew up.

I shook my head and decided some exercise was in order. The weather was still sultry and warm, but I needed some air. I hadn't been riding or seen Wellington since the accident. Clicking on the dishwasher, I rang Mary at Holly's stables to book a ride and dashed upstairs to get changed.

"Stacie!" Mary grinned and she slapped me on the back as I locked the car. "About time! Wondered if we'd ever see you again!"

I smiled apologetically. "I know, I know. How's Wellington?"

"Are you recovered? Wellington is fine. He'll be thrilled to have a visit."

He was. He put his ears forward and whickered at me as I apologised and held out slices of apple as a peace offering. I then saddled him, and we went slowly, gently, out for a ride.

I took Wellington along the bridle path, and then into open fields, cantering along well-worn paths. My thighs ached after about half an hour, but I knew how much Wellington was enjoying the outing, so ignoring my moaning muscles, I kept riding. The sun played peekaboo in the clouds, and the wind blew gently through the trees, making the shadows dance. Which was why I didn't immediately notice her.

Wellington did, however. He whinnied and shook his head. I frowned.

"What is it, Wellington? What… oh!"

The figure at the side of the trees was small, with a dark brown cloak and a white cap. It was the same spirit I had seen in the churchyard. The slender figure was clear and looked solid; I started as she acknowledged me. She nodded her head, and I glimpsed a lock of auburn hair, almost shocking against the dullness of her clothes. I reined in Wellington and he stood, snuffling.

I wasn't sure what to do. I nodded back and a smile lit up her face. I stared, but somehow, I wasn't scared. Not of this slight creature, with the laughing eyes and bright hair. We stood looking at one another for what seemed a long time.

Slowly, I dismounted, holding Wellington's bridle tight. I didn't fancy the walk back if he bolted. I glanced at him and wondered if he could see exactly what I did. I heard a chuckle, and I almost dropped the reins at the sound.

"He sees me clear enough," said the girl. I sucked in a breath, willing my knees to stay locked. The language seemed thickened to my ears, like hearing the words through cream. I swallowed. I might have muttered at the cat before this, but a conversation? That was something very new. I cleared my throat.

"Does he hear you?"

"Aye, I believe so."

There was a pause.

"I'm not sure what to say," I said eventually. "Should I know you?"

"Nay, perhaps not," she replied. "But we are cousins."

Cousins? My mind chased thoughts around.

"I wondered if I'd stopped seeing… um… things, or people like you." I was awkward and my words were clumsy. The girl didn't seem to mind.

"Yes, we have been absent. But whether you see us or no, we're always with you, Eustacia. You are not alone."

A deep shock unsettled my stomach.

"You know my name?"

"Aye. Eustacia means 'fruitful' does it not?"

A spirit who not only knew my name but understood what it meant in Greek. Good grief, Gran would have a fit when I told her. My hands tightened on the bridle and Wellington snorted.

"Who are you?" I said.

"My name is Sarah Bartlett, but you will discover that soon enough, I warrant."

"What do you want?" I paused; it sounded rude. I rephrased. "What can I do for you?"

She smiled a little sadly.

"I am here to give you aid and ask for yours in return. While my destiny was set in my time, my story is still unfinished. Your own fate is still unfolding, so make your decisions with care, Eustacia. I and others will watch over you, but you must cleave to your heart's desire."

I opened my mouth to ask further questions, but in the distance, I heard a dog and the high treble voices of children. I glanced away to the path and when I looked back, Sarah had gone.

"I will come again. Remember, cleave to your heart's desire," a voice brushed past my ear, and I swung round to empty air.

The breath whooshed out of me, and I leant against Wellington to gather my wits. He snorted softly, and I patted his neck.

"Yes, we should be on our way too if there's a hound coming."

Awkwardly, I swung myself onto his back and kicked his sides. We walked back to the stables, my mind in a whirl.

Gran looked at me, astonished and rather excited.

I shook my head, still wondering at what had just happened. "Yes, I realise I sound like some TV serial, but it really happened. If it didn't, I'm not sure what Wellington was seeing, and he most definitely was seeing and hearing something."

Gran considered.

"You said she was at the church? And is she the first spirit you've ever had a conversation with?"

I nodded, still astounded that it had happened.

"What did you say her name was?"

"Sarah Bartlett."

"I don't recall anyone of that name from our family tree, but perhaps I haven't gone back far enough. And she said you were family? A cousin?"

I nodded again.

Gran moved to her computer and switched it on. Settling herself into the chair, she gestured for me to take a seat.

"Can you remember what she was wearing?"

"A brown cloak, a cap of some kind. I think it was supposed to cover her hair, but it seemed loose."

"Can you place her clothes in time? Elizabethan? Regency? Victorian?"

"No idea; her cloak covered most of what she was wearing." I thought back to the time I had seen her at the church, but the details slipped away from me.

"Did she appear rich?"

"No, like a maid. The cloak looked like rough wool, although I didn't get close."

Gran typed something into the internet.

"Was she wearing anything like this?" she asked.

I glanced over her shoulder. Nothing seemed similar. She clicked on another page. And then another. It went on for a few pages.

"Hmm, that looks more like what she was wearing," I said, pointing to one image. Gran peered at the text.

"'Weaver, circa 1595'," she read. She typed in another range of dates and clicked search.

"That's it!" I said, my eyes zooming in on the line drawing of a woman wearing a cap. "I'm pretty sure the cap was like that."

"Right, sixteen hundreds then," she said, scribbling a note.

"Do we need to find out who she is?"

"Yes, and if she's a distant cousin, I'll at least be able to go backwards from your mother and father. I've got back to the early seventeen hundreds." She said this with a thread of pride. "But I must go back further. Now, let me show you what I've found out about your lovely guest."

"What? *Nate*?"

She clicked on a document.

"Indeed. It was easy. I looked up his bio on the university website, and with a bit of patience on one of the ancestry sites, and searching for press articles, I found some reports of his parents' accident and their deaths."

"Gran!"

"Oh, hush, nothing's secret on the web, and he said at the dinner table that they died when he was twenty. I admit I didn't tell you I was doing it and given how you're looking at me now, I dare say you would have stopped me. Anyway, his parents' death gave me a starting point. It helped of course that his father was a global expert on eighteenth-century history and his mother was a writer. Once I had copies of their death certificates, I was on the trail."

"But why all the searching?"

"You haven't been able to find out anything about him, have you, from conversation?"

I rolled my eyes. "Not only is he incredibly private, but I've also got Ellie breathing down my neck every time I try to speak to him!"

"Well, I wanted to know more about the ancestors he mentioned," she said. "I can't put it any more strongly than a feeling, but it does *feel* important."

I shared that feeling. I looked at the screen and rubbed my hand across my face. "I'm a bit creeped out by it, if I'm honest. Like we're stalking him." My eyes caught a date. "You've traced his family back to 1758?"

"Mmm. It gets more difficult, obviously, the further back you go, but his relatives were often in education – writers, researchers, professors…" She trailed off. "I know it's a little intrusive. But one," she said, ticking off the points on her fingers, "you feel weird around him. Two, you used to see ghosts, until Nate arrived. Then they all disappeared. Three, when he goes away, they reappear. That makes him interesting. And four, you've been seeing visions which seem to want to interact with you; the man while you were riding, and now this young woman, Sarah. Who incidentally has appeared to you previously. *That* hasn't happened before."

I looked up.

"No. No, it hasn't. And yes, I feel weird. But it might just be indigestion."

She rolled her eyes. "Search for more information on Sarah. You look at the ancestry sites, I'll investigate the parish records. She may hold the key to all this."

CHAPTER TWELVE
STACIE

The atmosphere struck me the moment I walked in the door. The silence was thick, expectant. I frowned and dropped my bag at the door.

"Ellie? Anyone here?" I called through the house.

There was a noise in the living room and I followed it. Ellie was sitting on the sofa, a strange look on her face.

"Um... hi. Is everything okay?" I asked.

Ellie's lips twisted in a slight smile. She unwound herself from the sofa and stood up. Her normally tight jeans showed skin at the waist. "Fine."

"You look a bit... strange."

"I'm fine."

I raised my brows and said nothing. She turned back to her book, so I gave up and retreated to my room.

Seb had emailed the details of the restaurant, a place I'd never been to. I'd heard nothing else from him, although the date was tomorrow night.

I was deep into my wardrobe, searching for a pair of shoes languishing at the bottom. Which is why I missed Ellie's knock at the door.

"Stacie!"

"Oh, sorry. What's up?"

Ellie stared at the sandals, distracted for a moment.

"Different for you, aren't they?"

I looked at the shoes. Cream high heels trimmed with black beads.

"I'm going out to dinner with Seb."

She took one of the sandals from me and examined it. "Wow. Where is the Right Honourable Seb taking you to give these an outing?"

"He's been away, and I haven't left the house for days. So I wanted to dress up a bit."

Half the truth, I thought. She giggled, sounding like my sister from years ago.

"Certainly not your normal footwear," she said, flopping onto the bed on top of the dress I had been considering. I pulled it out from under her with determined patience.

"You didn't come here to talk about my shoes. Did you want me?"

She hesitated, and then her words came out in a rush. "Are you out this week at all? Other than tomorrow."

My eyebrows rose.

"In the evenings? Just tomorrow, with Seb."

"Right. Just tomorrow?"

I frowned. "At the moment. Why? Are you planning a seduction?"

Faint colour rose to her cheeks.

Oh, my God, she is, I thought.

"Ellie, I don't fancy walking into a scene of lewdness and undress."

"No! Don't be stupid."

"He's a bit old for you, isn't he?"

The lightness left her face, and her mouth thinned. "What on earth would you understand about it? Oh, sorry, I forgot, you had a fling with a head teacher twenty years your senior, didn't you?"

The floor shifted beneath me. She flushed red at my glare.

"A fling isn't how I'd describe it. And how do you know about it anyway?" I asked evenly.

"Pat Clark filled me in when I came to the summer fair. I assumed that was why you were moving schools. Are you running away?"

Pat Clark taught history and had the loosest tongue in the country. I despised him. He didn't seem to give a shit for the kids in his care, or the quality of his teaching which hadn't changed in about twenty years. I folded my arms.

"Running away? Ellie, I'm moving to a new job with the chance to train. I bet Pat Clark didn't tell you that I smacked Neil Hathersage, did he?"

"No, he didn't." Ellie sounded shocked.

"So shall we agree that you have incomplete information?"

"So you *hit* the senior person in your school? God, I'm surprised they didn't sack you!"

"After he tried to bloody grab my boobs, I was completely justified!"

"Did you tell Grange Hall?"

I ignored this. "I'm busy, are we done? If you're going to make a move on our house guest, which is in really poor taste, if you ask me, currently I'm out tomorrow night."

"Thank you."

She left. With a dry mouth, I found something to wear for the following night. Then I reached for my mobile phone.

My hands were shaking as I dialled the number, and I cursed Pat Clark and Neil Hathersage. The tone sounded for a few rings.

"Grange Hall School, John White speaking."

"H-hello, it's Stacie Hayward," I said, and I cleared my throat.

"Stacie! What can I do for you?" John's voice boomed down the line.

"Do you have a few minutes? I'd like to talk to you about... about something personal." I took a breath.

"Sounds intriguing. Should this be face to face?"

"Well, I didn't want to impose, and it won't take more than a few minutes."

"Okay then. What's the problem?"

"You asked me at the interview why I wanted to leave Woodlands and I said there were no promotion opportunities there and that I wanted the training. While that was true, it wasn't quite the whole truth."

"Oh?" John White's voice grew sharper. Don't screw this up, Stacie, I said to myself, and rushed into my speech.

"A member of staff made a pass at me which I rejected, and I found myself more or less ostracised, and regardless of how brilliant I was as a teaching assistant, I would never be supported for promotion."

The tumbled words seemed to fall into the silence.

"Ah. Why are you telling me now, rather than at interview?"

"Because I wanted the job, and I was afraid you wouldn't hire me if I told you everything."

"What's changed your mind about telling me?"

"Because this is a small county with a close-knit education community, and I imagined you'd hear at some stage. And then you'd be hacked off that I hadn't told you."

"Is there anything else you need to tell me?"

I screwed up my eyes and took a deep breath.

"I smacked him across the face when he made the pass."

There was a long pause. "Interesting. Do you still want the job?"

"God, yes!" I lowered my voice with an effort. "The reason I'm telling you is that, well, if I was in your shoes, I'd want to be told by the person I employed," I said, not knowing if my confession was going well, or not.

Another pause.

"Well, between us, Neil Hathersage has history," John said slowly.

I didn't even need to tell my new boss who it was, I realised.

"So did you know?"

"Only after I'd offered you the job. I considered you were worth the risk, and so did Glynis, who you did the demonstration lesson with. She agreed with me that you were the most naturally talented teacher she'd seen in years. Although I didn't know you'd landed him one."

"Does that make a difference to your decision?" I asked, dreading the answer.

"Um… I'm rather pleased you clocked him, if I'm honest, although I will deny that statement should you ever mention it again."

I sagged with relief, clutching the phone like a drowning woman.

"I'm so sorry—"

"Enough," he cut me off. "I'm about to go away and I should be finishing this paperwork. I'll see you at the end of August. And, Stacie, don't hit anyone at Grange Hall will you?"

I stared into space for a long time after I'd ended the call. New start, new start, I chanted to myself.

<hr />

"Stacie! Are you eating with us?"

Ellie's voice sounded high, and I frowned. Dinner smelled delicious; beef Wellington, I understood. Completely over the top for a midweek dinner and apparently thrown together at breakneck speed. I threw aside my book and swung my father's chair away from the desk.

When I arrived in the dining room, Ellie was fussing around the place settings. Nate was still at the university.

"Can I help?" I asked, looking over the carefully laid table. Napkins, delicate wine glasses and serving spoons. Not casual dining, then.

"No thanks, I've got it covered."

I stood, wondering whether to go back into Dad's office and wait for her to call me, but decided that would relegate me to teenager status. I sat in an armchair, listening to Ellie clatter pans and rattle cutlery. After five minutes with no further conversation, I retrieved another book from my room.

I met Nate coming up the stairs, carrying his rucksack and a water bottle. There was a bit of dithering as I made to go past him. I'd always been superstitious about passing on the stairs, and he pressed himself to the wall at the half-landing. I slid past him and clattered rather ungracefully downstairs.

"Was that Nate?" demanded Ellie.

"Yes, he just came in," I muttered, opening my book and sitting down. Ellie left the room, and I focused on the page, trying hard not to listen to her now fluting voice and the deeper murmur of Nate's replies.

"Thirty minutes," she said to me as she returned to the kitchen.

The meal was an interesting mix of truly delicious food and tension so tight it destroyed my appetite. Nate seemed to be completely oblivious. Ellie was charming and attentive and Nate lapped it up, and although she didn't make him laugh, she got appreciative glances and the odd smile.

"You're quiet this evening, Stacie," Nate commented. I jumped, not expecting anyone to bring me into the conversation. "Is everything okay?"

"Oh! Yes, everything's fine, thanks."

"Stacie's nervous about her new job," said Ellie, looking at me over the rim of her wine glass. "New place, new people to meet, to win over."

"Really? Is that so hard?" He looked genuinely interested. Ellie laughed and Nate glanced at me, finally tuning in to the tension around the table.

"Yes, I saw a terrific opportunity at a new school and went for it!" I said, cutting a piece of beef Wellington. "I'm getting proper training in a job I love, at a higher salary. What's not to like? And the head teacher told me himself that he was thrilled that I was joining his team."

Ellie frowned, and I looked straight at her.

"He perfectly understands why I saw his school as the place to build my career," I said with quiet emphasis. "We both agree it's a good match."

Nate's eyes narrowed. I considered him. He was really good looking. He'd made such an impact on my sister, I wondered what the effect would be on his students.

"What's it like for you to join a new university?" I asked him. "Any nerves?"

Nate paused. "Well, I know my stuff inside out, so, no, I'm not nervous about the teaching."

"What about your students? Not everyone wants to teach, they'd rather just do research," I persisted. Ellie's lips tightened.

"Obviously," Nate said. "My students provide me with as much stimulation as my research does."

What an interesting phrase, I thought. "You're, pardon me for saying so, fairly young for a professor. Has that caused you any issues? Hero worship, that kind of thing?"

"Stacie!" Ellie protested.

"What?" I put on my innocent face. "It must be a real pain to be swatting away the attentions of eager young women, if that *is* an issue, of course." I turned back to Nate, who frowned.

"I've learned to handle it," he said.

"Really? What do you do?"

"Stacie, do shut up," said Ellie urgently. Nate looked between us as though watching a tennis match.

"Do *you* need to swat away the attentions of eager young women, Stacie?" he asked, attempting to lighten the atmosphere.

I grimaced. "No, just overweight men in positions of power."

"Unpleasant," he said evenly.

"So what's your secret?" I asked him.

"I have a single, unbreakable rule," he replied. "I never become involved with any students." I noticed that Ellie's hands, about to pile plates, stilled.

"If they persist?"

"I talk to them, explain my position as one of trust, outline my duty of care. If they don't listen, I have them transferred to other courses."

Not sure that would sort the issue, just make it less problematic for you, I thought.

"So you've never fallen for any of your female students?" I asked. "Or am I making a huge assumption, and actually you're gay?"

I could hear Ellie's intake of breath. He laughed.

"No, Stacie, I'm not gay. I like women of all ages and types – as long as they're not students." He raised his brows as if to ask if that was all.

"You make it sound so easy. It's not always, you know." I played around with the cutlery on the table. "When someone holds your promotion prospects in their gift, your job even, it's much less straightforward."

Nate breathed in sharply. "Is that what happened?" I glanced at him. "At your last job? Did someone make a pass at you? Is that why you left?"

For a moment I couldn't make my brain form any words. At last, I said, "Yes. I left because I wanted to train and there was no chance of that where I was after… what happened."

"They denied you advancement because someone came on to you?"

I nodded.

"And you did nothing?"

Other than smack him? I narrowed my eyes. I owed him no explanations, so I just said, "What are you trying to say? Let's hope my replacement has more guts than I did, is that what you mean?"

"Maybe. Running away to a new job is hardly going to rectify his behaviour, is it?"

"I said that to her," put in Ellie from the kitchen.

I hung on to my temper. "Hang on! You're suggesting that *I* should be responsible for his actions? That it's my responsibility to train him in basic standards of behaviour? He's a bloody head teacher! Perhaps you should talk to him about a version of your *rule*?" I forced out through tight lips. I pushed back my chair. To my surprise, he stood up and caught my arm as I stalked past him.

"Stacie, hey, I'm sorry. That was unjust of me, I know nothing about the circumstances."

"No, you don't," I said. "You are in no position to judge me *at all*."

"No."

His quiet agreement took the wind out of the force of my anger. I stood irresolute, the warmth of his fingers on my arm. Ellie sighed as she returned from the kitchen.

"If you've finished turning dinner into a soap opera, would you like pudding or not?" Her voice sounded bored.

"Please don't let my crass comments put you off your sister's delicious cooking, Stacie," Nate said, and his hand caressed my skin. A shiver slithered up my spine at his touch.

Ellie's porcelain skin flushed with pleasure at the compliment, and I realised Nate had soothed me and ensured Ellie didn't feel neglected at the same time. I swallowed and pulled away from him.

"Sorry, it's all got a bit heated, hasn't it?" I said, moving back to my chair. Ellie passed me a dish full of meringue and fruit without a word. Nate talked about a film I didn't know, and I sank quietly into reflection. I glanced at my arm, and it seemed I could still feel his fingers touching my flesh.

CHAPTER THIRTEEN
SARAH

Sarah lifted her gaze from her weaving to find Dorothy's watery blue eyes on her. She raised her eyebrows.

"There's talk…" started Dorothy and then stopped to swallow. She tried again. "There's talk about you bewitching Parson Dillington. They say you have drawn him to lust after you."

Sarah sighed and tried to keep calm.

"And how do they say I bewitched him?"

"That you have given him a love potion in the strawberries you took to the festival. He ate most heartily of them, they say."

Sarah bent her head to her work again.

"Did I bewitch all who ate the strawberries? The parson was not the only one to eat. You did. The alehouse keeper did. Heavens, even Mistress Whyte ate of the fruit! Is she in love with me also?"

Dorothy tutted.

"Mistress, you know how folk talk. There is no word from your aunt?"

"None, and I believe none will come, Aunt Hester is likely too frail to undertake the journey."

Dorothy shook her head and Sarah, realising that her weaving would not progress with her servant brooding over her, asked if she would check the fence around the hens. Muttering, Dorothy did so and Sarah was left alone. After a quarter of an hour, she finished the piece and tied off her threads. She shook it over her knees, noting that the cloth was even and although unfinished, smooth and even. She was worth her wage.

She arched her back to ease its stiffness and rose from her seat. There was a knock at the door. She tensed and then relaxed. She threw it open to find a smiling Abigail with Rebecca in her arms.

"Are you at leisure? I thought it late enough…"

"I have just finished the last piece and would welcome company, especially such company as this young lady!" Sarah gathered Rebecca into her arms and nuzzled her neck beneath the soft collar, making the child giggle and squirm. Abigail smiled and shut the door.

Their chat was comfortable. Abigail spoke of Parson Dillington's charitable and holy deeds in the village, and Sarah waited. And soon enough, Abigail came around to it.

"Sarah, you have not been at church recently. Is aught amiss?"

"I was there Sunday."

"Aye, but I saw you not at midweek service, nor on Friday," Abigail said gently. Sarah continued to tickle Rebecca.

"I was not well midweek, and on Friday I tended to Joshua Philpott, who broke his leg ploughing."

"Aye, I heard that. What dreadful news! And Beatrice about to give birth again? Whatever will they do without the harvest? The family will surely starve." Abigail was diverted momentarily, thinking no doubt of the Philpott family with its seven children and worn-down wife. Sarah kept quiet, but Abigail soon recovered her theme.

"Your absence has caused much gossip," she said hesitantly. "You should attend soon, otherwise folks will consider you heathen."

"Do they not already?"

Abigail was silent for a moment. "People say unkind things, but few know you as well as I."

"Are you not tainted by our acquaintance? Will people call you 'heathen' too?"

Rebecca whimpered, and automatically Abigail held out her arms for the child, turning a distressed face to Sarah. "Nay, don't look so fierce! I love you! Thomas loves you! Rebecca loves you!"

Sarah stood up with a short laugh.

"Have a care what you say! Apparently, I am bewitching my neighbours into loving me. So love me not, Abigail. You would be safer."

The door opened, and Dorothy stood, looking red in the face. Behind her, the tall shape of the parson was silent and still.

Abigail stood and curtseyed, Rebecca beginning to cry in earnest. Sarah gathered her composure. Dorothy darted away.

"Good evening, Parson. Is all well?"

"If you mean by that, Mistress Bartlett, that we are all fit, yes, we are," said the parson, coming into the room and seeming to fill it. He turned his green gaze to Abigail. "Good evening, Mistress Lester. I take it your child is recovered from her fever?"

"Aye, sir! Mistress Bartlett is so skilled, I would trust my child to no one else. Heaven has sent her."

Sarah looked down, praying that Abigail would say no more. The parson gave Sarah a shrewd look.

"You embarrass your friend, Mistress Lester. But indeed, she works miracles with her potions and cures, does she not?"

Abigail, who was no fool, simply smiled. "God blesses her endeavours."

"What brings you here, sir?" said Sarah, rather desperately.

To her relief, Abigail sat down again and soothed the fretful Rebecca.

The parson looked uncomfortable. "I wanted to know if you had considered our last conversation further, but this is not the time to discuss it."

Sarah kept her face blank and willed Rebecca to quieten, to encourage Abigail to stay. A few seconds later, the child was quiet, sucking on a wooden ring given to her by her mother.

"No, this is not the time," Sarah agreed.

"I will call again, but I certainly hope to see you in church soon?" Parson Dillington's voice was soft, but the implication clear.

"I will be there on Sunday." He nodded his head and smiled. She dipped a curtsey, and he left.

Sarah dropped to her chair as though someone had taken the air from her lungs. Abigail watched her. "What conversation?" she asked.

Sarah smiled bitterly. "He is in league with Thomas in that he thinks I should wed."

Abigail leaned forward eagerly. "And so you should! I do not understand your opposition to marriage! While you are young, you can do all things but what happens if you ail? And grow old? And do you not want children of your own?"

"I will manage. I have managed so far and I can always bring in help. And why do I need children of my own when dear friends will let me cosset theirs?"

Dorothy snorted from the pantry. Sarah raised her voice. "And indeed, why do I need help when my sweet Dorothy is here to tend me?"

At this, Abigail huffed and swung Rebecca onto her hip. "Saints preserve us!" she muttered. She walked to the door and then stopped and turned. "Be not a stranger to our house, Sarah, we love you and care not who knows it!" And she left, with Rebecca blowing bubbles as she closed the door.

Dorothy came in to find her mistress with tears on her cheeks.

THE VISITOR

Sunday brought more torture. As the parson had bidden, Sarah went to church as late as she dared to ensure she was at the back. But even so, it seemed to her all eyes turned as she stepped through the door and stung her skin like nettles.

She stiffened her knees and slid into an empty pew at the back. She had sent Dorothy on ahead of her, and the servant was sitting elsewhere in the church.

When the parson stood at the front, she was grateful that his gaze did not seek her and the pain in her chest, leaden and heavy, eased slightly. She unclenched her hands and saw the half-moon marks of her nails in the leather of her Bible.

The parson's voice filled the church and once again, Sarah found herself entranced by its cadence. She armed herself with a cloak of indifference and took communion, seeing nothing but the pale, elegant hands of the parson and the stones of the church floor. She stopped her ears to the whispers which followed her as she walked and made her mind a cool, white blank.

She sat perfectly still, her face turned towards the altar while the villagers filed past when service was finished, ignoring the nudges they gave one another.

"Sarah, are you ready to leave?" asked Thomas's deep voice. She turned her head.

"You should go on ahead," she said, with a smile.

"Nay, lass, I am content to wait."

She looked at him, massive and grave, his kind face creased with concern, and shook her head.

"You should go on ahead," she repeated. "You know how precarious my position, Thomas. I would not have you touched by the feelings against me. Rumour spreads."

He sighed.

"If you would but marry, it would offer some protection!"

She stood, her hands shaking.

"You think so? The village will malign me regardless of a

husband! There is no protection from the injury done through tittle-tattle and malice."

Thomas stared at her.

"So go, Thomas. Send Abigail my love, but leave me, please."

After a moment, he walked slowly out of the door.

Sarah walked to the altar, looking up at the crucifix.

What world is this that evil can be done so easily? she wondered, looking at the calm, pale face of Christ, streaked with blood under the thorns. She pondered His feelings of the fate that awaited him. Had He known what would come to pass?

Someone cleared their throat behind her, and she spun around. The parson stood at the door, the light from outside streaming in behind him, casting his face in shadow. Sarah narrowed her eyes, and it crossed her mind that she was looking at an angel, come to demand her debt to God. She swallowed and bobbed a curtsy.

"Sir."

"Mistress Bartlett, I was waiting to speak with you."

She stayed silent and nodded.

Parson Dillington walked towards her slowly, as though she was a nervous bird that would fly at sudden movement.

"Have you considered further my suggestion that you wed?"

"Yes, sir. There are obstacles to this."

"What might they be?"

"I have no suitor, sir. I had one, Ned Brighton, but I wanted time to grieve the loss of my mother and father, and he grew impatient."

His eyes were bright and keen, fixed on her face. She fidgeted with her Bible.

"There is no other beau?"

"No, sir."

"But you are a desirable match, Sarah. You have your farm—"

"Aye, sir. And cherry and apple orchards, and chickens and a cow. I'm aware of how 'desirable' I am."

His eyebrows rose at her tone.

"You sound bitter, mistress. Are you not grateful for your lot, which God has blessed you with?"

"Oh, yes, sir. So grateful I could not bear to give it up."

He frowned and seemed at a loss.

"You speak boldly. You do not agree that a woman should render all she has to her husband?"

Sarah bit her lip and considered her answer. "Aye, sir. The Bible tells us so, and thus I would prefer to remain single."

To her surprise, his lips tweaked at the corners. "You are an interesting woman, Mistress Bartlett."

Sarah gazed at the tiled floor.

"But none of this protects you from malicious tongues." His voice gentled, and she looked him in the face.

"I know this, sir. But you forget. I am a healer. I see the bruises and the broken bones and the cuts of those beaten by their husbands. Who would protect me from my husband? No one. I am his chattel, he *owns* me."

"Marriage is an honourable state, Sarah."

"As is my chastity." He fell silent, his face flushing. Sarah felt hers heat in response and dared not speak further. Parson Dillington's eyes seemed to glow and the tic under his eye twitched. She curtseyed.

"I thank you for your concern, parson. I will not wed."

And then she left.

❦

She couldn't settle. She walked up and down the room, sat, picked up a book, put it down, stirred a potion, touched her spinning.

"Mercy on us!" Dorothy eventually cried out. "What ails you, mistress, that you are so restless?"

Sarah had no answer, and finally, she sat by the fire and

waited for the knock at the door. It came at around nine, when the last rays of the sun had dimmed.

The parson stood there. Dorothy looked at them curiously and then, her face clearing, talked about an errand and left the cottage.

Sarah gestured to a chair, and the parson sat down. There was silence.

"Mistress Barton, my mind has reflected on our conversation in church. In truth, I have thought of little else these past few days," he began. Sarah gripped her hands together in her lap.

"Your ideas are unfeminine. Your stand is contrary to the word of God, who ordained that men and women should wed for the procreation of children and for mutual comfort." She stared stonily at him.

"Whilst your opinions shock me, your heart is good." She smiled briefly. "And therefore I come in good faith with a possible solution." His voice dropped. His eyes fixed on the fire, stuttering in the hearth.

Sarah looked at him, feeling her heart pound. She pressed her lips together tightly.

"As you know, I am widowed. The bishop has given me his blessing to wed again. Prudence is at an age where a woman's guidance would benefit her greatly. You are intelligent, and I believe we should suit. I come, therefore, to ask for your hand in marriage."

His green eyes lifted to her face and she strove, for both their sakes, to keep her expression bland.

"I am honoured by your proposal, sir, but I must decline."

"Why?"

The word rang out in the stillness, and she heard his torment adding to her own.

"We *should not* suit, sir. I am solitary and unused to company. And did you forget what I said to you on Sunday, sir? I am not like to be the property of anyone."

"I have thought of that," Parson Dillington said smoothly.

"My lawyers will draw up papers which allow you to keep your cottage and orchard. You will retain their use and can do with them as you will."

Sarah gaped at him. "But that would be madness! Have you heard what the villagers are saying, Parson Dillington? That I have somehow bewitched you! If you do this, they will see this as proof of my powers!"

"I care not for the opinions of the village!"

"But *I* do!" Sarah stood up, breathing rapidly. "You said I need protection. At least there we are in agreement! But not like this. This way you make an exception, and *such* an exception that cannot but excite comment! It draws attention to me in such a way that can only harm me!"

"With me as your husband and protector?" he said incredulously.

She laughed, a bitter sound echoing around the room.

"Oh, you do not know the power of Mistress Whyte and her friends! Your cloth may protect you, but not me! *You* will be bewitched, but I will be the spell caster!"

She sat down, twisting her hands.

"No, sir. I cannot accept. Not under those terms – not under *any* terms! I cannot marry you."

There was a pause.

"Cannot? Or will not?"

Sarah closed her eyes to stop the tears.

"I am destined to remain unwed, sir."

His face looked like stone and she grieved for his pain, the angel Lucifer, cast out of Heaven.

"Then I shall bid you goodnight, Mistress Bartlett."

CHAPTER FOURTEEN
STACIE

From the patio, I heard the thin, pleading note in Ellie's voice and winced.

"Oh, say yes! It'll be fun!"

"Ellie, I can't spare the time." Nate's voice was gentle but firm. "I have a chapter to complete at the end of this week, and I'm already behind."

There was a brief silence as Ellie judged the likelihood of changing Nate's mind – or pissing him off.

I looked at the page in the textbook, giving no sign that I'd heard the exchange. The sun had moved in the sky. There was a prickling on my arms and shoulders, and I forced myself to get to my feet and pull the deckchair under the umbrella.

The scent of honeysuckle tinged the still, hot air. A door closed, and I looked into the dimness of the sitting room. Ellie stood in the centre of the room, alone. She hugged herself and sank onto the sofa. I rested my head on the back of the chair and sighed. The seduction didn't seem to be going all that well.

My phone buzzed at me, and I groped on the floor for it. It was Seb, and I sat up, and then sank back, cursing myself for my foolishness. It was a brief text.

See you at 7?

My lips tightened. Seb's texts normally covered several screens. Well, two could play at that game.

Fine.

I wondered how much fun this was going to be.

❦

"H-hello. How've you been?" I said, standing by the table in the restaurant. Seb jumped and rose to his feet, closing the menu.

"Stacie! I didn't see you!" He kissed me on both cheeks and held out a chair for me.

So formal, I thought.

I settled into my seat and inspected him from underneath my lashes. He looked older than I remembered him. He caught my gaze and smiled tightly, and I smiled back at him.

"Shall we order?" he said and picked up the menu again.

"Oh, right." I made a pretence of looking through it, my eyes not focused. When the server came, I chose the first items that wouldn't choke me as I ate. My stomach revolted at the plates of food around me. Eating anything should be interesting.

We circled around the conversation like there was an unexploded bomb in it. He asked about my prep. I asked if he'd seen the latest message from Jo. The food arrived and we both picked at it. Seb ordered two glasses of wine and then left his untouched. I drank mine almost in one gulp.

I was struggling to eat any of my main course when I lost patience and put down my knife and fork.

"Seb, what on earth is going on? We're acting like strangers!"

Seb finished his mouthful of food.

"What makes you say that?"

I stared at him.

"Oh, let me see. You disappeared for weeks? You didn't

respond to my texts? Or calls? All I could think was that you were so pissed off with me over the holiday, you'd washed your hands of me! I thought we were friends!"

He shook his head and took a drink of water.

"You pissed me off, sure," he said. "I didn't see why going on holiday with me was such a big deal."

"But—"

"I understand that you're saving for the deposit for a house. But I've done as much as I can to make it as cheap as I could, offered to sub you, and still you threw it back in my face. I concluded that you didn't want to go. And if that was the case, I'd rather you said so straight out."

"It wasn't that! Of course, it wasn't that!"

"So what was it? That you don't want to be beholden to me? What's that about? To quote your earlier words, I thought we were friends. Stuff like that doesn't matter. To me, anyway."

"But it matters to me!" I said. "For you to 'sub' my holiday doesn't work for me at all! Don't you know me well enough to understand that?"

He clasped his hands on the table.

"I hoped you'd know me well enough to be sure that I would never take advantage of you for that. Anyway, I needed to put some space between us to sort it out in my head," he said, taking another sip of water. I noticed his hand was shaking.

"And?" I croaked.

"I've decided that I need to tell you that from my side, we're not friends anymore."

The floor seemed to fall away from me, and the noise of the restaurant receded, leaving the silence roaring in my head. A sharp pain speared my chest. I wondered if it was my heart breaking.

"What?" I whispered.

"We're not friends from my side, Stacie, because I'm in love with you and have been for months."

He let out a deep breath, his face pale.

My mouth fell open. My brain didn't compute, I couldn't speak, couldn't move for the sensation that swept through me.

The server arrived at the table to ask if everything was alright with the main courses, and Seb answered automatically. The server left, and there was silence again.

"Stacie?"

I pushed back my chair and threw my napkin on the table and he glanced up, startled. I crossed to his chair, put my hands around his face and kissed him hard.

"Ditto," I said, when I raised my head. He looked dazed, and I slipped back into my seat, aware of the curious eyes of the other diners. Finally, he laughed and stretched his hand over the table.

"Really?" he said, lacing his fingers through mine.

I nodded. "I have been for ages! But you always seemed to have a girl on hand, and I'm so different from the women you date—"

"Statuesque blondes?"

I nodded. "I never dreamed you would see me as anything other than a friend," I said. "So, I stayed a friend. But I've always wanted more. And I so missed you when you went away!"

A small smile lit his face.

"Or was that the idea?" I asked, sitting back. He held onto my hand.

"Partly, but I was wondering how I could make you see I was serious!" he protested. "Jo told me months ago that I should tell you straight out, but I was sure you'd get the message eventually. And I was terrified you'd just express polite regret and then we wouldn't even be friends either!"

"So we've been circling around each other trying to be friends?" I put the word friends in air quotes and he nodded, grinning.

"Looks like it."

I shook my head, contemplating the strange ways of the

world, and he smiled. A true Seb smile, which lit up his face and crinkled the skin around his eyes.

There was another pause, and then we both picked up our cutlery.

I found myself ravenous. It seemed to be the same for Seb, and we finished eating in what seemed like record time. As the server cleared the plates, he asked if we would like coffee or dessert.

"Perhaps we could have coffee at my house?" Seb asked. My pulse, having recovered its equilibrium, now jumped again. I nodded, unsure of myself.

As we rose to leave the restaurant, he said, "Nice sandals. Haven't seen them before."

It occurred to me, as I drew up alongside Seb's car, that in all the time I had known him, I had never been to his house before. We'd met in bars, restaurants, even Jo's messy flat. But never Seb's house. As I peered through the darkening evening, it was bigger than I expected, with a long sweeping drive.

I climbed out, locked the door and turned just as Seb unlocked the front door and switched on the hall lights. My eyes widened.

"Bloody hell! What do they pay you, Seb?" I muttered.

Nothing like my salary, obviously. The house had three floors and his huge front door led to a massive hall. Lots of blonde wood everywhere and pictures covered the walls – everything from blown up Marvel cartoon covers to Jackson Pollock-like pieces. I shut my mouth with a snap. Given my reaction, perhaps it wasn't surprising that he'd never invited us. Working-class Jo would never have let him hear the end of this luxurious setting.

"Come in!" Seb said from the kitchen door. I glimpsed black countertops, gleaming aluminium, and white cupboards.

"Thanks," I said, wondering if I should take off my shoes. I bent down to undo the straps on my sandals, kicking them off and padding into the kitchen.

There was an awful noise as Seb ground some coffee beans in a funky machine and the aroma swirled around me. I hitched myself onto a high stool and watched uncertainly. He turned to me.

"Not very comfy, those stools. Want to come into the sitting room?"

I slid down with a sigh of relief and followed him into a spacious, wide room, dominated by an enormous TV screen at one end. It was untidy – books and papers strewn about, dirty gym kit in one corner, a tie draped over the arm of one of the deep green sofas, used mugs and a wine glass on the large coffee table. Seb whipped the tie off the arm of the sofa and swept papers into a pile.

"Sit. Do you still take your coffee black?" I nodded.

"And strong, please," I added.

"I remember." He grabbed the dirty crockery, grinned and went back to the kitchen.

I took in my surroundings, recognising slightly battered luxury. I touched the leather of the sofa, soft under my fingers and worn from lots of bottoms. The rug in front of the pale marble fireplace had a few tassels missing, and I smelt a faint tang of wood smoke. The books on the endless bookshelves looked well-thumbed. At ease, I nestled in further. It was the last setting in which I would have imagined sharp-dressed, needle-witted Seb.

He came in with two huge mugs of coffee.

I thanked him. A brief sniff told me it wasn't strong enough, but I smiled. There was a pause.

"So, what shall we talk about?" Seb said, placing his mug on the coffee table.

"How about, how do you live in this palace?" I asked. "Do you live here alone?"

"All alone," he said, making a mournful face. "Yes, it's my house, I bought it with the returns from my investments."

I nodded but didn't know what to say. Investments? He had that kind of money? His eyes twinkled.

"Are you considering whether I'm suitable?" he said.

I blushed. "Sorry, I didn't mean to be intrusive."

He laughed.

"Oh, don't go all stiff on me, Stacie! I don't care! Ask me anything!"

I ran through what I had learned of Seb over the months since Jo had introduced us. I knew his politics (left-leaning), his favourite foods, his football team, and he'd told us something about his family. He liked strange foreign films – I'd been to a few and left bewildered by them – and that we shared a love of psychological thrillers. He was serious about his teaching, one of the things I loved about him. Seb liked house music, and he played tennis very well; he had beaten me several times. And then there were the facts which didn't tell the whole story, and which I'd puzzled over: his clothes, the sports car and now this house.

"Well, you look rather better off than most teachers," I said. "I suppose I've always known it, but I've never stopped to wonder how you do that."

"Mum and Dad bought me a portfolio when I was sixteen rather than give me an allowance," Seb said promptly. "It seemed hard when all my mates were buying CDs and new clothes, but I learned to invest as I grew older. It's been keeping me in decent holidays and cars for years. And I own this house."

"Oh."

"Now I've established my prospects, shall I tell you the stuff I thought you'd want to hear? Like when I knew you were special?"

Despite a wry reflection that he didn't understand quite how special I was, a warm glow spread through me. He'd said he loved me. It was extraordinary. "Go on then."

"It started when rumours of this amazing teaching assistant made me curious. But really, it was when you came into the staff room with tissue paper glued to your hair. When Pat Clark told you, he expected you to get all embarrassed, but you fell about laughing!"

"And that was when you fell in love with me?"

He shrugged.

"No, it's been more slow burn than that. But you showed Clark to be the twat he is. Even if you hadn't been hot, I adored you for that."

I was hot? He adored me? I shook my head to marshal my wandering thoughts.

"Jo always talked about this endless line of perfectly turned-out blonde women," I said. "And I even met a couple of them. Remember Becky?"

We both grimaced at the memory and then laughed. Becky had been so determined to be a model, that she rarely smiled in case it gave her laughter lines and she ate only fish starters in restaurants. She didn't last long.

"And you... You always looked like you'd stepped out of a magazine shoot," I added.

"And I fell for the woman with tissue paper in her hair." Seb smiled and held my gaze. I looked at his mouth. He took the hint and kissed me.

My senses cheered. I felt as if I'd come home, and my hands clenched around his shoulders. I inhaled his scent: warm and musky. A noise which might have been a purr came out of my throat. Seb raised his lips from mine and rested his forehead against mine, breathing heavily. His fingertips trailed over my cheek and I leaned into his hand.

He groaned.

"Jeez, Stacie!" He pulled me onto his knees and kissed me again.

For a few moments, I was a little wooden. It had been a while, after all. But his hands stroked my back, and the flattering 'hmm-ing' noises as he kissed me, reassured and relaxed me. After some minutes of wonderful kisses, I pulled away.

"Seb..."

"Shh... don't fret. I've waited bloody months for this, I imagine I could wait a bit longer before I get my hands on your luscious bod."

I relaxed again, but his erection pushed the cheek of my bottom as I sat on his lap. With a sigh, I rolled onto the sofa. He looked confused and I took his hand.

"Taking it slowly?" I said, flicking my eyes to his lap. His face cleared, and he sighed.

"Yes, probably best."

We sat and we talked of nothing, of everything. He brought out a bottle of wine and more coffee. Later, we ate a cheese toastie.

"Stacie?"

"Hmm?"

"It's half past three."

I blinked. "Christ, is it?" I looked at the clock on his mantelpiece and then shrugged "Oh well. I suppose I should be going."

Seb stroked my hair. "You don't have to. I have a spare room. And it has a door that locks."

I laughed. "Will that be necessary?"

"It might." He looked at me seriously.

"Next time," I said, from under my eyelashes, surprised to see a faint tinge of pink creep up his cheeks. He moved and kissed me hard on the mouth.

"I'll hold you to that."

CHAPTER FIFTEEN
SARAH

Sarah felt the prickle at the back of her neck and froze. The woman who was serving her looked at her askance. Sarah forced a smile to her lips and handed over her pennies. She put the apricots into her basket and, drawing a breath, turned around.

Prudence was watching her from across the marketplace, and Sarah shivered at the look on her face. She forced herself to nod and then walked across the cobblestones to get a pitcher of beer.

"Mistress Bartlett, how do you do?"

Sarah turned to face the young woman.

"Well, I thank you. I trust you are well also?"

"Yes, my pains have completely disappeared. It is almost magical," Prudence said, raising her voice and choosing her words with care. Sarah's mouth was dry.

"My tea has good qualities. Many women in the village have found it helpful."

Prudence just looked at her, and after a few moments, Sarah nodded her head and, stiffening her back, walked away.

As she walked, others glanced at her and then looked away.

Her fingers grasped the handle of her basket so tightly, the willow creased her palms. She forced herself to walk at her normal pace down the road until she reached the cottage.

She caught sight of a flash of brown and white in the orchard. The children were scrumping again. The breath hissed between her teeth. It was too early for windfalls; the children were stealing. She shouted a warning at them and, listening to the laughing and running feet, she walked up the path. She closed the door with a thump and breathed out.

"Mercy, what ails you, mistress?" Dorothy asked from the pantry. "You look pale as death!"

Sarah pushed herself off the heavy wooden door.

"I'm just a little faint."

Dorothy hurried towards her and pushed her into a chair, muttering. She thrust a mug of beer into Sarah's hand and stood with her hands on her hips.

"Mistress, this cannot go on! You are wasting before my eyes this past sennight! You eat less than a bird, you do not sleep, and when you do, I hear you crying into the dark!" she said. Sarah hung her head and sipped her beer.

"And all this since the parson came to call," she added shrewdly. Sarah looked up to see Dorothy's beady eyes fixed on her and blushed. "Did he ask to wed you?"

Sarah sighed. "He did."

"And? What answer did you give?"

"I refused him."

Dorothy tutted. "Mistress, are you right in the head? Think not that I'm deaf to the gossips. I hear them right enough! And I see the looks cast at you, all the time while taking your potions! This village is sour and bad, and the parson would have protected you!"

Sarah put the mug down.

"Dorothy, I cannot marry him."

"Why, mistress?"

Sarah was silent, deciding what to say. Finally, she said: "It is not my fate. And it is not his."

Dorothy opened her mouth to speak and Sarah continued. "And I have been thinking. You should visit your sister soon, in Chichester. I can spare you for a month or so, and you should go as soon as it can be arranged," Sarah added, plucking at her skirt.

"Mistress!" Dorothy grabbed the back of a chair, her face now white.

"Nay, I am not displeased," Sarah said hastily. "I am aware you have not seen her these four years and your nephew must be, what, nearly nine by now? It is high time he was reminded of his aunt!"

Dorothy sucked in a breath.

"You are sending me away?"

Sarah shrugged and smiled at her maid.

"Only for a short time, sweeting. You will return in two months and all this will have passed."

"Will it, mistress?"

Sarah nodded, tightening her lips.

"It will."

The silence settled in the room.

"I will pack my things," Dorothy said, blinking back tears as she rose, squeezing her mistress on the shoulder.

Sarah left the cottage to examine the orchard for damage.

There was a hammering at the door later that afternoon, and Ed Tilley, a scrawny youngster, fell into the room as Dorothy opened the door.

"Me mam asked for you to come! It's me sister!" he gasped to Sarah, his eyes panicked. Sarah rose at once and reached for her basket.

"What ails her?"

"She's 'avin' fits and the like, her eyes all wrong!" Ed said.

She paused for a second and then turned to him. "I will come now, but go gather leaves from the elder tree by the lane. Do you know it?" He nodded. "Fetch me two good handfuls. Here, take this cloth and put them in there. Then go home with them. Hurry!"

He whirled around and Sarah continued to put her herbs into her basket and then grabbed her cloak. Dorothy watched as Sarah tied the strings.

"Have a care, mistress," she said.

"Aye, I will. You should leave as soon as you can – today."

"Must I, mistress?"

"Yes, you must, fool!" Sarah scolded. "You know it is for the best!"

Dorothy held out her thin arms, her cheeks wet. Sarah paused and then fell into them, as the sobs moved Dorothy's thin chest.

"God be with you," she whispered between her tears.

"And with you." Sarah kissed her and left the cottage without a backward glance.

※

The door flew open as Sarah raised her hand to knock again. A wild-eyed man stood there, his face stricken.

"Thank the Lord!" he said, standing aside to let her pass.

"It's Oliver, is it not?"

"Aye. I thought ye might not come, the missus is sore afflicted."

Sarah glanced around at the scruffy room. There was a thin keening from a side room, and she entered to find a plump woman wringing her hands by the narrow bed.

"She's gone!" she wailed. "She's gone!"

Sarah knelt by the girl who was still as stone and quickly found a pulse.

"Nay, she lives still. I may be able to help. What has she eaten these past three days?"

"Nothing different from us. We think she be possessed by the Devil!" wept the woman.

"Nonsense," Sarah said, opening her satchel. "I think she has eaten something that is causing this." Frowning, she turned to the white-faced child, seeing the sticky froth at the corners of the girl's mouth. She was pulling out some mint when Ed ran through the door panting, clutching the big kerchief with elder leaves in it.

"Good," she smiled at him, taking the glossy green leaves. She turned to the mother. "Now, can you boil me some water in a small pan? Put a handful of the leaves in it and when it is boiling, strain the liquid through a muslin. And open the window. I need light and air." Sarah thrust the leaves into her hands. The woman gawped at her and then turned to do as she was bid.

Ed stood irresolute in the doorway.

"Could you find me a clean cloth? And cold water?" asked Sarah. He nodded and ran away.

Sarah perched on the edge of the pallet and put her hand on the child's forehead. It was burning and her lips tightened.

The scent of the mint leaves rose to her nostrils as she crushed them in her mortar. Ed came back with a clout and a bowl of water. Sarah nodded and dipped the cloth in the water, then rubbed it into the crushed mint leaves. She gently cleaned the corners of the girl's mouth.

"What is her name?"

"Jane," replied Ed.

"Jane, can you hear me?" Sarah said softly. "Come, sweeting, come back to us."

Jane was unresponsive, and Sarah gently lifted the eyelids. The pupils were huge and black, and Sarah sighed. She loosened the ties of the girl's dress, allowing air to the neck and throat.

"Open the shutter, please," Sarah said again. Ed leapt to do her bidding, flooding the room with the bright afternoon light and some blessed fresh air.

"Ask your mother if the liquid is ready."

He ran out and Sarah's fingers sought the pulse at the thin wrist. There was a beat, slow and faint, but a beat.

She sensed him before she saw him, and she tensed.

"Mistress Bartlett, how does she?"

"She is very sick, Parson Dillington," she said, without turning. "I may not be able to save her."

The parson moved into the room, dwarfing it and towering over her. "What can I do?"

Leave me, thought Sarah briefly. "Chase Mistress Tilley for my potion. It will make the child sick and may purge the poison from her stomach."

"You are certain it is poison?" His deep voice settled in her bones.

"No, I am not, but this way we will know. I fear she may have eaten mistletoe berries. The children were scrumping from my orchards and I noticed that mistletoe had been torn from one of the trees earlier."

"Is that fatal?"

"Yes, sir. It can be."

He turned to call for Mistress Tilley, who came running in.

"Oh, sir, can you save her?"

"Have you prepared the potion as instructed?"

"Yes, sir, but we think she might be possessed by a demon! She has been shouting all kinds of ungodly things and foaming, sir, at the mouth! Can you get the Devil out of her?"

"I will be here to shine the light of God on your daughter," he said soothingly, as Sarah gritted her teeth. "But bring me the potion."

The woman returned after a few minutes, carrying the liquid in a beaker.

"Have you clean sheets?" Sarah asked, trying not to be curt.

"Lord, is she like to die?"

"No, she is like to be violently sick."

Sarah saw the parson's mouth turn up at the corners before he became grave again.

"A bowl then, Mistress Tilley?"

"It is more violent than that, Parson," Sarah said, clearing her satchel to one side and taking an apron from it. She turned to see him looking slightly alarmed. "You might want to withdraw, sir."

Sarah wrapped her apron around her dress, and the mother stared at her with wide eyes and then held out the beaker. Sarah took it and carefully raised Jane, lying still and pale on the pallet. She wrapped an arm about her and put the beaker to her lips. The child gave a cough, and some liquid seemed to slip down her throat. Sarah tightened her grip on Jane's shoulders and continued to drip the potion into her mouth.

"Now, Jane," she said softly. "Drink this down."

Jane moaned, and Sarah tipped the beaker again.

"That's it," she said encouragingly. She watched as Jane's eyes fluttered open.

"Praise be!" said Mistress Tilley, clutching Ed, who looked wide eyed. The woman then screamed as Jane's face contorted and she began to retch.

"Gently, Jane. You will be sick and then be much better. I hope..." said Sarah, holding her tight. The child turned piteous eyes on her and then began to heave.

The vomiting seemed to last hours, although in reality, it was only a quarter hour. Ed watched in admiration as green-yellow bile ejected from Jane's mouth, almost reaching the end of the bed. Finally, the heaving subsided, and she lay back, gasping and exhausted. Closing her eyes briefly, Sarah loosened her arm and stood up, flexing the muscles to get the blood flowing again. She bent and dipped a cloth in the mint-flavoured water and gently wiped Jane's mouth.

"She will be well, presently, I think, but she should drink – mead, if you have it, weakened with boiled water. Take care to boil the water," she said in a low voice. Mistress Tilley clutched the arm of her husband, who had crept into the room.

"Praise be to God!' she said in a hushed voice.

"Amen," said Parson Dillington.

"I could swear she had been given over to the Devil!" Mistress Tilley continued.

"Could you now, Mistress Tilley?" Prudence said from the door. Sarah stiffened but continued to pack her bags with steady hands.

"Prudence! What business do you have here?" Parson Dillington asked, surprised.

His daughter looked at him with innocent eyes.

"The business of the Lord, Papa. What else should I do?"

Sarah carefully folded her stained apron, so it did not sully her satchel as she packed it away.

"Father, did you not see her drive a devil from this child? It came from her mouth and flew out from the window!"

Parson Dillington's jaw dropped open. Sarah gritted her teeth and reached for her mortar.

"And see, not a word to defend herself!" Prudence cried, pointing at Sarah.

"Aye, it's true, she did want the window open," said Mistress Tilley. "Was that for the Devil to fly out?"

"No doubt, Mistress Tilley!" Prudence nodded.

"Prudence, you will be silent." The ice-cold voice of the parson whipped out and Sarah, fastening her cloak at her throat, shivered. "Leave now. I will deal with you at home."

"Father, you are spellbound!" Prudence wailed. "You, a man of God! She is in league with the Devil and she has bewitched you! I have seen how you grow pale, and fast, and are awake long into the night! I know you walk around before dawn!"

The parson looked thunderous, his handsome face contorted with anger.

"Prudence, do as you are told! You have stretched my patience enough."

The girl burst into tears and ran out of the room. Sarah pulled the cloak closer around her. There was silence. The boy Ed began to snivel.

Sarah moved quietly to the door. The parson reached out a hand to stop her, but his hand dropped at her look.

The Tilleys flattened themselves against the wall as she passed, and she swallowed the tears, gazing into the middle distance.

She forced herself not to run, but to walk steadily back to the cottage, neither looking at anyone nor speaking. The light was fading from the sunny day and she looked at her shadow on the ground as she walked. She opened the door, closed it gently, and leaned on the solid wood. Dorothy had done as she bid, and the cottage was empty. She sat down to wait for the next act to begin.

The magistrates came two hours later. Sarah was still in her cloak, although she had unpacked her basket and the cottage was neat and tidy. She flinched at the banging on the door.

Samuel Cootes filled the doorway, his stomach hanging over his belt. His eyes, like currants in uncooked dough, gleamed as they saw her. Behind him, less enthusiastic, was Joseph Sanderson.

"Sarah Bartlett, we are here to arrest you for witchcraft!"

"Are you?" asked Sarah mildly, as she picked up her Bible and turned back to him.

"Aye, Mistress Bartlett! You will be taken to the assizes and tried for your comportment with the Devil! And I see you are quiet. No doubt you expect the foul one to conjure you away!" He leaned in, and she caught a whiff of sweat and ale.

"I am ready, sir," she said calmly.

He grabbed her roughly by the arm, to the protests of Joseph Sanderson.

"Sam, be gentle. She has not been tried yet."

Sarah shot him a grateful glance as Sam's malicious fingers dug into her flesh. She put the hood of her cloak over her head, but he pulled it off, dislodging her cap. Her hair, red and gleaming, came free from its pins and fell to her shoulders. Joseph gaped.

"She has hair like flames," he muttered.

As Sam hustled her through the door, Sarah saw Annie Whyte, sucking her teeth and watching the proceedings. Sarah put up her chin and Mistress Whyte turned away with a satisfied sneer.

"Evil, I've always said so," she said to anyone who would listen. Other villagers, informed by whisperings and a fine-honed sense for a burning, appeared at their doors, watching her with wide eyes. Sarah saw Abigail throw open the door to her cottage and heard her cry of alarm.

"Sarah! What is amiss?"

"She is arrested for witchcraft, Mistress Lester," said Sam, scowling. "What have you to say about it?"

"Sarah Bartlett is no witch!" Abigail cried.

Sarah shook her head in warning, but before Abigail could say anything further, Thomas came from the smithy. His eyes glanced over the group – Sam's hand on her arm, Joseph and Mistress Whyte still talking – and understood it all. He strode over and pushed Abigail back into the cottage, slamming the door. Sarah relaxed.

The walk through the village seemed endless, but at last, they came to the gaol. Samuel thrust Sarah into a cell, gloomy in the half-light, and shut the door with a bang. The key grated in the lock, and all was silent.

CHAPTER SIXTEEN
STACIE

I struggled out of bed at nine thirty and crawled to the kitchen, expecting the house to be empty. I stumbled downstairs in my bare feet, in search of coffee.

"Good morning," Nate's voice came from the top of the stairs.

"God! You made me jump!" I said, my hand against my thumping heart. I peered up. His eyes gleamed at me from over the bannister.

"Sorry. Good night?"

None of your business, I thought.

"Great, thanks."

"What, did the Honourable Seb declare himself at last?" came the voice of Ellie from the kitchen door. I remembered her seduction plan. It hadn't gone well, judging by the tartness in her face and voice.

"If there's coffee, I'll have some," I said, wrapping my robe around me a little tighter.

"Ooh, woman of mystery!" sniped Ellie, looking grumpy.

I stretched my mouth into a smile, poured coffee and took a sip. I wanted to shower and do some thinking. As I walked up the stairs, I met Nate coming down and his glance slid up my bare legs. My pulse skittered at the look on his face.

"Excuse me," I said, waiting for him to get out of my way. He stood for a couple of seconds before stepping aside.

I shut my bedroom door, out of breath.

He'd left by the time I had struggled into my clothes. Ellie sprawled on a chair in the lounge with a book.

"So, how was the fabulous Sebastian? I always thought he'd be great in the sack."

"I wouldn't discuss it with you even if I knew, little sister," I said, sipping my coffee. "The seduction scene with Nate didn't go to plan, I take it?"

She sat bolt upright.

"What did he *say* to you? God, the—"

"You're in such a foul mood, I presume it was merely embarrassing," I interrupted.

She stared at the carpet.

"We had a nice dinner," she said.

Failure of any kind wouldn't sit well with Ellie; she wasn't used to it. I kept quiet, not knowing quite what to say.

"He needs to get to know me a little better," she said, almost to herself. She focused back on me. "Are you seeing Seb again?"

"Yes, we're meeting tonight."

"Mmm… keen."

I considered. "Yes, I am."

⁂

The day crawled by, for once, my attention not held by my work. I mooched about the house, shuffling papers and not reading books until, at last, it was time to change. I took the stairs two at a time.

"Dear me, aren't we eager?" was the remark from Ellie. I turned my hand on the door of my room.

"Ah well, gives you another opportunity to get Nate into bed, doesn't it?"

Ellie's lips tightened, and her colour rose. "Will you be home tonight?"

"No idea, so try to keep it down, eh?" I closed my door.

There was a text on my phone.

I might be early. See you when you're ready.

"Me too," I muttered, casting an eye at the weather and slipping into a sleeveless summer dress. Would my upper arms wobble? I held out my arm and patted the flesh. Hmm. Firm enough.

I glanced at my face in the mirror and it looked *alive*, my eyes sparkling. I giggled. And giggled some more at the unfamiliar sound. I turned to my handbag and chucked a lipstick into it. On impulse, I grabbed an additional pair of knickers and stuffed them next to my purse.

It was quarter to seven; our reservation was in forty-five minutes. It would take me ten minutes to get to the pizza place. I sprayed some perfume in my hair and grabbed my bag. I wavered for a moment and grabbed my car keys. We could always eat early, or sit at the bar with a drink.

I met Nate.

"Out again?" he said, holding the door. I smiled. "See you later?" he asked when I said nothing.

"Maybe." I laughed before the door closed.

※

I arrived at the pizza place just sixteen minutes later, breathless as I tumbled through the door. I saw Seb at the back of the restaurant and also the young girl in a high-waisted dress who kissed her fingers and winked at me. With a wink back, I threaded my way through the tables to Seb.

He was turning his knife, point over point, on the table. As I watched, he checked his watch. I waved, drawing his attention.

His face lit up, and he rose. The girl waved at me and then vanished.

As I reached the table, his hands reached out and his long, firm fingers smoothed my skin. He gazed at me and my body grew warm.

"Hi."

"Hi."

There was a pause. I grinned, and the awkwardness vanished. He poured me a glass of wine, and I grabbed it like a lifeline.

"What are you having?" I asked, scanning the menu. I wasn't that hungry.

"Haven't thought yet," he replied. "I'm not sure how interested I am in the food."

My glance darted to his face, his eyes intense. I swallowed. "Um..."

He smiled and picked up his menu.

"I feel like a teenager!" I confessed after we'd given our order. "Shows how long it is since I dated. You'll need to let me know if I'm getting it wrong."

He laughed. "You won't get it wrong, Stacie."

"Is it like riding a bike?"

He grinned as my cheeks flushed at the slight innuendo. Like the gentleman he was, he disregarded it. "How are you? Is the prep for the new job going okay?"

I nodded, scrabbling for safer conversational ground in a public place, but recalled the work I hadn't done today because I hadn't been able to focus. "It's fine. I'm excited about it. I'll get it completed soon, I hope."

"Why is it taking so long?"

Well, you're not helping, I thought, taking a sip of my wine.

"We have a new bloke from Dad's university staying with us, which is a bit of a nuisance, and if having a stranger in the house wasn't enough, Ellie's slavering over him."

"Sounds unpleasant."

"You have no idea. She asked me when I was going to be out of the house earlier this week."

"Why?"

I gave him an old-fashioned look, and after a second, his brow cleared. "Ah. Ugh."

I nodded, saying nothing.

"Are you worried about it?"

I nodded. "He's… He makes me feel weird. There's something… off about him. Or perhaps I'm just prejudiced about Americans."

His eyebrows tweaked.

I took another drink. "I don't know. I've not seen Ellie like this before."

"What, in love with someone other than herself?"

"That's what Gran said!" I laughed and then sobered, playing with the stem of my wine glass. "She's so fixated. Like she might *hurt* someone who gets in her way. I might be imagining things."

"Let's hope so. She's scary enough as it is, without being a psycho."

I laughed and decided we'd spoken enough about Ellie and Nate, and it was time to concentrate on being here with Seb. I'd secretly wanted this for so long, I could barely believe it was happening.

Be cool, Stacie, I said to myself, trying to clamp down on my giddiness.

At the end of the meal, the server asked if we wanted coffee.

Seb looked at me, and I smiled. "No thanks, we'll just have the bill. We can have coffee at yours, can't we?"

☙

At his house, Seb fumbled with the key, swearing under his breath until the door opened. I walked into the hall and he closed the door, leaning against it as I turned.

There was a long pause.

"Um… coffee?" I said, my palms sweating.

"Of course," he said, pushing himself off the door. I followed him into the kitchen and a tense silence built as he made the drinks and I waited. There were butterflies in my stomach.

He put the mug in front of me.

"Shall we sit somewhere comfy?" I said, after clearing my throat. He nodded and led the way to the sitting room. We sat at either end of his enormous sofa.

There was silence.

"Could—"

"If you—"

We both stopped and laughed.

"Come here," I said, patting the space next to me. Seb slid along the leather and I took his hand.

"I'm glad you're here," he said in a low voice.

"Me too." I kissed him.

He groaned, pushed his hands into my hair, and deepened the kiss. My pulse rocketed, my skin blooming with sensation. The buckle of his belt was digging into my belly and I wriggled. I heard him groan, and I locked my arms around his neck and pulled him close. His lips left my mouth and nibbled at my neck, and I caught my breath.

My hands ran down the length of his lean torso, and I pulled the shirt from his trousers to touch his skin, smooth and warm. He closed his eyes for a moment and then looked at me.

"Stacie, this may be too soon but, would you like to come to bed?"

"I thought you'd never ask," I breathed.

He laughed and rose to his feet. I grasped his hand, and he led me up the stairs.

His bedroom was dark. As he led me through the doorway, I hesitated and he looked at me.

"Stacie? What's up?"

I gulped. "Look, I haven't done this for a long time and my last boyfriend told me I wasn't very good at it."

He stared, his eyes gleaming from the hall light. "You've not been dating the right men, Stacie." And with that, he drew me to the bed and sat me on the edge. He took both my hands, and I wondered if he could hear my pulse thundering.

"Relax. We'll do whatever you want, and nothing more. Okay?"

I nodded. He eased me back onto the crisp white duvet, and I could smell the fabric conditioner. I smiled. He'd changed the bed, I'd brought clean underwear. We both wanted this.

He kissed me; my forehead, my neck, my cheeks, my lips. His shirt came undone, the skirt of my dress was around my thighs, the only sound in the room was my sighing. I brushed my hand across his crotch and he groaned.

"I'm wearing too many clothes," I said and turned over so he could unzip me. The straps fell from my shoulders, my breasts tumbled into his hands and he nuzzled them with his lips. I groaned. He pulled the dress down my thighs and draped it over a chair. He gazed at me, and I wrapped my arms across my body. He pushed them gently down.

"Oh no, you don't. You're bloody gorgeous, don't hide."

Pink in the face, I smiled at him. "You're overdressed."

Mere moments later, he stood in front of me naked, his erection nodding. I grinned and held out my arms. He moved into them and lay beside me, cupping my cheek with his hand.

"I meant what I said. We don't have to have sex. We can play, if you'd rather."

"I'm not sure I know how to play," I said in a low voice, my mouth drying.

"Then let me show you. Lie down and close your eyes. No peeking."

I did as I was told and his hands, his lips, and his body brushed all of mine. My back arched in response. When he eased my legs apart and settled his shoulders between them, I looked up in panic.

"Eyes shut," he repeated.

"But—"

"Lie back and think of England, Stacie."

When his fingers brushed my inner thighs, I jumped but squeezed my eyes closed.

"Good girl," I heard him murmur and my lips tweaked.

"Don't be patronising, Seb," I warned, and he chuckled.

Then his mouth started nibbling the soft flesh of my stomach. I squirmed as the moisture pooled between my legs.

His hands wrapped around my thighs and with a sigh, which I hoped was pleasure, he began to lap at me. When my orgasm came, I lifted off the pillow and cried out, gasping and pushing his mouth away, unable to bear it any longer.

When I opened my eyes several moments later, Seb was grinning at me.

"Good game?" he asked, looking smug.

I recovered my breath. "Do you want to play too?"

The colour rushed to his face. "Yes, please." His voice sounded hoarse as he climbed up the bed to lie beside me.

I pulled my hair to one side and teased his nipples with my teeth. It didn't take long to move down his body. He grabbed my shoulders.

"You don't have to, Stacie."

"Try not to be scared, I'll be gentle," I teased, as powerful and sexy as I had ever been in my life. He chuckled under his breath.

I licked and stroked and then took him into my mouth, watching with satisfaction as his hands clenched the duvet cover.

"Not sure I can cope with much more, Stacie," he murmured after a few minutes.

"How disappointing," I said, sitting back on my heels. "Do you have a condom?" He lunged for the bedside table.

I groaned as I slid down him. It had been a long time. I could hear the hiss from between his teeth.

"Good God, you feel amazing."

I moved, and he groaned. The tingle between my thighs bloomed and my breath came in quick gasps. His clever hands reached between my legs. I orgasmed with a slow moan, and then his head went back into the pillow, and he gave a loud groan.

I rolled off him and curled into his arms while my heartbeat slowed.

"You didn't have to move," he said into my hair.

"I thought I might be too heavy."

He sighed.

"No, Stace. You really haven't been dating the right men."

I smiled and snuggled closer, replete, happy.

CHAPTER SEVENTEEN
SARAH

Sarah arched her back to ease the ache and rubbed her hands over her chilled arms. She'd lost count of the hours they'd had her locked in the cell but could see that the dawn was coming as the shadows lightened and the darkness turned to grey.

Her stomach rumbled. She'd had nothing to eat since the previous day.

As if reading her mind, Joseph Sanderson returned. Sarah turned and pushed her hair under her cap as best she might.

"Good morrow, Mistress Bartlett," he said, pushing the jug and loaf through the bars. She had to strain to hear his gruff voice. She bobbed a curtsey and then fell on the bread.

"You have the parson to thank for your breakfast," he added, and she swallowed.

"Please pass on my gratitude," she said, and then she stilled.

"'Tis nothing," said Parson Dillington, coming into the small antechamber. Joseph touched his cap before backing out.

There was silence and the parson watched as Sarah finished the bread and took a deep draught of the beer.

Wiping her mouth on her sleeve, she sighed and sat with her back against the wall, pulling her gown and cloak around her legs.

"Your situation is perilous," said the parson. She nodded.

"Aye, I fear so. Your daughter has much to answer for." He stiffened, and then his shoulders drooped.

"But you are innocent of the charge of witchcraft, are you not?"

Sarah smiled.

"What does that matter? I have enemies, and the folk here are superstitious. And, as you have said, I am alone and without protectors."

He moved closer.

"I would have protected you and can still do so. But you must confess."

She stared at him. And then laughed.

"I have done nothing wrong and I never lie. But even if I have nothing to confess, they might torture me until they kill me anyway. Whichever way it happens, they mean me to die."

"But if you confess, I can exorcise you!" he said, gripping the bars. "But you must confess, Mistress Bartlett!"

"I have nothing to confess, therefore I will not."

Parson Dillington frowned.

"Why not? What would it serve you, other than pain?"

"I do not lie, and I will not be beholden to you, Parson Dillington."

He snorted. "Beholden? In what way would you be beholden?"

"I would be in debt to you for my life, and I will be in debt to no man."

"I am at a loss to understand you. Surely your life is worth more than your pride? And God would forgive the sin of untruth!"

She looked straight at him.

"I will be in debt to no man, and I never lie," she repeated. "And have a care; defending me will only increase my reputation as a sorceress. Did you not mark what Prudence said? That I had bewitched you?"

The parson flushed. "She is just a child."

"Not so much of a child that she doesn't know when another woman is threatening her role in your life," Sarah observed. Parson Dillington stiffened, and she waved away whatever he was going to say. "If you would grant me one boon, Parson Dillington, I would ask that you visit Thomas Lester, the smithy, and his wife Abigail and beg them not to attend my trial, or defend me in any way. If they do, they will suffer from it."

"Of course, but your friends will not desert you."

"They must. Speak to Thomas, he will understand. Abigail is too passionate, too quick to speak." She paused and dashed away a tear that had fallen on her cheek.

His eyes bored into her, and he clenched his hands. "Something must avail," he muttered.

She shook her head. "This is my fate, sir."

"I know the justice who will be sitting. I will speak with him."

"Who is it?"

"Justice Peter Darcy."

She laughed, a strange sound in the dim misery of the cell. "Ah yes, a man liberal with his promises of mercy to get those accused to confess, and unscrupulous about breaking them," she said, thinking back to Margaret Eames, whom nothing could save – and certainly not Justice Darcy.

Parson Dillington frowned. "You seem determined to die. Are you aware that such action is deepest sin?"

"I am not determined to die, sir, but I am prepared."

He looked at a loss but grasped her hand. "I will speak with Thomas."

And he left her in the gloom, watching the light of the day grow stronger.

THE VISITOR

She held her head high as Joseph led her into the room. Her nostrils flared as the stink of the crowd washed over her.

Her whole body ached. The women examining her for the witches' mark had found nothing, but they had been rough, pinching and shoving her. Her face flamed as she remembered her indignity, stripped naked while they stood in a ring around her. She clamped down on her rising anger. To be angry would not serve her here. She must endure it.

Justice Darcy sat on a raised platform, a tall, thickset man with small eyes and a large nose. With him was another man, skeletally thin with skin as white as a corpse. She drew a deep breath and took her place on the stand, and the noise from the crowd erupted. She glanced at the mob and knew she would get no mercy from them. Mistress Whyte's piggy eyes glittered with malice, and her cronies sat with her. What hope she might have had from Parson Dillington, died. She stiffened her back and faced the justices.

"Sarah Bartlett, you are accused of the most foul crime of witchcraft. How do you plead?"

"I am innocent of any crime." Sarah's voice was firm.

"Let us hear the evidence and we shall decide," he said, his face sneering. "Mistress Lawrence, step forward."

Agatha Lawrence stood up, twisting a handkerchief. Her brown eyes looked huge in her face. Her voice quavered as she swore on the Bible.

"Tell us what you saw," Justice Darcy said, leaning forward. "Be not afraid." He smiled at her, revealing small, yellow teeth.

"I was at the wife of the smithy; Mistress Lester and her child were content. But when Sarah Bartlett arrived, the child did cry and wail and fell sick with a fever."

"And?" Justice Darcy prompted.

"I saw a black cat."

"Her familiar? An imp of Satan?"

"Yes, sir."

Sarah stared in disbelief, her mouth dry, as the words fell

into the silence of the courtroom. Murmurs from the crowd rose like chattering sparrows.

"Does the child live?"

"Yes, sir." Justice Darcy looked disappointed and Mistress Lawrence strived to redress her worth. "I left as soon as I saw the imp, but it was only when Mistress Bartlett left, that the child recovered."

There was nodding from the crowd and muttering.

"Rebecca is well because of my care!" Sarah burst out. There were catcalls from the villagers in the courtroom.

"Silence!" Justice Darcy snapped as Mistress Lawrence shrank back at Sarah's voice. The noise died away.

Sarah closed her eyes. It was futile. The justices hadn't even called the Tilley family yet, and she felt already threatened. And then there was Prudence.

"Continue," the justice urged.

"Nothing more, sir." He nodded curtly, and she took her seat, congratulated and petted by friends.

"John Maudlin!" Justice Darcy called. Sarah frowned, not recognising the name.

To her horror, the man who had accosted her at the festival swaggered up, leering at her. How had he been called to give evidence? Who had known him?

The man confirmed his name and swore on the Bible that his testimony was true.

"John Maudlin, tell us what you saw," said Justice Darby.

"I met this woman on the eve of the Damask Rose, wandering in the woods," he began.

"Wandering in the woods? Alone?" put in the other justice.

"Aye, called on her familiars to attack me, she did."

"What happened?" Justice Darcy asked.

"I were set about by huge black birds, coming to her call."

"And then?" Justice Derby pressed, leaning forward, his small eyes intent.

"Then I came along," Parson Dillington's thunderous voice came from the back of the court, to the gasp of the crowd. "You were chasing this woman, and she was fleeing you. There was no witchcraft to save Mistress Bartlett, it was pure chance I was there! Remember your oath, sir." He strode to the front of the room and glared at John Maudlin, whose face mottled red.

"Silence! Wait to be called!" the second justice cried, and Justice Darcy nodded.

"You will have your turn, Parson. Continue, Master Maudlin."

"I left the woods," said John Maudlin. "I took myself home to pray and thank God for a lucky escape. What would've happened to me had I consorted with a witch?" He crossed himself and the crowd murmured in agreement.

Parson Dillington rolled his eyes, and his lips tightened. Sarah felt herself turn cold with fear. She looked down at her trembling hands.

More people took the stand to testify against her. Neighbours, who had used her skills to heal them, now protested they had seen evil things with wings fly around her door, that she had turned their milk sour, that their cattle had died at her whim. Sarah tried to remain stalwart but grew more and more dismayed at the vitriol directed against her. When she protested against the 'evidence', she was silenced by Justice Darcy.

Then Mistress Tilley was called to the stand and the courtroom tensed in anticipation. Sarah wondered how Jane did, and looking around the room, saw Oliver Tilley, looking ill at ease.

"Mistress Tilley, you have sworn on the Bible," Justice Darcy reminded her, as she nodded, round-eyed. "Tell your tale."

"My daughter Jane fell ill after being bewitched by Mistress Bartlett," she said in a rush. "She cursed the children—"

"While they were in my orchard, stealing my fruit!" Sarah cried.

"The accused will be quiet! Mistress Tilley, continue."

"They were walking through the field behind!" said

Mistress Tilley, flushing pink. "They might have picked up a few windfalls."

Sarah stared steadily at her.

"I could tell something was amiss," she continued, shifting her gaze to Justice Darcy. "Not a half-hour after she came in, my youngest, Jane, were fittin' and shakin' like she were possessed by the very Devil!"

There was a swooning sigh from the courtroom, and Mistress Tilley crossed herself.

"And then?" said Justice Darcy.

"My Ed fetched Mistress Bartlett, although had I known she were the cause of my Jane's distemper, I'd have never allowed her in the house!"

Heads nodded in the room. Sarah could feel her nails digging into her palms.

"She asked twice for the window to be opened so that the Devil could fly out," she added. The crowd whispered and tutted.

"And what happened to the child?" asked Justice Darcy.

"My back was turned, but I'm sure she asked the Devil in kind words to come back to her. Then such a dreadful sight as the spirit was cast forth by my poor Jane! 'Twas only because the parson was present that we could be safe, I'm sure!"

Sarah turned to Ed, with her eyebrows raised. He blushed scarlet and ducked his head. His father continued to look grim and uncomfortable.

"And the Devil flew out of the window?" asked Justice Darcy.

"He did, sir, leaving mess and vileness all around. Then Prudence Dillington came and accused Sarah Bartlett of witchcraft, and of bewitching her father."

At this, the whole courtroom seemed to sit up. Justice Darcy looked surprised and cast a glance at Parson Dillington, whose face was as stone.

"Indeed?"

"Aye, sir. And of making him pale and sleepless, and lacking in appetite."

"What happened then? Has the good parson been bewitched?"

Mistress Tilley twisted her hands together.

"Sir, I know not. The parson seems a good man and offered to keep us safe while the witch was in our house. But he sent his daughter home and seemed angry when she spoke."

Justice Darcy looked narrowly at the parson who looked haughtily back at him.

"I see. Thank you, Mistress Tilley. We shall have Prudence Dillington's testimony next."

"Will the accused be given a chance to defend herself from these treacherous and superstitious lies?" Parson Dillington asked in a voice of ice.

"All in good time, sir, if indeed anyone will speak for her."

None would if they had hope of safety, thought Sarah, feeling the tears prick her eyes.

"I will speak for her," said Parson Dillington, and Sarah shook her head in dismay. The justices whispered among themselves, and Justice Darcy nodded at the parson.

"So be it. But can we trust your testimony, sir, if you have been bewitched by this woman?"

Parson Dillington clenched his teeth and said nothing. Justice Darcy nodded in satisfaction. "Meantime, we will speak with your daughter, Prudence."

Prudence took the stand, her face as calm and white as paper. Her gaze, however, chilled Sarah to the bone. The child looks mad, she thought.

Prudence began her story. Parson Dillington had not been the same father she had known since coming into contact with Mistress Bartlett; his appetite failed, and she listened to him pace the floors at night. Prudence surmised that as a man of God, he had been cursed by the witch and was not in his right mind.

"Mistress Bartlett has attended to you, has she not?" asked

the second justice. Prudence looked startled, and then a mottled stain of red crept up her throat. She nodded.

"What ailed you?"

As Prudence was lost for words, Sarah spoke.

"It was women's problems, sir. Mistress Dillington recovered with a hot brick and a warm drink."

As she expected, the justice scuttled away from the subject, but then returned to Jane Tilley.

"You were present at the Tilley house when Jane was ill, were you not?"

Prudence nodded.

"What did you see?"

Prudence paused, and Sarah saw the moment her gaze hardened.

"I saw the evil spirit fly out of the child and out through the window. I thought Mistress Bartlett wanted it to escape because of my father's presence. When I challenged her to deny she was a witch, she said nothing."

The justices nodded.

"And she bent her powers on my father to stop him hearing my words!" she added, her face twisting. "He became angry and sent me away!"

"Did he beat you?"

"No," she admitted. "But his heart is cold towards me now and it is all *your* fault!" she screamed, leaping to her feet and pointing at Sarah with a shaking hand. "You have cursed me. My father no longer loves me!" She sank to the floor, sobbing.

Parson Dillington dropped his face into his hands and Sarah watched with tears pricking her eyes as the parson stood to help Prudence, and then stepped back as her body jerked and convulsed.

"She is possessed by the Devil!" someone cried. John Dillington watched, aghast, as his daughter writhed. Then he strode towards her, lifting her from the floor.

"Prudence!" he thundered, shaking her, and her head

flopped about like a rag doll. "Control yourself! This is an ill humour, nothing more!"

"See how he defends the witch!" Mistress Whyte shrieked. There was uproar, the noise from the room deafening. Sarah winced as she clapped her hands over her ears.

Angry as he was, the parson still had his wits about him and changed from shaking his daughter to hugging her. The justices banged on the desk and the noise finally quietened. The parson stroked the dun-coloured hair of his daughter, so different from his own.

"My child, be yourself," he said, so softly that Sarah had to strain to catch the words. "We will be as we were. If you continue, more harm may befall your father than you know." He continued talking in this vein until Prudence came out of her fits.

"Parson Dillington, how does your daughter?" demanded Justice Darcy when Prudence finally sat up, pressing her face into the parson's shoulder.

"Better, I thank you, sir."

"Even as you see her powers against your daughter, you are prepared to speak for the accused?"

There was a long, long silence. The parson looked at Sarah and with a small smile, she shook her head. If he spoke, he might die with her. He drew a breath.

"I need no one to speak for me," Sarah said at once, turning to the justices. "I am innocent of harming anyone. The 'Devil' that Mistress Tilly and Mistress Dillington imagined was simply the purging of poison. Jane ate mistletoe berries with the apples she stole from my orchard and these caused her to be ill. My remedies made her vomit. There was no Devil."

"Are you in league with Satan?"

"Indeed, I am not."

"But how can we trust your word, Mistress Bartlett? The Devil is a subtle master and even now tempts us to believe you," Justice Darcy growled.

"It is the truth, sir. I tell nothing but the truth."

"And what of the possession we have just witnessed?"

Sarah took a deep breath.

"I cannot speak for the jealous ramblings of a child who sees her father fall in love with another woman."

The room roared in disapproval.

"Do you deny you have bewitched him?" The second justice shouted to make himself heard above the noise. "Would a man of God love a mere wench with no family or connections?"

"He is still a *man*!" Sarah responded. "In the end, I am little different from the woman he married! Why should he not love me?"

"You are a disgrace to our sex!" Mistress Whyte called, and many of her cronies shouted in agreement. "You are immodest, forward and saucy."

"Silence!" said Justice Darcy, and the noise died down.

"You have been accused of witchcraft, and although you say you have not done harm, you have not denied that you are a witch," he said slowly. His eyes glittered. "I charge you that you *are* a witch and that your sorcery is manifest through your healing."

Sarah kept silent.

"And you always tell the truth, do you not?"

"I do, sir."

"Are you a witch?"

"I will not defend myself from charges driven by children's wantonness and personal slights," Sarah said calmly, knowing the end was near. She saw, from the corner of her eye, the parson's face grow pale.

Justice Darcy looked smug.

"Sarah Bartlett, you do not deny it. I pronounce you a witch. In accordance with custom and the law, I sentence you to death by burning. May God save your soul."

The words echoed in Sarah's ears along with the cheers from the crowd. It was too much. Her legs buckled, and she knew nothing more.

CHAPTER EIGHTEEN
STACIE

"I think you need to see what I've found in the ancestry site I've been looking at," I said to Gran as she opened the door.

"You sound grim. Are you illegitimate?"

"I've found Sarah Bartlett."

"Have you? Good, because I've found some stuff that's rather worrying. You go through and I'll make some tea."

She pushed me into the seat at her desk, and I turned on my small laptop.

I began to look through ancestry sites when I was trying to trace my spirits, although at the beginning, when fewer details were online, it took a lot longer. Now, with so many resources on the internet, looking through the maze of information was faster. I was proud of my efforts. I had traced the Bartlett family back to the fifteen fifties, starting with Joseph and his sister Hester. Then there was Joseph's wife, Elizabeth. Two brothers had died in infancy.

I followed the bloodlines of the chart I'd pulled up on my screen. Both Joseph and Elizabeth had died in the same year. Sarah had died the following year. Sarah had been only seventeen when she died, something which, when I first saw it, had shocked me.

My eyes drifted down the chart, following Hester's family. The families were large, and children died young. Hester appeared to have married twice, both of her husbands considerably older than she was. The generations flowed down the years until we reached my great-grandmother, then my grandmother, then my mother. And then Eleanor and me.

Gran listened intently as I talked her through it, sipping tea.

"You've outdone yourself this time. I can't believe you actually *found* Sarah from all those years ago!"

"I know. And isn't it shocking she died so young?"

Her face turned serious, the usual humour gone from her eyes.

"Yes, that's what I discovered – how she died," she said, putting the mug down carefully. I looked at her as she rifled through some papers covered with her untidy scrawl. I noticed lots of red pen and asterisks.

"First, let me show you Nate's family tree," she said.

"Nate? What has he got to do with Sarah?"

Gran opened a window on her desktop and another family tree graphic appeared.

"This is Nate." She pointed to Nate's name, Nathaniel John. Then she traced the family back through the years, telling me who were the teachers, the writers, the academics and the doctors. My ears caught the change of professions as she moved further back in history – from teachers and doctors to priests and reverends.

"The last time we spoke about this, I had traced Nate's family back to the eighteenth century, and I decided I wanted to see how far back I could get. I've actually followed the lines back to the fifteen hundreds."

"Impressive," I murmured, wondering where this was leading, but with a growing sense of unease.

"At that time, his family was based in England. Nate's ancestors were from Oxfordshire and, as he said, there's a long line of clergy. One of them, John Dillington, moved to a small village called Leyton, apparently not that far from your house."

The name of the village puzzled me; it didn't seem familiar. "He's mentioned in a surprising number of letters from the period." Gran shuffled through her papers, pulling out copies of papers with old English text on them. I took them and squinted, trying to make out the words.

"So, 'Parson John Dillington, our most holy brother, hath this day delivered a sermon to the righteous, so bathed in the light of God that those hearing his voice did weep.' Blimey!"

"Mmm. There's lots more where that came from – talking of his preaching as the very sound of the angels, and such like. But this is what I wanted to show you."

Gran pulled out another piece of paper. I looked at the title, making out the words from the heavy, ancient lettering.

"Court proceedings?"

"Read on, Stacie."

I scanned the paper, stopped, and began again.

"*Witchcraft?* This is a trial for witchcraft? But who—" and then I caught the name. "Oh my God!"

I read on in growing disbelief.

"'The court, having heard Sarah Bartlett deny she hath entertained foul spirits or familiars was persuaded by the testimony of one Alice Tilley who said that having cursed her child Jane for taking apples, Jane fell ill and like to die and Sarah Bartlett did conjure a spirit from her mouth, which flew from a window. She was also accused of bewitching Parson John Dillington by Mistress Prudence Dillington...' I paused. "Who? Who is Prudence?"

"His daughter."

I shook my head, trying to clear it.

"Let me get this straight. Sarah Bartlett, someone distantly related to me four hundred-odd years ago, stood trial for witchcraft, accused by the parson's daughter? And the parson is a distant relative of Nate Williams? Is that right?"

Gran nodded. I let out a big breath.

"And that's not all," she added quietly.

I looked up.

"They found her guilty and she was burnt to death at the stake."

The blood drained from my face.

Suddenly, the room was hot, very hot, and smoky, with the crackle of logs beneath my feet. I looked at the ceiling and it was the sky; blue, bright blue, scarred by the black clouds rising into it. The smoke stung my eyes, making them run with tears, and I choked, gasping for breath.

"Stacie! For God's sake, Stacie!" A sharp slap on my cheek and I came to on all fours on the rug. Gasping, I bent my head and tried to control the blind panic that shook me.

"Drink this," said Gran, pushing a glass of cold water into my hand. I sat back on my heels and drank it thirstily. Gran looked pale. I finished the water and carefully climbed to my feet. I cleared my throat.

"Sorry. Not sure what happened there. Must have been the shock of hearing…" I couldn't finish the sentence.

I sat down, and so did Gran. There was silence.

"Burnt? As a witch?" I said eventually, hardly able to believe it.

She nodded.

"I… I felt it."

Gran looked alarmed. "Are you okay now?"

I nodded but truly wasn't sure I was okay. I focused. "So. Burnt as a witch?"

"Yes. I've double-checked. They buried her in unconsecrated ground just outside Leyton. You're descended from Hester, Sarah's aunt."

"What happened to Nate's ancestor, John Dillington?"

"Ah, well," said my grandmother, moving back to her papers after casting an anxious glance at me. "According to letters between the deacon and the parish, it sounds like he had the Jacobean equivalent of a nervous breakdown. When he finally recovered, he travelled to America to preach but also to become something of a campaigner after he left for America. I found his name on the passenger list of the *Mayflower* and his name is all over several pamphlets, demanding better evidence in witchcraft trials. He died thirty-seven years later, with a long list of good works behind him."

She shuffled her papers, plucking one and peering at it. "Ironically, he set up refuges for poor single women. He's mentioned in the Salem witch trials, protesting that some of the testimonies were false. I even found him mentioned in an American history of religion, as responsible for saving more than a hundred women from burning."

"And Prudence?" I said, hearing my voice harden.

"Engaged before her father left for the New World, married while he was still travelling, as far as I can tell. I'm not clear why she didn't go with him."

"And what happened to *her*?" My throat felt dry and scarred, and I took another drink of water.

"She lived to the comparatively ripe old age of sixty-three."

"Lucky her," I said.

Gran put her hand on my arm.

"Stacie, what did Sarah say to you, again?"

"She said something about her destiny." I thought hard. "She said her destiny was set, or something like that. And she warned me to be careful about the decisions I made."

"Hardly helpful. Aren't you always careful about the decisions you make?"

I frowned.

"Did she mention strangers? Or Nate?" Gran persisted.

"No. Not that he's much of a threat," I mused. "He's just an academic, albeit a good-looking one. Ellie's been doing her best to charm him into bed since he arrived."

"Is it *Ellie* he's interested in?"

I laughed, glad of the respite from thinking of Sarah.

"Well, he's certainly not interested in me! He's more interested in finishing his book."

As soon as the words came out of my mouth, I brought to

mind his face and eyes as I had stood before him, wrapped in a bath sheet.

Gran contemplated me.

"You underestimate yourself, Stacie." Her brow furrowed. "I don't know. I just think that there are coincidences piling up, and I'm rather unnerved by it all. I'm going to keep looking through the records, in case there's more to learn, but in the meantime, please take care."

·

As I was returning my garden tools to the shed, the sound of Nate's motorbike grumbled in the air and I tensed. It was just after four. He was early. Ellie was out somewhere.

"Hey, Stacie! Fancy coming to view a house with me?"

I turned and saw Nate with his helmet in his hands, his leather jacket unzipped. His attempts to be friendly had meant trying to include me in conversations. It wasn't going down well with Ellie.

"Um…" I wanted to refuse and prepared to say something about going out for a ride, when he smiled. At the sight of that smile, a jolt of attraction zapped through me.

"Aw, come on! You can't be so busy that you can't spare me an hour to visit this house! And you still haven't had a ride on my bike!"

At this, I laughed.

"I don't have any biking gear!" I gestured at my shorts and he looked up and down my bare legs.

"You have nothing to wear?" He rolled his eyes. "I have a spare helmet. Just wear decent boots and your jeans. And a jacket, if you have one."

I hesitated.

"Please? I really need a second opinion on this place," he added. I ran through other excuses and could find none which wouldn't sound exactly what they were: excuses.

"Okay, I'll get changed," I finally said. He grinned and

goosebumps rose on my arms. I turned and ran upstairs to change.

Ten minutes later, I found myself on the back of Nate's powerful bike, the throb of the engine under my thighs. I had my arms around his waist, the smell of his leather jacket filling my nostrils. I was firmly told to hang on as we drove away. I was startled by how clear his voice was in my helmet.

"I only got the details from the agent about an hour ago. It's not even on the market yet!" he said.

"Where is it?"

"Lewsbury. Do you know it?"

He took a bend rather faster than I would have liked, and my breath hitched in my throat.

"Yes. Yes, I've heard of it, it's only a few miles from us," I stuttered.

"Is it a nice place?"

"I don't know, I've never been there."

"Oh?" Nate's voice was curious. I forced myself to concentrate and looked away from the road. A brief experiment with my eyes closed while riding made me feel sick. I opened them and focused on the back of his helmet.

"No, I haven't. Not sure why."

The greenery flashed past and my arms tightened around his waist as he seemed to speed up. I could feel the strong core of him through the biking jacket, and the seams of his leather trousers pressed against the inside of my thighs. Against my will, I responded to his warm, hard body. I heartily regretted agreeing to ride the bike with him, and I breathed more freely when he throttled down. He put the kick step down on the bike and, exhaling hard, I swung my leg over the back of the bike and stood while my shaky legs recovered.

Nate pulled his helmet from his head and put it on the top of the bike while I fumbled with the strap on my own. He brushed my fingers aside and gently released the strap. I shook my hair out and saw his pupils dilate. He held my gaze.

Oh shit, I thought, and swiftly swung around to face the

building. It was a double-fronted house and looked old. A sense of unease grew in me.

Nate pulled out the paperwork from his jacket pocket, smoothing out the creases.

"It was a rectory, originally. Built in the sixteenth or seventeenth century, the real estate agent said."

"Wow."

The estate agent drove up in a flashy red mini, parking on the pavement. A hard-faced woman in her mid-thirties with blonde hair and a bored expression climbed out, and pulling her skirt down her thighs, tottered towards us. This was Janice, and talking almost non-stop about the heat, the location and the traffic, she opened the front door. Nate stepped in. I stood on the doorstep and such dread swamped me, I couldn't move further.

"Stacie?" Nate asked, looking worried.

"I'm not feeling well. I'm not used to the bike. I'll stay outside and get some air."

"I wanted to know what you thought about the house!" Nate protested.

"I'll be in when I've had some air," I said firmly. "I'm sure you wouldn't want me to throw up, would you?"

Nate gave me a concerned glance and then turned to follow the estate agent who was already talking about the house.

I sank down onto the front step and breathed deeply. The hazy sun glinted through the trees and stroked my cheeks. The rectory was at the end of a lane, the church visible from the front door. Smaller cottages faced each other down the lane, each well-kept and neat. A car rolled by. A plane flew overhead. Gradually, I gathered myself and telling myself not to be an idiot, I turned and stepped inside the door.

Take care.

The words snapped my head round. No one was there. I almost ran to find Nate and the agent.

"...the present owners have done significant modernisation, but many of the original features, including the fireplaces, are just as they were," she was saying. I arrived in the room they were in, trying to calm my heartbeat.

"Are you better?" asked Nate. I smiled and said nothing. I looked around at whitewashed walls, low ceilings and beams. It was overstuffed with chairs, sofas and shelving units, but I could imagine it more sparsely furnished and probably more comfortable. The vast fireplace dominated the room. He looked at me expectantly.

"Good size," I said, for want of something to say. Nate looked pleased.

"Yeah, I thought that too. I have a lot less furniture than this, other than books, of course."

The agent herded us through the rest of the house, chatting on about central heating, character features and listed status. It was when we turned into one of the bedrooms that I turned cold. This wasn't the master bedroom, but one of three rooms on the first floor. Ice trickled through my veins and the words of Nate and the agent fell away. I looked around and there was a fierce fire burning in the grate, and heavy brocade drapes around a bed. There was a chamber pot and a wooden chair, the floors were dark and bare. I shook my head, barely believing what was in front of my eyes.

"Stacie?"

Nate's voice came from a distance and when I blinked, the fire, bed, everything, had disappeared.

"Wha…" I grasped the edge of a wardrobe.

"Are you okay? You look kinda strange. Do you need to sit down?"

"I'll get you some water," said Janice, peering at me and then clicking her way downstairs.

I sat on the edge of the bed, looking hard at the pretty floral duvet cover and trying to slow down the whirl of thoughts in my head. What was this place? What was I seeing? God, was I finally cracking up?

Nate took the glass from the agent and waved her away.

"I'll see you downstairs," she said, reluctantly. Nate smiled at her and she softened. "Take your time."

There was silence when she left. I sipped the water. The minutes ticked past.

"Better?" Nate asked, on his haunches beside me. He was too close, I thought.

"Mmm," I said noncommittally. There was another silence, and his breathing changed. As I watched, his hazel eyes gleamed and my heart rate kicked up. He edged closer, his hands on either side of me on the bed. Despite my best efforts, my gaze fixed on his lips and I tensed, wanting to move away and yet locked in place. Nate's pale hair glinted in the light. His head dipped towards me and my eyelids drooped.

Beware, Eustacia. Sarah's voice whispered in my ear.

I gasped, and Nate sprang up and backed away, his face confused.

"I think I just need a bit of air," I said as calmly as I could, and taking a firm grip on the glass, I walked steadily downstairs. His eyes followed me as I walked away.

I stood next to the bike for fifteen minutes as Nate viewed the rest of the house with the agent. My mind was carefully blank.

Janice came out with Nate and they chatted while she locked up. They shook hands and she waved at me as she passed, jiggling her car keys.

"Hope you feel better soon!"

I nodded and raised a smile. Nate walked slowly towards me and I tensed. He looked at me carefully.

"Are you interested in the house?" I asked, rushing to fill the silence.

"I *hope* I've bought it," he replied. "I've offered the full asking price."

My jaw sagged, and I snapped it back up.

"Congratulations," I said faintly.

We drove back in near silence.

CHAPTER NINETEEN
STACIE

Time to plan our holiday, sweet pea. Shall I come round? said the text from Seb as I walked in from the stables. My heart sank. To add Seb into the tension in our house at the moment would be interesting; like adding air to custard powder. I wasn't sure that Ellie was speaking to me yet after the excursion to Lewsbury the previous day.

And I still hadn't made sense of what had happened. There had been that cold knot of fear as I had entered the house. Not to mention my vision in the bedroom, which chilled me as I remembered it. And finally, Sarah, who'd interrupted… something. I still wasn't sure what.

"My spirit chaperone," I muttered, trying to clear my head as I tried to decide how to respond to Seb. In the end, I offered to cook for him and received a huge heart via text. I would keep quiet about the almost-kiss with Nate. Now, a day later, it seemed like a dream.

I clattered downstairs to see Ellie staring out of the sitting room window at the garden.

"Ellie, Seb's coming around tonight and I'm cooking for us. Shall I cook for you too?"

She turned her head. "Let me guess. Spaghetti Bolognese?"

I grinned. "Failsafe. I can cook it in my sleep."

"I'll miss, thanks," she laughed. "When do we expect lover boy?"

"About eight."

She nodded and made to turn away, but I continued. "Look, Ellie, why don't you get out of the house. Go for a ride! I'm sure Napoleon would be thrilled to see you. Get some air. You're looking pasty."

Surprised, Ellie jumped up to peer at herself in the mirror.

"Pasty?"

"Like you've been ill."

It was true. Her skin was its normally flawless self, but shadows were deepening under her eyes. Her face had a brittle quality.

"I haven't been riding for a while," she mused. I kept silent, crossing my fingers. "Yes, I'll call Holly's and see if I can take Napoleon out. Although I won't be long," she warned me.

"I promise not to be hanging upside down naked from the light fittings when you get back."

I was in the pantry checking ingredients when she ran down the stairs.

"Take your phone! And if it's not charged, you're on your own!" I called.

"Noted!" she called. The door banged, and I was alone.

༺ ༻

The Bolognese sauce was bubbling nicely when someone opened the front door. Nate. We had skirted around one another since the trip to see the house, and I paused my herb chopping as he poked his head into the kitchen.

"Hi."

"Hi," I said, concentrating on the herbs.

"Smells good. Spaghetti?"

I nodded and carefully brushed the herbs into a bowl.

"Yes, I have company this evening," I said.

"Right," he said. There was a pause. "I may go into the village to eat then."

I looked at him. Good manners screamed at me to invite him.

"I can recommend an excellent Italian if you like?"

"Thanks, I'll find a pub."

I was struck by the coolness of his tone and rushed to seem less rude. "Why not ask Ellie? She's out riding at the moment, but I'm sure she'd bear your company."

Nate looked at me for what seemed a long time. "Yeah, maybe."

I rubbed my arms as he walked away, trying to warm them against the goosebumps which had appeared.

About an hour later, as the sauce sat on the stove, becoming the kind of Bolognese that only delayed eating can produce, Ellie returned, smelling of the stables.

"You look better," I remarked, looking up from the newspaper and eyeing the colour in her cheeks. She smoothed her hair.

"Mmm, I feel better," she said. "I'll get cleaned up."

"Nate's upstairs," I said. "He's going into the village to eat."

"Is he now?"

Her eyes sparkled, and she marched to the bathroom.

Hoping that I'd done the right thing, I tried to focus again on the article. There were murmurs upstairs, Ellie's laughter, and then the sound of the shower again.

I headed outside to the garden. The air clamped tight around my head and the heat of the day was still settled among the greenery. I missed the lad in the lace collar; all of my ghosts, in fact.

The sky was a bright, deep blue, and I sank into a chair to watch the swifts swooping over the bushes and grass, catching insects. It should have been peaceful, but somehow the atmosphere was brooding, uneasy.

"Are you slacking?"

I clenched my teeth.

"Sorry," Nate said, not sounding at all sorry. "You looked miles away."

I smoothed the skirt over my knees and said nothing.

"I came to ask you the name of the Italian you recommend. Ellie's going to join me for dinner."

Ah.

"Pasquale's," I said. "It's by the old bank, not far from the Brown Cow pub. The pasta is homemade and wonderful."

"Is the sauce as good as yours?"

I stared.

"Um... yes, I think so. Although they use more garlic," I said, watching the slow smile spread across his mouth. He was staring hard at me. My eyes flicked to Ellie, pausing by the window. Even from here, I could tell she'd pulled out the big guns. Floaty, almost backless dress, delicate sandals and her hair up. Classy and beautiful.

And yet, here he was, staring at me as though I might be on the menu.

"I think Ellie's waiting for you." I gestured, and he turned. I thought he sighed.

"You ready?" he called. "I take it you don't want to go on the bike?"

Ellie laughed and dangled her car keys at him. "I don't think I could wear this on the bike!" She swished her skirt around her knees and pouted at him.

I looked on as my sister literally came to life under Nate's hard, hazel eyes.

"See you later," I said, walking towards the house.

The house was deadly quiet. I slammed some music on and turned it up. The Arctic Monkeys were booming through the house so loudly I missed the doorbell ringing at first.

"I'm sorry! Volume's too high..."

Seb grinned at me and drew me into his arms.

"I take it we're alone?" He nuzzled my throat. I tipped my head back and closed my eyes briefly in bliss.

"Mmm… but not, sadly, for long. Ellie and Nate will come back at some stage. I promised her we wouldn't be *in flagrante*."

"You're such a spoilsport," he complained, and I grinned, slipping away. "Smells good."

We talked of nothing much as I finished the food and he set the table. I changed the music to something classical. Seb was clearing the last of his sauce with a piece of bread when complete happiness swept over me.

I offered coffee and chocolates but Seb took my hand and drew it to his lips.

"Sounds perfect. When do I get to taste you again?"

I drew a sharp breath as my insides melted. He pulled me towards him and I stood between his thighs as his arms snaked around my hips. He nuzzled my belly.

"Mmm. You smell… hot." I laughed and pushed him away, still flustered.

"God, enough! Let me get you something to nibble on other than me!"

Seb sighed theatrically and followed me into the kitchen.

"If we're not doing anything more interesting, we need to get organised for the trip," he said. "It's only two weeks away."

My hands paused as I was stacking the dishwasher. At that moment, the front door opened.

I frowned. "I thought they'd be out for hours yet."

But no, here they were, Ellie looking slightly grumpy, Nate's face a picture of blandness.

"Erm… hello. We're just about to have coffee," I offered awkwardly, my eyes darting between the two of them.

Seb stepped forward and held out his hand, introducing himself.

The two men measured one another up.

"Nice to meet you," murmured Nate.

"Finally, you declared your hand, Seb?" Ellie said, perching on the sofa arm. Seb grinned at her.

"Some things are worth waiting for," he said, flicking a look at me. Ellie snorted and eased off her high heels.

"How was Pasquale's?" I blurted out.

"Good, although I've no doubt the Bolognese sauce *isn't* as good as yours, Stacie," Nate said. Seb stilled at the caress in the American voice and I saw Ellie's head whip towards us.

"No?" I said as lightly as I could, reaching out to smooth my fingers down Seb's arm. "Never mind, it's a family favourite so when I get Ellie out of the kitchen, doubtless it will be on the menu and you can compare."

I busied myself with sorting out coffee, leaving an awkward pause in the sitting room before Seb started a conversation, and then heard the low-toned response of Nate. As I pushed down the plunger on the cafetière, I heard Ellie laugh.

"Oh, Seb's been hanging round Stacie for ages!" she was saying as I walked into the room. Seb grinned at me lazily, but Nate was off his chair and taking the tray from me before I could protest. I said nothing but smiled back at Seb.

The conversation was a little brittle after that, and I drained my coffee as soon as I could.

"Shall we plan then?" Seb suggested.

"Plan what?" asked Ellie.

"Our trip to Australia," Seb said, standing up.

Ellie's eyebrows rose. "Really? I thought you were impoverished teachers! Have you been hiding fivers under the mattress?" she mocked.

Fuck off, I thought, walking out of the room without a word. Seb caught me at the bottom of the stairs.

"Chill, sweetheart. Stop letting her get to you."

I swung around and just stopped myself from swearing at him. He looked calmly at me.

"She always knows how to wind me up," I murmured. "You'd have thought I might have learned by now."

We trailed upstairs to my room and for the next hour, we talked travel plans, stop-overs and car hire. My mind began to wander, and I offered to get more coffee.

I walked through the living room, and I paused, sensing tension. Nate and Ellie were sitting close together on the sofa.

Ellie smiled at Nate and stretched her arms above her head, her breasts straining against her shirt.

Without a word, I got two mugs of coffee and headed back to my room.

"You look like you've seen a ghost!" Seb said, looking at me.

Oh, I wish! I thought to myself, putting down the mugs with a thump.

"What's up?"

I paused, wondering where to begin. My mind ran over my ghostly conversations. Sharing with Gran was one thing, sharing with Seb, a scientist, quite another.

"I think Ellie's close to getting her wish," I said finally. Seb frowned and then his face cleared.

"You caught them making out?" he grinned. "Were they both naked?"

"No, of course not! It's just…"

"What?"

What could I say to explain? How could I even say it? He would think he was talking to a madwoman.

"I… I… we know so little about him. And she's still quite young."

"Doesn't he come with references a mile long from the university? I didn't like him much – a bit too familiar with you, if you ask me – but he's an unlikely axe murderer, surely?" Seb looked at me with his head on one side. "Just chill. Ellie's more than capable of handling her love life, she's only three years younger than you!"

I nodded, unconvinced. We talked a little more, but Seb eventually got to his feet.

"You're looking knackered. I should go."

"I wish you could stay."

"Can't I?"

I'd never had anyone stay over at my parents' – never had the opportunity. But I would be uncomfortable with both of them away.

"Would you mind if I said no? But I'll come over to you tomorrow and we'll finish the planning."

He kissed me and the warmth reached down to my toes.

"And you'll stay?" he asked, his forehead on mine.

"Definitely."

The living room was empty as I locked the front door after waving him off. I turned off the lamps and walked to the kitchen, reaching for a glass and opening the fridge for milk.

Nate was standing silently at the kitchen door when I closed the fridge. The milk slopped above the glass.

"Fuck!"

"Sorry."

There was silence as he just looked at me as I wiped my hands.

"Did you want anything?" I said.

His lips twisted, but he shook his head.

"Okay then. Goodnight."

I forced myself not to run up the stairs but there were tingles down my back as though he was staring at me as I walked. Inside my room, I shut the door and listened.

He passed my door, and a moment later the guest room door closed.

๖ฺ

Pain sliced through my leg, and a cry echoed around the room. I glanced down. Nothing.

I leapt up, looking around as though the walls of my room would explain everything, and a moment later, I was throwing on my jacket and running out of the house, turning my ancient car towards my grandmother's house.

"Gran!" I called as I opened the door.

"Stacie! Oh, thank God!" Her voice came faintly from the living room.

She was lying on the floor, her face white and her leg twisted beneath her. I rummaged for my phone and rang for an ambulance, keeping my voice calm with an effort as I reached for her hand.

When the operator told me the paramedics were on their way, I knelt beside her and placed a cushion from the sofa under her head.

"What happened?"

"I didn't see the stool." Gran gasped in pain as I shifted her too far. I winced for her and patted her arm gently.

"How long have you been on the floor?"

"I don't know exactly. Fifteen, twenty minutes? I thought I'd be here hours! I was going to return your call when I tripped." She lay back, her upper lip beaded with sweat.

"Are you cold? I'll get you a blanket," I said, and ran upstairs to the bedroom. The memory of the pain and the cry I had heard crowded into my brain, but I pushed them away; there would be time for reflection when Gran was sorted.

The ambulance men were kind and calm and cheerful, giving her morphine before lifting her gently onto the stretcher but I saw her face cringe as they moved her. I left a message for Ellie before I jumped into the car.

Despite the prompt arrival of the ambulance, it was still three hours before they saw us. Gran was in a lot of pain, drifting in and out of consciousness, and I began to make a fuss with the hospital staff. She'd just gone to X-ray when Seb arrived. He hugged me hard, and I fought back tears. There was still no word from Ellie.

X-rays confirmed she had broken her femur, and eventually, they put her leg in a pot. She looked frail in the hospital gown, her face colourless from the pain, despite the morphine. She wanted to go home and reluctantly, the doctors agreed.

I finally got her into her own bed nearly six hours after I'd walked through the door.

"I'll see you later, Gran'ma," I said, kissing her forehead. She nodded and patted my hand. Tears threatened and I turned and left.

Seb pulled me into his arms as soon as I'd locked the front door. I dropped my head on his chest and cried quietly.

"Shush, it's okay. She just needs to recover from the shock," Seb said, after a few minutes. "She's fit and healthy and she'll be fine."

I nodded, swallowing fresh tears, and took a deep breath.

He walked me to my car. "Will you be okay?" he asked. I managed a smile.

"Of course. I need to get back to find out where the hell Ellie is and why she didn't answer my calls."

"Shall I follow you?"

"No, I'll grab a book and come back here to keep an eye on her."

I was seething by the time I got back to the house and this hit full-blown rage when Ellie's laughter drifted in from the garden.

I stood at the door, hands on hips as I watched Ellie flirt with Nate, who watched her lazily with a beer in hand.

"Did you get my messages?" I asked as she turned to face me.

"What message?"

"The four – no, five – messages I left on your voicemail and one on the home phone."

She frowned.

"No, I've been charging my phone, so I turned it off. I haven't checked the answerphone. What's happened?"

"Gran's broken her leg."

Her face froze. "What? How?"

"She fell."

"Oh, no!"

"Is there anything she needs?" Nate said, standing.

I waved him away. "No, they've put her in plaster and she's at home in bed. I could have done with some support at the hospital."

Ellie looked upset. "I'm really sorry, Stace! I didn't think to check my phone."

I looked at her, still angry. "No. I thought you must be busy."

There was an awkward pause and Ellie flushed.

All the air whooshed out of me. I was exhausted. "Anyway, now you know. I'm going back to Gran's once I've grabbed some stuff." I turned away and climbed heavily up the stairs to my room.

CHAPTER TWENTY
STACIE

Seb stared at me, speechless. I bit my lip. He drew a deep breath.
"Can I just check if I've understood you?"
I nodded, steeling myself.
"After all the planning and discussion about the holiday, you're now pulling out? To look after your grandmother, who isn't ill, but in plaster, and who seemed well on the road to recovery when I visited her earlier. Not to mention your sister, who admittedly, appears to have had a personality reversal, and seems determined that you should go on holiday and is prepared to watch over your grandmother. Have I missed anything?"

I shook my head. My parents weren't returning as Ellie had insisted she and I could care for Gran. I had been furious but overruled by Gran, who hated a fuss.

"So, given that your grandmother isn't badly hurt, and that there are other people to care for her, I can only assume you don't want to come on holiday with *me*."

"It's not that—"

"Then what is it?"

I recognised the hurt in his face and wondered what he would say if I told him that something seemed so off-kilter I was unsure where to put a foot next.

"Tell me, Stacie."

His voice was hard.

"Look, Seb, I've already said I'm saving my money for a deposit for a house. And with Gran immobile, and Ellie besotted, I'm just not sure this is the right time for me to take off on holiday. And I'm not sure about Nate—" I broke off as he jumped to his feet with a disgusted snort.

"What *is* it about this bloody American, Stacie? Other than Ellie has the hots for him?"

I drew breath, but he interrupted me.

"Or is it *just* Ellie that's got the hots for him?" he said, white and angry. My eyes widened, and I blew my cheeks out in frustration.

"Don't be bloody ridiculous!"

He leaned back and examined me. After a long, long moment, he got up and handed me my bag and wrap without a word.

"What's this?" I stared stupidly at him.

"You're not telling me the truth. There's no future unless we're honest with one another."

Well, he had that right. I certainly wasn't telling him the whole truth, just selected rational highlights.

"Seb, I—"

"Leave it, Stacie."

"But you're wrong!" He said nothing and my temper flared. "Just a minute here. If I'm guilty of anything, it's that I've changed my mind about going away. Haven't I got the right to do that? I understand you're disappointed, but for God's sake don't blow it up into anything else!"

He glared at me and I stood up, slinging my handbag over my shoulder.

"Right," I said. "I'm sorry to be a pain, but I can change my mind, and I *am* changing my mind. If Gran had been more seriously injured, I wouldn't have dreamed of going away."

"But she's not! She's just broken her leg!"

"She's hardly a young woman!" I shot back. "If your mother had fallen and broken her leg and was alone, would *you* fly fifteen thousand miles away?"

"Ellie is around too!"

"Only as long as she's not shagging the guest!" I shouted. "Have you seen the way she looks at him? I wouldn't trust Ellie to remember her own name if they started an affair!"

We scowled at each other for a moment, and then Seb looked away with a sigh.

"I'm sorry. I thought it would be great for us to go together, and I'd made it possible, despite your finances. I didn't factor in your fucking sister and her love life."

"Are you still going to go?" I asked.

"My brother's expecting me. And you!"

"Will I see you when you get back?" I asked quietly, ignoring his last comment.

There was a pause so long I wasn't sure he'd answer me.

"I don't know. Shall we see how it goes?" His voice was so cool, it didn't sound like Seb.

I gulped, shocked at how painful his words were to me.

"I'm truly sorry," I said, through a dry throat.

He shook his head, but before he could say anything, I kissed him hard. He responded, and the embrace was clawing, angry. At last, he pulled away.

"Was that something to remember you by?" he asked, panting.

I raised my chin. "Only if you don't call."

His face closed, he showed me out. I turned from the car to wave, but the door was shut.

When I rang him two days later, he'd already left the country.

The first week after Seb left passed in a haze. Conversations were indistinct and I could barely tell the difference between one day and the next, so lumpen was my mood.

Gran, now more confident with crutches and a horde of friends and elderly admirers from her bridge club popping in and out, noticed it immediately.

"So what happened?" she demanded.

I told her briefly about Seb and the argument.

"You used me as the reason you ducked out of a fabulous holiday? I'm not such a poor creature! Why didn't you tell him about your ghosts and what's going on with your dratted sister and Nate?"

"Gran, Seb is a scientist! He'd think I was insane!"

"Would he?"

"Well, if I was in Seb's shoes, I'd certainly think twice about getting involved with someone who potentially had a serious mental illness!"

"Are you in danger of underestimating him?" Gran frowned at me. "Not everyone's like your parents!"

"Well, anyway, he's gone. He's cross with me, and with himself, a little. He told me he'd planned for everything apart from Ellie and her love life, but I'm uncomfortable about having everything done for me."

"Are Ellie and Nate sleeping together yet?" Gran asked.

I wrinkled my nose. Ellie was looking like a cat in a vat of cream and glowed with anticipation. Nate was looking grim and serious.

"Not yet," I said gloomily. Ellie had been denied very little in her life to date, and I didn't imagine Nate would hold out against her determined seduction. The idea repelled me in some ways, but the thoughts were too tangled in my head to work out why.

"Hmm," Gran said, hoisting herself from her chair. I rushed to help. "No, no, Stacie, I can manage! Don't fuss."

"I wish you'd let me help!" I said crossly. "What are you doing?"

"Getting my iPad," she said calmly, slotting it under her arm and making her way to the dining table. She looked at me again. "So what's stopping him taking what Ellie is putting on a plate?"

"I've no idea. They normally fall at her feet, and she walks all over them. Perhaps he doesn't want her *because* she's so available!"

"Is it anything to do with you, Stacie?"

I opened my mouth to deny it then stopped, the words untrue. "I don't know," I sighed, fiddling with some pens on the table.

"How is he with you both?" Gran persisted.

"Watchful," I said after some reflection. "Like he's playing chess or something, planning his next move." I shook my head. "God, I'm sounding like a DH Lawrence novel, I can't bear it!"

"But something has kept you here, Stacie. I keep wondering about Nate's house."

"The agent was going on about its original features. It looked quite old but no different from lots of houses in this area."

"Where was it?"

"Lewsbury. I don't know it, never been before, weirdly."

"Yoo-hoo!" came a voice from the front door.

"Is that you, Francine?" Gran called as a petite, birdlike lady came in bearing a cake tin.

"I've brought you over some – oh! I'm so sorry, I didn't know you had company, Catherine."

Knowing all further discussion would be at an end, I protested I was just leaving and kissed Gran goodbye.

"You call me if you need anything," she said pointedly.

"Shouldn't I be saying that to you?" I smiled, my face muscles stretched for the first time in days. She waved me away, and I left, heading to the stables so I could stay out of the house a little longer.

Two hours later, my legs sore and stiff, I let myself into the house, relieved to find it empty. I made my way upstairs and ran a bath. I looked at my phone, hoping that Seb would be in contact. Nothing.

"Oh, for God's sake, get a grip!" I muttered to myself, adding lavish bubbles to the running water. He might still be suffering from jet lag. Or he might not be thinking of me at all, but chilling with his family. I swirled the hot water around in the bath, wondering if I'd got it all wrong; whether I was losing my grip on reality. Was this a decision I had made 'carefully' as Sarah had asked? Should I have gone with him?

I looked at my face in the mirror, surrounded by steam. It didn't look like me. The hair was brighter, redder, the face thinner, the eyes more slanted. I stared harder, and the face smiled, almost reassuringly. It was Sarah.

Steam swirled over the mirror and then I was looking at my face, worried and with dark circles under the eyes. But now the resemblance between us was clear.

"I'm not sure whether to feel better or not," I said beneath my breath as I turned off the taps.

But twenty minutes later, up to my neck in scented water, something in me had shifted. I was certain that I had been right to stay here.

The front door slammed and I resisted the urge to put my head underwater. I glanced at the bathroom door, checking I had locked it. I swished the cooling water around me, soothing my aches and pains.

"Stacie?" My sister's voice came from the other side of the door.

"Yeah, what?"

"Just checking who was in there."

So Nate wasn't in. Good. I allowed myself another ten minutes as my skin wrinkled.

Ellie was hunting through the kitchen cupboards when I got downstairs. She looked up.

"Hadn't you better get some clothes on?" she said, taking in my bathrobe, tousled hair and bare legs. "Nate will be back shortly."

I opened my mouth to speak and then a key scraped in the lock. We both stilled.

Nate walked into the kitchen, stopping as he caught sight of us. His eyes flashed and pulling the lapels of the robe together to my neck, I excused myself. He breathed in deeply as I passed him.

As soon as I finished dressing, I made an appointment with a letting agent.

Dinner was going to be a tense affair, I thought, taking one look at Ellie's face when I came downstairs.

"Ellie, I'm not in for dinner, I'm seeing Gran tonight," I said, improvising on impulse.

I had no idea if Gran needed or wanted my help, or even if legions of her elderly admirers would be on hand to serve her dinner, but I didn't want to get between Ellie and her prey this evening.

"Fine," Ellie said. "Send her my love and tell her I'll be round tomorrow if she needs anything."

I texted Gran and received the message that she had been looking forward to fish and chips, and if I'd like to pick them up, that would save Edmund the trouble. I grinned. Edmund was a wickedly funny gay man who had lost his partner ten years ago and he and Gran were often to be found sampling various gins. Unexpectedly, my spirits rose, anticipating the evening in store. Until then, I'd retreat to the summerhouse with a book.

"Hey, Stacie," Nate said from the sitting room before I could make my escape through the patio doors.

"Hi." I paused, searching for something polite and quick to say. "Have the vendors accepted your offer on the house?"

"They have." He smiled at me and I responded almost against my will. "I'm waiting for the paperwork – which seems real complicated in England!" I nodded, inching towards the doors. "It was good to have someone with me to view the place."

I glimpsed Ellie hovering at the sitting room door.

"Glad to have been an extra pair of eyes," I said.

"When are you expecting the sale to complete?" Ellie put in.

"I'm not sure – a month? Given the age of the house, I'd be crazy not to have a surveyor's report, but, hopefully, that won't take long."

"You're welcome to stay here as long you like, of course," she stressed. He looked at her and then back at me.

"I'm grateful for your hospitality. I know it can't be easy having a stranger living with you."

"Oh, you're not a stranger, are you?" Ellie smiled.

"Anyway, that's great news about your offer," I said into the pause that followed. "I'm off to the summerhouse to read a bit before I go to Gran's."

"Do you fancy a beer in the garden?" said Ellie to Nate, and I escaped.

The summerhouse was warm and stuffy. Despite strenuous efforts, none of the windows would budge, so I threw open the door to let air in.

"I must have a go at them," I tutted to myself. The last 'decorator' my mother had employed appeared to have painted the windows shut. I heaved one of the armchairs near the door and flopped into it. The sun kissed my face, and I opened my book.

I had peace for perhaps twenty minutes.

"I wondered if you'd like a gin and tonic, or a beer?" Nate said.

"Um…" I wanted to say no, but again, my Britishness made me hesitate; it might seem rude.

"Or some wine?"

"Actually, I'm fine," I said, putting down my book. "But thanks for the offer."

To my dismay, instead of returning to the house, he stepped into the summerhouse and sat down. Even given the size of the summerhouse, which held two large sofas, my chair and a couple of tables comfortably, he seemed too close.

"Cosy."

"Yes, it's a great spot for a bit of privacy," I said pointedly. He smiled apologetically.

"I wondered if you were completely recovered from your dizziness? After the bike ride, you looked real pale. It wasn't my driving, was it?"

I shook my head with a smile. "Yes, completely recovered. I might have been in the sun too long before we went," I said.

He nodded, looking at me closely. "I was worried about you."

"No need. I'm fine."

"But you're not going on vacation any longer?"

I winced. Now that was a wound I didn't need poking. "No."

"Why not?"

"Gran's fall changed my plans. I didn't want to be on the other side of the world if she needed me." Again, not all the truth, but certainly part of it.

"I hope you don't mind me expressing an opinion, but that seems extreme," he said. "Your grandmother seems fit and healthy and with lots of friends to help. I met some of them today."

"What? You've been round to visit her?"

"I took her home after dinner that time, you know? I have a good memory for places, so I dropped in on her today, to check how she was."

The gesture flummoxed me. Nate was speaking again.

"It's none of my business, of course, but given the support your grandmother has, I'm curious why you didn't go with… Sebastian, is it?"

"Yes, you're right. It *is* none of your business."

Nate looked as surprised as I felt at my straight, unvarnished answer.

He hesitated. "Stacie, I don't know if you felt something

when we went to the house…"

My heart sank. God, that almost-kiss coming back to haunt me.

"…but I did."

My head jerked up. He looked at me intently.

"Nothing happened," I said breezily.

"But I wanted it to."

Now his directness took my breath away.

"I… well, I'm with Seb," I said, stumbling for words. He put his head on one side.

"Really? He left kinda quick. Almost like you'd fallen out."

"Not sure how you reached that conclusion."

"He must have been disappointed you didn't go with him," Nate pressed. I'd had enough.

"We *both* were."

He continued to regard me, and I kept my face neutral with an effort.

"That's a great shame," he said softly.

"Thank you. Shouldn't you get back for dinner?"

He smiled, getting to his feet in one smooth movement.

"I can take a hint. But before I go… believe me, Stacie, when I say I like you – a great deal – and I think we could be good together. And I'm not sure what's keeping you around, but I'm certain it's not because your grandmother has broken her leg."

Ellie called from the patio doors.

"Are you coming, Nate?"

"Think about what I said," he said as I tried to marshal my thoughts. "I'm probably not your normal kind of guy and in fact, you're quite different from other girls I've dated but I know how to have fun." He walked off, and try as I might, I couldn't keep my gaze from his tight buttocks and long legs.

You're certainly *not* my 'normal kind of guy' I thought, wryly. Even though you have glinting hazel eyes and a body to die for. I groaned aloud.

His words circled around my head for the next ten minutes. Eventually, I rose and headed out.

CHAPTER TWENTY-ONE
STACIE

Something had disturbed me, and I started awake, my heart thumping. I glanced at the clock. Half past four.

Every nerve straining to catch the next noise, I lay in bed. I must have been immobile for another five minutes before I breathed more freely. I slid my legs out of the bed and tiptoed to the window. It would soon be dawn.

As I peered into the lightening gloom at the garden, I relaxed. It had been a fox, or a cat. I saw the shape on the lawn and I sucked in a breath.

The figure looked up at the window and I drew back.

"Shit," I muttered. "Shit, shit, shit!"

I grabbed my robe, remembering a comic sketch I'd seen some years ago, where the comedian wondered why, in horror movies, people just about to be murdered *voluntarily* walked into dark corridors and threatening woods, and looked behind closed doors. It had seemed funny then. I stood looking at the handle of my bedroom door for about a minute before reaching for it.

The house was silent as I padded downstairs, and my blood was thundering in my ears as I walked to the patio doors. The figure was motionless on the lawn. He looked like Nate, but his cloak and strange hat told me it wasn't Nate, but someone else.

John Dillington.

He seemed to stare straight at me; the light was so dim, it shadowed his eyes. My fingers fumbled with the lock on the doors, but I finally slid them open.

The chill of the early morning seeped through my robe, and I wrapped my arms around my body as I stepped into the garden. The dew wet the sides of my feet, grass tickling over my flip-flops. We stood there, watching each other. Time seemed to stop.

I took a step forward. And then another. Despite my growing feelings of unease, his presence compelled me to move closer. I dug my nails into my palms and the pain made me pause. I looked at his face, still in shadow even as the sun lightened the sky. He smiled, and my stomach clenched at his severe beauty. I took another step. At last, I was standing six feet from him.

"Are… are you John Dillington?" I said, my throat dry.

"I am he."

His voice was so glorious, it was like the stroke of velvet across my skin. I shook myself, trying to concentrate. Think, Stacie, don't be distracted. I forced more words from my dry mouth.

"Why are you here?"

"I come to make amends," he murmured, suffering etched into the lines of his face.

"What for?"

"My cowardice for the last time I should have protected you. For you are in danger again."

My pulse racing, I swallowed.

"I'm sure I'm perfectly safe…" My words trailed off as he stepped towards me.

"No, *you are in peril*," he said, in tones like thunder. I gaped at him, not knowing what to say. I was struck by his resemblance to Nate. The planes of John Dillington's face were the same, but harsher. Where Nate had muscle, John seemed to be made of bare bones. His green eyes sucked me in.

"I know I must keep to my path, follow my heart's desire," I said, repeating what I could remember of Sarah's words, and he smiled, and my breath hitched as the smile transformed his face with a severe beauty.

"You are a good child, but you do not need to walk that path alone," he said, the timbre of his voice licking my nerves, soothing them. "I will protect you this time and we both shall have our heart's desire, Sarah!"

He held out a hand towards me, and I looked at it stupidly. His fingers were pale and long. He stepped towards me and without knowing what I did, I raised my hand.

Sarah?? He had mistaken me for Sarah! A shard of light reached my brain. I snatched my hand away and John Dillington looked at me, startled. I shook my head and backed away. Distressed, he held out his hands towards me and then, with a groan of pain, disappeared into the early morning light.

Like a puppet whose strings had been cut, I fell to my knees.

The ground was damp beneath my palms as my head swam; I grabbed the blades of grass and hung on as I steadied my breathing and waited for the world to right itself.

I didn't know how long I was on the ground, but when I raised my head, the sun had started to cast shadows over the garden and birds were singing. I sat back on my heels, looking at the trees, before I staggered to my feet.

Back at the house, I reached for a mug and, on automatic pilot, I brewed some coffee. The clock on the mantelpiece chimed. A quarter to six.

I was cradling my mug and staring into space when Nate came downstairs. He was in running gear, his powerful thighs encased in stretchy Lycra. He stopped at the kitchen door as he saw me.

"Good morning," he said, his voice wary. "I haven't seen you up at this hour before. Is everything okay?"

I took a swig of my coffee and looked at the tee shirt pulled over his broad shoulders. I gave myself a shake.

"Just couldn't sleep."

He looked at me.

"You look a bit… weird."

So would you if you'd been talking to ghosts before five thirty in the morning. My smile seemed to crack my face.

"Like you said, this isn't my usual hour to be awake. Coffee?"

He nodded, and without a word, I handed him a mug. He sipped and leaned against the door jamb. His scent tickled my nose, bed-warmed, with a tinge of lemon.

"What are you doing today?" he asked. Not wanting to continue the small talk, I stood up.

"I imagine I'll go back to bed at some stage," I said, putting my mug in the sink and then wished I'd chosen my words more carefully as his eyes flashed.

With a bright smile, I walked past him. He caught my arm.

"Stacie?"

I stood still, not looking at him.

"I imagine I'm doing this all wrong, but…" He stopped and took a deep breath. "Are you sure you're still 'taken'?"

My head whipped round, and I could see yesterday's stubble on his chin. The scent of him filled my nostrils and his eyes locked with mine. I swallowed. Slowly, he bent his head and kissed me.

My mind was blank. I was incapable of moving a muscle. As if I might run away, he placed his coffee on the counter with care and grasped my hands.

"I don't force myself on girls, and you're not my normal type, but I like you very, very much. I'd like to get to know you better. Come out with me?"

Mute, I just looked at him and he kissed me again, harder this time. His lips were firm and dry, his mouth tasted of coffee and toothpaste. His hands pulled me closer and my body moulded against his, the muscles harder than I had thought.

Beneath my robe, my skin seemed to spring to life. Not knowing what I did, my hands came up to grip his shoulders and a murmur of appreciation sounded from his throat.

The toilet flushed. Ellie. I pulled away with a gasp. *You are in peril.* The words smashed through the fog of my senses.

"What?" he said, breathing heavily. He looked a little confused, as though forgetting where he was.

Make your decisions with care, Eustacia. "This isn't right," I muttered, turning away.

He grabbed my arm, stopping me. "*What's* not right?" he said, frustration edging his words.

"I'm sorry," I said, tugging my arm. "I know I seem like a tease—"

"You think?" His words were hard.

"But honestly, this isn't a good idea."

"Give me one good reason it isn't a good idea."

"You're a guest in our house…"

"Believe me, I'm trying to get out as fast as I can!"

"You know nothing about me -"

"Something I'd remedy if you'd give me a chance!"

"- and Ellie loves you."

He stared at me in the sudden silence.

"What?"

"My sister thinks she's in love with you. *She* wants you! Can you imagine what it would do to her if we started dating?"

He laughed, a short, bitter laugh.

"Jeez, I'm not even sure how we got here, but—"

"Shush!" I hissed. "She'll hear you!"

He grabbed my shoulders and pushed me against the kitchen door.

"I don't care what Ellie wants! I care what *I* want. And I want you, not her."

And then he kissed me again. I struggled against his rough mouth, lifting my knee in warning, and I twisted away as his hands slackened. I turned on my heel and ran upstairs on tiptoes, as quietly as possible. I closed the door of my room and locked it.

For about a minute, there was silence and then the front door opened and closed, his feet hitting the gravel as he began his run. I fell onto the bed and closed my eyes, wondering at the events of the last two hours.

Muttering to myself that I'd be lucky to get another wink of sleep, I fell asleep within five minutes.

☙

"Good God, no wonder you look like death warmed up!" said Gran that afternoon after I'd told her of the morning's events. I tried injecting some levity.

"It makes a bit of a change to be so in demand. Two blokes before seven in the morning! Although I can't count one because he's been dead for hundreds of years."

"I'm not sure this is a laughing matter," said Gran.

"But what does it all mean?" I said. "Why is the Right Reverend turning up all of a sudden? What on earth was he talking about, 'making amends'?"

"Let me find the notes I made." Gran grasped her crutches and rather shakily walked to the dining table. Among the cards, flowers, and a half-eaten chocolate cake, which looked like Francine's work, was a file of papers.

Muttering, she sorted through the papers, covered with her elegant writing. After a moment, she pounced on something and peered at it.

"Hmm. That's worrying."

"What is?"

"The date of Sarah's death. It's in a week."

I stared at her.

"What?! He's here for some kind of *anniversary*?" My voice rose, and I cleared my throat and tried for a deeper register. "Are you sure of the date?"

"Yes, the court records say it was August eleventh when she was... when she died."

The bile rose from my throat, and I caught a whiff of wood smoke, and I turned and went to the kitchen and drank straight from the tap. I returned to the sitting room, and we stood looking at one another.

"Well," I said.

"Yes, indeed."

Silence.

"God, what on earth am I supposed to do?" I said, my head aching with unanswered questions. "*Am* I in peril? *What* peril?"

"I don't know, Stacie. I'm wondering if you ought to have gone with Seb."

"But then what? Nate's still here, Ellie's still here, and eventually, I'd come back from wherever I went. That seems like running away and that's not my usual style. It might even make whatever might happen *worse*!"

Gran pursed her lips.

"Would it? If you weren't here, perhaps Nate would fall in love with Ellie."

I wrinkled my nose. From this morning, I knew Nate didn't want Ellie – he wanted me. Wow, what a turn-up for the books. I forced my mind to concentrate on the date. August 11 was just days away – and then what?

"John Dillington said he was here to make amends for his cowardice," I said. "What cowardice? Do we have any idea what that means? How was he cowardly?"

"I have no idea, Stacie. I've looked at the official records, but they're too light on detail. Seeing as I'm confined to the house, I'll investigate some more."

I nodded. Knowing what had happened in the past might hint at what was coming. In the meantime, I needed to be careful, very careful.

I slipped into the house, hoping to get to my bedroom unseen.

"Is that you, Stacie?" called Ellie.

"Yeah, just me," I said, my foot on the bottom stair. Ellie wasn't having that.

"Don't go, I want to talk to you."

I sighed and trailed into the sitting room where she was curled in an armchair, a book face down on the arm. I sank onto the sofa.

"What's up?"

"Are you okay?"

I stared.

"What? Yes, I'm fine, why?"

"Was that you this morning, really early?"

Oh shit, I thought. I hope she didn't overhear our conversation. I wiped my face of expression.

"Yes, I couldn't sleep. I was even up before Nate!"

"Mmm. He said."

"But I'm fine," I added into the loaded silence, smiling and wondering what *else* he'd said. She peered at me.

"You look knackered."

"Yes, I'll have an early night."

I stood up, ready to leave.

"What did you and Nate talk about?" The question sounded forced from Ellie's throat.

"Basically, the conversation we've had just now. How he didn't usually see me at six in the morning, how I couldn't sleep, et cetera."

She looked hard at me, her eyes glittering as though wet. God, she's so young, I thought.

"Right."

"But I'm all right, there's no need to worry," I said, attempting to smile. "It's just the weather. We could do with a good thunderstorm to clear the air, don't you think?"

Ellie said something indistinct as I stood and escaped upstairs.

CHAPTER TWENTY-TWO
SARAH

Sarah shivered in the early morning light, pulling her cloak more tightly around her. There was silence, and she strained to hear other signs of life. She had lost track of the hour, but judged it to be about five o'clock, the grey light bringing shape to the walls of her cell.

Soon they would come for her.

Her tears caught in her throat and she forced them down. She must be strong; she knew there were things she could do to ease her passing. And others to come depended on her. But the eyes on her, the jeering crowd, ah, that image pained her.

It was a strange sensation. Her head seemed full to bursting of thoughts, but she caught none of them, her mind blank and white. She took a mouthful of tepid, stale water.

Voices drew near. Carefully, her limbs stiff from the cold and the hard floor, she stood up.

"A condemned prisoner is allowed a last meal! For Christian charity, man, let me through," the parson said to the guard. She straightened her dress and put her shoulders back. The key scraped in the lock and the parson strode into the cell, carrying a basket.

Glancing around quickly, he called to the guard. "Sir, two stools and some fresh water so she might wash and be clean for the word of the Lord."

"The she-devil will need more than water to clean 'er!" But the guard eventually returned, grumbling, with a bowl of fresh water. Sarah said nothing as he placed it, none too gently, on the floor, water slopping over the sides and into the straw. A moment later, he brought two stools. The parson thanked him gravely, and the door slammed shut. Sarah stared at him.

"Will you not be seated?" he asked gently. "I have food and ale."

Sarah bent to the bowl of water and rinsed her hands as best she could, shamefully aware of her filth. She wiped her hands on the clean cloth he handed her.

"Thank you, sir."

He said a short grace and then passed the fresh bread. She sank her teeth into it; it was still warm, and the taste almost made her swoon. She sighed and closed her eyes. His snort made her open them again.

"I take it they have not fed you well?"

"They have not fed me at all!" she retorted, wiping her mouth. He handed her the beer, and she drank thirstily. He had brought cheese and ham, too. A feast.

He waited until she stopped eating and had drained the last of the beer.

"How are you, mistress?"

She shrugged.

"Well enough. I am frightened, but I would be a fool not to be."

"There is no need for you to face the fire, Mistress Bartlett! I can save you, if you would just confess!" he said urgently.

She smiled.

"What would you have me confess? My sins? They are some, but not as many as others. You would have me speak truth but the truth will not, I fear, set me free."

"Why did you not tell the judge I had offered you marriage?"

Sarah started. This was not a question she had expected.

"Because he did not ask," she said reluctantly. "He would have simply counted it as more evidence that I had bewitched you, and I knew you in sufficient danger already."

Parson Dillington was silent for a long moment.

"You *have* bewitched me," he breathed. She dropped her eyes, her heart swelling. "Ever since the first moment I saw you in the marketplace, you have been constantly in my thoughts. Marriage was essential to sanctify my impure thoughts. But you would have none of me."

"Marriage is not my fate, sir."

"But you care enough to want to keep me safe?"

She caught his eager tone. Part of her longed to give him that truth. But that would not help. Her plight was sealed, and it would launch him on his own path. So she chose her words with care, as close to untruthful as she had ever been.

"You have treated me well, sir, and I am very grateful. But believe me, when I say, I cannot marry you."

He stood up so swiftly, he knocked the stool over.

"Could you not bear me enough to save your life?" he cried. "Am I so hideous that you could not stand to make me your husband to deliver you from the pyre that they are even now building in the market square?"

She gasped at his cruelty and immediately he fell on his knees beside her, grabbing her hands.

"Mistress Bartlett! Sarah! I beseech you. Confess your sins that I may exorcise you. I can go to the judge and say it is so and you will be saved! And then marry me. Marriage will be a protection from jealous folk! I care not if there is no passion. We can grow together as companions in the Lord."

"But what of your daughter?"

"Prudence will become accustomed," he said grimly. Sarah laughed, pulling her hands away.

"You believe so, sir? I would be afraid for my life, she hates me so!"

"She is a good girl and will submit to her father's authority."

Sarah shook her head, smiling despite her situation.

"But, sir, even if Prudence did as she was bid, I fear I may be too independent for marriage and thus set her a poor example."

Parson Dillington looked intently at her, his eyes gleaming with desire. Her heartbeat stuttered.

"Do you mistake your feelings, Mistress Bartlett? I feel your pulse flutter when we are close, and I see reflected in your eyes some semblance of passion. I feel it, I am sure."

She stood, breathing heavily, searching for a safe response.

"Do not presume, sir, because I am alone and without family, that you may treat me uncivilly!"

"You are alone, without family, and in peril!" he growled, standing to face her. "I am in earnest, Mistress Bartlett, and with reason! Does the fear of death not move you at *all*?"

"Of course it does! I am near faint with terror!" Sarah stamped her foot, her tears filling her eyes.

"So why will you not let me help you?"

"Because I cannot lie, and my truth will condemn me!" Sarah cried in frustration.

He made an inarticulate sound and before she could move, he grabbed her shoulders and pressed his lips to hers. Sarah was unmoving for a moment, his fingers burning her flesh through the stained fabric of her dress. Her body yearned towards him, the power of it surprising her.

It would be so easy, she thought. To avoid the pain, the shame. Who would blame her if she took, for once, the simpler journey? Her hands crept to his shoulders, their width greater and muscles stronger than she expected. She relaxed.

Then his teeth grazed her lips and with the pain she shuddered, her dreams rent apart. Had she forgotten those who would suffer if she wavered from this course? Those who would die *as she did*?

His mouth gentled, and he raised his head.

"Sarah -"

She swung away, wrenching herself free.

"Please go."

The silence stretched on, filled with the sound of his breathing as he fought for control.

"I beg your pardon!" he said at last in a mortified voice. "I am a brute to have forced myself on you in such a manner. I beg you, forgive me."

Sarah bit her lip.

"Forgive me!"

She sighed, her breath clogged with tears.

"I forgive you, Parson Dillington, but you must go."

"I am here to absolve your sins."

"And assault me?"

He was silent for a moment.

"I deserve your approbation. I humbly beg your forgiveness. But there is a greater forgiveness that I am here to deliver. Will you not allow me to hear your confession?"

She gave him a clear-eyed look.

"Sir, I have nothing to confess."

He looked shocked. "That is blasphemy. We are born in sin."

Another silence.

"I do not lie."

His face took on a crafty look.

"Then tell me truthfully, Sarah, do you feel nothing for me?"

"Are you not duty-bound to ask me if I am a witch, sir?" she responded, avoiding the question. Too late, she realised this was the wrong question.

"Are you a witch, Mistress Bartlett?"

She smiled bitterly.

"Goodbye, Parson Dillington. Pray for my soul."

He stared at her, the truth dawning at last. Then he left without saying another word.

※

The tears had long since dried on her face and Sarah was very tired. She dozed, dimly aware of noise from the street which filtered through the window. She had been visited by the crows, who had pecked miserably at the bars on the window, and she had softly sent them on their way. The owls hooted gently to her in mourning.

The sun was well up when a familiar voice spoke outside the cell.

"I demand to see the woman who has bewitched my father!" Inwardly, Sarah groaned.

"The witch is to see no one, Justice Darcy say so," was the response. Sarah could almost imagine Prudence having a temper tantrum.

"But I wanted to tell her that my father is returned to himself!"

"Well, mistress, I can't stop you shouting and mayhap she'll hear 'ee," said the guard, coaxingly.

"I would tell her that my father has told me that he loathes the witch!" Prudence shouted, her words piercing the thick door of the cell. "He told me that she is past redemption, believing she has no need of forgiveness! He told me that he believes she will burn in the fires of hell!"

"Well, Mistress Prudence, she shall burn on earth today, that's certain! She will be accustomed to it!"

There was shared raucous laughter between Prudence and the gaoler, and Sarah heaved as a wave of fear rolled over her as well as something deeper, more painful.

The sound of the voices grew fainter and Sarah sank down on the stool again, more lonely than ever. And while she had thought she had no more tears, one fell on her cheek and she tasted saltwater on the corner of her mouth.

CHAPTER TWENTY-THREE
STACIE

"Top up?" said Ellie to Nate. He smiled a little absently as she refilled his wine glass, and his glance flicked to me. I looked back at the newspaper and then threw it aside to escape to the garden.

"Don't trail in mud, will you?" Ellie said as I slipped on my battered garden shoes.

"No, Mum," I said, escaping from the stifling atmosphere.

The storm the weather forecasters had been promising us for days still hadn't materialised, but I was willing to bet my secateurs that rain was on the way. The weather had clamped an iron helmet around my head, and a nagging headache throbbed at my temples.

I scanned the rose beds with little hope of seeing the young boy with the ringlets. He wasn't there. I sighed and began to deadhead the roses before the bleached daylight faded.

Gran was still hunting for more information about the events surrounding Sarah's trial. I was still very much in the dark about what, if anything, would happen to me on August 11. I was on edge, looking for danger behind every corner. I had seen nothing, not even slippery steps or mislabelled tablet bottles. Although Ellie was certainly throwing me looks that could kill.

It might all be nothing, I mused. All this fretting for nothing. I grabbed a handful of spent geraniums and sliced through the stems.

"Wow, has it upset you?" Nate said from behind me.

"God! Don't *do* that!"

He put up his hands as I waved the secateurs at him.

"Sorry, but what did the plant do to you?"

"It'll have a second flowering this way," I said shortly.

"You looked miles away."

"Yes."

"Anything I can help with?"

Could you disappear from my life?

"No, I'm fine, thanks."

"You seem to be sleeping better."

"I sleep with the window open."

"Yeah, the weather's kinda heavy, isn't it?"

"Mmm."

Nate stood watching as I hacked away at the geraniums. He made me nervous and after nearly nicking my fingers on the secateurs, I forced myself to concentrate. It became a competition – him staring; me looking studiously at the plants. After what seemed like hours, he sighed and walked away. As soon as he'd disappeared into the house, I sagged with relief.

The geraniums looked scalped. I cast a glance at the sky, now slate grey.

"Rain," I muttered. "We need rain."

As if in response to a prayer, I caught the faint sound of thunder in the distance. Thank God. It would be here soon and then perhaps the fog in my head would clear and I could work out what to do.

When it came, the rain was heavy. The noise on the skylight in the kitchen made conversation almost impossible.

I breathed a sigh of relief, as the bands around my head dissolved. I sipped at my coffee. The downside, of course, was that I was now stuck in the house, and the only place to retreat was the bedroom. I did so, ostensibly to watch television, but I was uneasily aware of Nate's eyes following me as I left the room. Ellie's face was blank. As I climbed the stairs, he announced he was going to Mother's library to prepare some notes.

Channel-hopping provided no more amusement than I anticipated it would, and when Gran called, I answered with relief.

"Hi, Gran. How are you? Any news on the dastardly Reverend Dillington?"

"Ha! I'm fine, Stacie. I was calling to see if you've found anything. I'm still looking."

"I've asked for some stuff from the British Library," I said, watching the rain batter the window. "But they said it would be a couple of days. It's some letters from someone who was named in the trial as a witness."

"That sounds promising. If I find anything, I'll send you an email. I don't want you driving in this weather," she said, sounding serious.

After the call, I was restless and went downstairs to get a drink. As I was about to reach for the coffee, I caught sight of the wine bottle. I shifted my hand to another cupboard.

Swinging my legs onto the sofa, I sipped the glass of wine with a sigh of appreciation.

"As bad as that?" grinned Nate from the doorway.

I nodded.

"Absolutely. And not looking as if it's improving anytime soon," I said.

"What can I do to make it better?"

"The wine's doing a grand job, thanks." I drew up my legs and tucked the skirt securely around my feet.

He walked into the room and sat on the end of the sofa, a little to my dismay.

"I don't see you drink often," he observed.

"She's got the softest head in the county!" Ellie chipped in with a laugh as she emerged from the study. The laugh sounded brittle to my ears. "A cheap date is Stacie."

Nate glanced at her but said nothing, and I shifted uncomfortably, drinking more wine. Naturally, I ended up trying to stifle a cough.

"See?" said my sister, grinning. "Hopeless with grown-up stuff."

"I think it's rather cute," Nate said easily, smiling at me warmly.

Ellie gaped like a landed fish.

"Well, on that note, I have a thriller with my name on it, so I'll see you later," I said, untangling myself from my skirt and standing up. I took the rest of the bottle with me.

The breeze blew tentatively through the open window, and an owl hooted. Although the rain had stopped and the night was now cool, I turned restlessly under the sheet. I flipped on my back. Then onto my side. I had a headache. Serve me right for drinking the best part of a bottle of red wine, I grimaced.

After punching the pillow and turning a few more times, I gave up and reached for my wrap. It was again about four am. I was going to be a wreck later. Resigned, I quietly opened my door and padded downstairs for, unusually for me, tea.

The light was still dim. I avoided looking at the garden, not wanting to be drawn into any encounters of the third kind this morning, thank you very much.

I put out my favourite teacup and saucer and when my tea brewed, headed to Dad's study to sit among the leather-bound books and slightly musty papers. I perched on the office chair, bought at great expense, while my mother scoffed at its ergonomic credentials.

I could smell Dad's familiar scent. I frowned. We hadn't communicated with my parents for a little while. I would text tomorrow, or rather later today. It would be about five thirty in

Italy and my mother wouldn't be pleased to have her sleep disturbed for chit-chat.

I switched on my laptop. Emails, mostly promotional stuff, filled my inbox, plus some instructions about my starting day at Grange Hall. I was just about to close my email when I noted something in the 'Spam' folder and idly, I opened the folder, expecting to just empty it. In it was a response from the British Library and I tutted impatiently, thinking how lucky it was that I'd checked. The message was polite, saying nothing, and I opened the file attached to the email.

I could see that it was a letter, faded and faint, from Agatha Lawrence to someone called Joan, in Cirencester.

I peered at the handwriting which, although neat, was cramped, with lines going up the side of the page, and horizontally. After a few moments, I recognised the letters in the unfamiliar script and began to read.

My dearest Joan

I commend myself to you, sweet sister, and pray that all is well with you and your family. I write a shamefully laggard thank you for the lace you sent last month, it will furnish my gown most handsomely. My delay in replying is caused by a commotion in the town, where, God save us all, we have discovered another witch who was burned Tuesday last.

Our parson, the God-fearing John Dillington, had been willing to speak for the witch Sarah Bartlett at her trial, but you may judge how amazed we were that the female had refused confession to our good parson. He said that although she may yet be delivered if God give her repentance, she, being obstinate, was prideful and destined for hell.

Sarah Bartlett had stiffly denied sundry times that she was guilty of aught but the jealous and spiteful attentions of the parson's daughter Prudence for reasons you may surmise, as the wench is well favoured. The daughter said the witch had drawn the parson to lust but this I give no credit to. The parson, having offered her penitence and having had it so pridefully dismissed, finally believed her a witch and condemned her before she went to the stake, where some were expecting her to be acquitted at the last. As it was, she burned without hope of redemption.

"So simply because she wouldn't let you hear her last confession, you swapped sides, did you, John Dillington?" I muttered as I forwarded the file to Gran. "No wonder you feel like a coward, bloody toeing the line instead of standing up to the mob."

I read the letter again, as if reading and re-reading would give me some insight into what happened in that dim, stifling courtroom. All this told me was that Sarah had refused confession. I wasn't clear why that seemed important, and my thoughts failed to knit together. After ten minutes, I gave up. I glanced in the mirror, half expecting Sarah to be staring back at me, but my own face, drawn and pale underneath messy hair, was all I saw.

The clocked ticked steadily, but my nerves were jumping after reading the letter. I wondered what time it was in Australia. I couldn't remember where Seb was on his trip. I'd lost track with all the drama here. I picked up my laptop, balanced the tea rather precariously on it, and headed back to my room.

Seb would be anywhere between eight and twelve hours ahead of me. I dug out my phone, cursed as I saw it was almost out of power, and spent the next five minutes searching for the charger. I clicked on the power switch, the noise loud in the pre-dawn quiet, and the battery icon on the screen pulsed. While it charged, I slid open the drawer where I kept my notebook and leafed through until I found the page on which I'd written the holiday details. Where was Seb now? Brisbane. I turned on the laptop and searched for Brisbane. Ten hours ahead of us, so mid-afternoon.

I sat and finished my tea. What if he didn't want to talk to me? What if he was taking part in some afternoon delight with some honey blonde Aussie miss who would tower over me with legs up to her armpits?

"Fuck it," I said to the silent room, and picked up my phone.

The tones sounded strange to my ears, too long, the wrong pitch. They seemed to ring out forever, and then Seb said, "Hello?"

Hearing his voice so clearly, almost as though he was in the next room, unnerved me, and I was lost for words for a moment.

"Hello? Stacie, is that you?"

"H-hi!" I managed, cringing at the shake in my words. "How are you? How's Australia?"

"It's an amazing place."

"Where are you?"

"En route to a hotel. I'm in the car at the moment."

"Oh, right."

There was a pause.

"Is everything all right?" he said, sounding polite.

"Um... not really," I said.

"What's the matter?"

"Just... I miss you. I wanted to hear your voice."

The silence yawned at me over more than fifteen thousand miles. I tried again.

"And things at home are horrible. Ellie hates me."

"Why? What have you done?" Seb's voice sounded hard.

"I'm *fighting off* her boyfriend," I snapped. "I'm doing everything I can to avoid him, and all she can see is that he seems to prefer me to her."

"A novel experience for Ellie."

"I'm not interested in him. I've *never* been interested in him, all I'm worried about is Ellie."

"Why?"

"She seems slightly... unhinged around him."

"Hasn't she always been a bit highly strung?"

I relaxed, hearing his voice warm a little.

"Perhaps. But the situation is complicated too..." I trailed off.

"How?"

Go on, tell him, I said to myself.

"Stacie? How are things complicated?"

"How… what would you say if I said I'm seeing ghosts?"

Silence.

"Well. Whatever I thought you were going to say, that wasn't it," he said slowly, making me wonder what he had thought I was going to say. "*Are* you saying that you're seeing ghosts?"

I took a deep breath.

"Yes. Yes, I am saying that. I've been seeing them since I was nine. And these ghosts now are connected with Nate."

"How?"

"Because they're his ancestors. And mine. It's all linked to some kind of cosmic coincidence, somehow. It's all very weird and a little frightening, and I'm not explaining it very well, but I'm *really* worried about Ellie's being besotted with this bloke."

The silence on the line stretched on.

"Seb? Are you still there? Do you think I'm crazy?"

"I'm still here. Is this why you wouldn't come with me?"

"Yes, it is." The truth, but not all the truth. I also didn't like being strong-armed, but just as we were starting to speak after two weeks didn't seem the right time to mention it.

"Why didn't you explain?"

"I thought you'd think I was insane. My mother did when I tried to tell her about my ghosts years ago."

There was a puff of exasperation on the phone.

"You put me in the same camp as your *mother*? Christ, that's insulting!"

"You're a scientist! How was I to know you'd be so—" I stopped. "Well, *do* you think I'm insane? Or do you believe me?"

Another pause.

"I don't understand but I've always thought there were stranger things in heaven and earth, et cetera." His voice sounded crisp. I vaguely remembered Gran had said much the same thing. I refocused on his voice. "Just because I teach chemistry doesn't mean I reduce everything to a bloody formula. I've no idea what's going on for you, but why wouldn't I believe you? I *love* you, for fuck's sake!"

My breath caught, happiness swamping me unexpectedly. "You do?"

"Good God, woman! If you were here, I'd bloody strangle you," he muttered. "Yes, Stacie, I love you. I've been in love with you for months. Or had you forgotten? Oh, for God's sake, don't cry!"

"I'm sorry!" I gulped. "I just didn't know how you'd respond to a girlfriend who goes around seeing dead people!"

He laughed ruefully. "I was an idiot, eaten up with jealousy for some blond Yank who was sniffing around you! That's what I thought you were going to say when you said things were complicated. I thought you might be falling for him."

"God, how often do I need to say it? I'm *not* interested! And, even if he was sniffing around me, why on earth would I just keel over for him? Give me some credit!"

"I'm sorry. I should have given you a great deal more credit than I did."

"Too right. Never underestimate me, Sebastian. Otherwise, you and me are going to have a lot of words in the future."

"Duly noted," he said, and even from Australia, the smile was in his voice. I smirked to myself. It would be all right. "Look, I'll be home in just over a couple of weeks and we can talk it all through," Seb said, his voice flowing like honey around my slightly battered spirit. There was a bit of a crackle on the line.

"Are you still there?" Seb's voice broke up a little, and I raised my voice slightly.

"Listen, Seb, I wish you were here – or I was with you! And for God's sake, don't worry about Nate, he's not important to me, you are!"

"This signal is getting worse. Look, I'll text when I get to the next hotel and we can talk again." His voice grew fainter. "I'll

THE VISITOR

be back…" The signal disintegrated, and I lost his full sentence, but I heard his parting words, "Keep safe!"

"Bye! I love you!"

I lay back. He believed me? The quiet of the night swept over me again and I smiled and hugged myself, remembering what he'd said. He loved me! Still!

The floorboard outside my room creaked, and I froze.

As quietly as I could, I rolled off the bed and crept towards the door which I saw, too late, was slightly ajar. Slowly, holding my breath, I reached for the handle and pulled it open quickly. I looked along the landing. No one was there, but I heard the soft click of a door shutting.

I carefully turned the key in the lock and lay awake until the alarm the next morning.

CHAPTER TWENTY-FOUR
STACIE

"But why should she refuse confession?" Gran said the following morning as I handed her a coffee. She was still looking pale but grew more agile on her crutches as the days passed. "Religion was much more important in Jacobean times than it is now and it must have been quite a statement to *refuse* confession before going to die. What's that bit in Hamlet, where he decides not to kill Claudius because he's at prayer?"

"I suppose it would depend on what she was being asked to confess to," I hazarded. "Perhaps she thought whatever she said, they'd use against her?"

"I wonder if Prudence was right and her father was in love with her and she was jealous?" wondered Gran.

"What, and Prudence did away with her by telling everyone she was a witch? Seems slightly farfetched!"

"Farfetched?" scoffed Gran. "Says the girl who sees and talks to ghosts."

"Yeah, point taken," I muttered.

"It might have been that he was afraid of himself. People got hysterical about witches in those times; the time of James I and his *Daemonologie*, remember? And we know that *after* Sarah died, he spent a lot of his time demanding more evidence in witchcraft trials." She rustled through some papers strewn across the desk, eventually pulling a page out and pushing it at me. "Did I tell you he also established shelters to give single women and girls some protection during the witch hunts?" she asked, and I nodded. "Perhaps the John Dillington you saw regretted that he wasn't as brave for Sarah, particularly if he was in love with her."

I thought back to the light shining in the parson's eyes as he'd spoken to me on the dark lawn. Yes, that might be the look of love. Or it could be insanity, which wasn't comforting. I stared out of the window at Gran's bright garden, bathed in the sunshine.

"How are things at home?" she asked me, her eyes searching my face.

"Tense," I said. "Nate's keeping out of the way, leaving Ellie free to ignore me completely."

"You were really close as children," Gran sighed. I remembered those days vaguely, but more vivid was the memory of Ellie realising she could do her sums faster than me. I had fallen off my pedestal with a bump and I was still feeling the bruises.

"She'll come round without water," I said, dismissing my younger sibling. "Listen, what are you doing about your birthday?"

She waved a hand at me.

"Oh, really, I don't want a fuss. I thought we'd all go to that French restaurant at Banbury."

"Sounds nice, do you want me to book?"

"It's already done, my dear. And I've booked a table for four."

"Is Edward coming?" I asked, puzzled.

She gave me a faint smile.

"No, I thought we'd ask Nate."

I stared. "Are you sure, Gran?"

"Absolutely. You need to keep your friends close but your potential enemies closer."

※

"No, don't *fuss*, I'm absolutely fine!" said Gran, on the edge of cross as the maître d' hovered around her. She was carefully negotiating her way across the restaurant.

"There!" she said, as she sank into her chair.

"Well done, Grandmother," Ellie said. "You're quite nimble on the crutches, aren't you?"

I looked at Ellie, wondering what the evening would be like. I pulled my wrap over my shoulders again to warm me against a sudden chill. It had been a difficult few days, rubbing the gloss from my conversation with Seb. Ellie was completely ignoring me. And whenever I had been in the house, Nate had been somewhere close, turning up with cups of coffee, asking advice on the house-buying process, drawing me into conversations he was having with Ellie. Despite the returning summer heat, the temperature in our house was Arctic.

Gran had invited Nate to the celebration, as she'd told me she would. As a result, Ellie had dressed to kill, in a black halter neck dress which fitted her so closely I wondered if she was wearing underwear.

Gran's eyes had sharpened when she'd laid eyes on Ellie, but she'd said nothing. She'd also looked at me.

"What's happened?"

"What?"

"You look… lighter… than the last time I saw you. What's happened?"

I opened my mouth to tell her that my weight had indeed gone down and she clicked her fingers.

"Seb. It's Seb, isn't it? He's been in touch."

I felt the heat rise to my cheeks. "Is it so obvious?"

She patted me on the shoulder. "Only to those who are looking, dear. Has that improved things with Ellie?"

I looked at my sister's back, retreating to the ladies' room.

"Yeah, you'd have thought, wouldn't you? But I'm not sure what's going on with her as we've barely spoken twenty words in the last three days."

"Ah. And Nate?"

"What about him?"

"How has he reacted to your suddenly blooming looks?"

The light went on in my head. I had solved the mystery of his more than close attention over the past couple of days. I fished out my phone and peeked at myself in the camera. It was obvious now. Even *I* saw my eyes sparkled, and my skin looked fresh and clear as if I'd had a wonderful night's sleep.

"Acting like he's sniffed some kind of pheromone," I sighed, turning off my phone.

"Good evening, Nate," said Gran over my head.

"How nice to see you, Catherine. Happy birthday," Nate responded. I blinked. He certainly brushed up well, wearing a wonderfully-cut suit and snowy shirt. His short hair seemed less brutish than normal, eyes warming while he kissed Gran's cheek. He turned to me.

"Hi." His smile hit me full force, and I stiffened.

"Hi. Good day at the office?"

He grimaced. "So-so."

"Hello, Nate," said Ellie's soft voice, winding itself around the table. Gran's eyebrows rose at the implied seduction in Ellie's voice.

"Hi, Ellie! You're looking very glamorous," Nate said.

Ellie sat down gracefully as a waiter rushed over to draw out her chair.

"Well, this is a special occasion. I like to make an effort, although I realise some people are more relaxed about these things," she added, her eyes flickering over me. I smiled sweetly. I had only a couple of 'good' dresses and this was the summer one. I'd had it for about ten years and it came out for most family parties. You could see it in the photo albums going back years.

"I heard from your parents earlier today," Gran intervened swiftly. "They rang to wish me a happy birthday, but the line was dreadful. I could barely make out what they were saying!"

"How's the trip?" I asked, thinking guiltily that I should have texted them before now.

"Very good, although I didn't speak to them for long – off to another lunch or something, your mother said."

"That's Mama for you, always looking for the next book deal!" Ellie said, looking around. "Where's the waiter? We could do with some wine."

The waiter, who'd been watching from the side of the room, appeared immediately. Ellie ordered white wine without consulting anyone and Gran raised her eyebrows.

"And what would *you* like to drink, Gran?" I said, twitching the wine list from Ellie's hand.

Gran ordered rosé and asked if Nate wanted anything different. He ordered sparkling water.

"Are you on the wagon?" she teased, and he smiled.

"Not at all, but I have a big meeting with my publisher in London tomorrow and I need to be up early. And on my mettle. He strikes a mean bargain."

"Have you finished the book?" Ellie asked.

"No, that's why it's a big meeting. I'm asking for an extension. I've been… distracted."

I swivelled to gaze at the other guests in the restaurant, suddenly finding them fascinating. I could feel Ellie's eyes boring into me.

"Well, buying a house is as distracting as it gets," Gran intervened again. "How's it all progressing?"

"At glacial speed, for no reason I can see. The survey's done, they've agreed the price, I'm happy to move forward. I'm completely baffled by the time it's taking."

"It's such a stressful time for you," Ellie sympathised in a syrupy voice. I stopped myself from rolling my eyes. "Apparently, it's the most stressful event after death and divorce," she added.

"Hell, I can believe it!"

Ellie's laugh tinkled across the table, and she patted his arm. "It'll soon be over and you can hold a housewarming."

Nate looked dumbstruck. "Yes, yes, I will. It'll be one way to say thank you for your hospitality."

He smiled, and Ellie seemed to bloom. Thankfully, the waiter arrived with the water and a lot of glasses. While he set them out, I exchanged glances with Gran. She looked a little exasperated. I knew the feeling as Ellie preened and posed in front of Nate, who, to give him his due, didn't seem to notice much. He looked on indulgently, as though Ellie was a favourite niece.

The food was delicious, but I began to feel queasy as Nate became more and more marked in his efforts to draw me into the conversation and Ellie drank more and more wine. Gran looked wary.

As she drank, Ellie became clumsier in her attempts to draw Nate's attention to her. How we got onto the topic of perfect partners wasn't clear, but to my dismay, here we were.

"Of course, when I married your grandfather, it wasn't the done thing for women to work," commented Gran at one point. "It was only because he wanted to support me to have a life outside marriage that I could work after Julia went to school."

"What did you do?" asked Nate.

"I joined the Civil Service and loved it. We needed the money as well, of course, and my wage made things a lot easier."

"My mother worked," said Nate. "What with Dad's work and hers, I never saw much of them."

"Did that change your views about women working?" Ellie asked, sipping her drink. He looked thoughtful.

"I guess that I'm blessed with a good salary and standard of living, and if I could, I'd want a partner who wanted to stay at home and be a mother to our children. If there's no financial need for her to work, why should she?"

I tried to imagine myself not teaching and failed. "Wow,

your partner had better *love* you, if she was giving up everything else!"

He smiled at me. "Well, yes. I hope I'd be worth the sacrifice – if there was any."

"Oh, absolutely!" Ellie trilled. I felt ill and put down my cutlery.

At last they cleared away the plates, and I could signal the waiter to bring out the cake. It arrived with due pomp and ceremony, seven large candles, and the waiters singing Happy Birthday. Gran beamed as the waiter revealed the cake and other diners in the restaurant applauded as she blew out the candles.

We picked the candles carefully out of the sticky chocolate ganache and the waiter took it away to have it cut.

"That is a *big* cake," Ellie said. "Too big for just us. And aren't you on a diet, Stacie?"

I smiled, wanting to slap her. Nate stared.

"She doesn't need to diet, Ellie. She looks great from where I'm sitting."

Inwardly I groaned and once again, Gran stepped in.

"Your sister is just fine as she is, Ellie, and if you don't mind me saying, I think you've had enough wine."

"Actually, I *do* mind you saying, Grandmother! I'm not a kid you can order around, you know!"

I could see the waiter returning with plates of cake, triumphantly carried at shoulder height on a tray, and I imagined him, clownlike, shoving one of them into Ellie's face. As I watched, he caught his foot on the strap of Ellie's handbag lying on the floor. Two slices of cake fell into Ellie's hair and the chocolate ganache, softened by the heat of the restaurant, slid down her bare back. She cried out, jumping up, only to slip on the other piece of cake which had landed on the floor. She went down, the crockery and glasses went flying, and after a moment's complete silence, there was chaos, with Ellie crying, waiters rushing around with cloths and brushes and Gran pressing her lips together and trying not to laugh.

I was horrified. *Was that me?* I wondered wildly. *Or was it really an accident?*

Nate tried gently to help Ellie to her feet, but she slapped him away and ran to the ladies'. The waiter, scarlet with remorse, and the manager, apologising, were all I could hear until Gran's voice quietly suggested I should go to her.

"Me? I'm the *last* person she wants to see just now!" I said. The manager caught his breath and Gran smiled at him.

"It was just an accident, and Ellie's not hurt. But perhaps we *could* have the bill? Stacie, see if your sister is all right, beyond needing to wash off the chocolate."

I dragged myself to the bathroom. Ellie, rigid with anger, was gripping the basin. She'd washed much of the cake from her hair, but there were still traces of chocolate down her back.

I sighed and tore off lengths of toilet paper. "Are you okay? Did you hurt yourself when you fell?"

"I'll have a few bruises."

I wet the paper and wiped the chocolate from her back. She gasped as the wet paper hit her skin.

"You'll need a shower when you get home."

"Obviously."

I kept my mouth shut as I took another paper towel and dried her back.

"There. Gran's asked for the bill, so are you ready to leave now?"

"Yes, I bloody am!"

She swung out of the door. I washed my hands and caught sight of my reflection in the mirror; hair redder than usual, sharper cheekbones. Sarah. One eye winked at me.

I fled the bathroom.

༺༻

I sighed as the door to Ellie's room slammed shut. I threw down my bag and poured a glass of whisky.

"Surely it's not as bad as all that," said Nate, amused. "It was just unfortunate."

I turned to him.

"Really? You don't think it's been a truly dire evening?"

He shrugged.

"Or that your attention to me, despite my telling you how Ellie feels, might not raise the tension a bit?" I added.

He held his hands up.

"Whoa, hold it right there. You think *I'm* responsible?"

I put the glass down with a snap. "I told you she fancied herself in love with you. I told you I didn't. You chose to ignore that information and try to charm me in the hottest summer we've had in years, and where the civilising force of my parents isn't around to dampen down the hassle you're causing. Yes, Nate, I *do* think you're responsible!"

"You can't be serious!"

"Indeed, I am! Christ, when is that bloody house sale of yours going to complete?"

"As soon as I can manage, believe me!"

"Good! Get a move on, please, before we all kill one another."

"Stacie—"

"I'm going to bed."

"What can I do?"

I stopped, caught by surprise at his question. Looking at his earnest face and deciding he was serious, I perched on the sofa arm.

"My sister is beautiful, highly intelligent, and believes herself in love with you. If you can't feel anything for her, can you just believe that I am not interested and stop trying to—"

"To what?"

"I don't know. Stop trying to involve me in conversations, ask my views, engage with me on anything but a superficial level!" I frowned, aware of sounding slightly ridiculous. Nate's eyebrows rose.

"Stacie, this is normal interaction! I've no idea how people have treated you in the past, but this is *not* singling you out!"

"You look stunned," Nate commented after I was silent for a moment, lost for words.

"Yes, I'm sorry." I stood up, feeling slightly off-balance. He looked hard at me.

"I haven't met anyone like you before. I find you incredibly attractive, warm, engaging, human, sexy—"

I made a noise in my throat and swung away to escape to my room. As I closed the door, I heard Ellie sob. I went to bed very uneasy.

CHAPTER TWENTY-FIVE
STACIE

I smiled at the text from Jo, who'd returned from holiday for a rest from her love affairs. She was returning soon, she said, and demanded to know what I'd done all summer.

I rubbed my eyes. I hadn't slept well. My brain was nowhere near awake enough to have *that* conversation by text. Another message pinged.

Has Seb finally told you of his undying lust?

"Yes, you traitor!" I muttered. "You bloody *knew* and said nothing! What kind of friend are you?"

Yes. He's in Oz at the moment.

WTF??? Why aren't you with him??

Just about to sign a lease on a house I texted back, a grin on my face. *No cash.*

Bloody typical. But splendid news on the new pad.

Ellie clattered into the room, looking like death. Her eyes were black rimmed where she hadn't bothered to take off the make-up.

"Coffee?" I said. She nodded, seemingly unable to speak. I placed a strong black coffee in front of her.

I picked up my phone and wrote an email to meet the letting agent later that morning. There'd been silence for perhaps fifteen minutes when she opened her eyes and said, "Thanks."

"How are you? How's your knee?"

"Fine. It's fine."

"Right."

She studied me and I stared back. "What?" I said, irritated.

She sighed. "I mean, you're pretty enough, but…" She shrugged her shoulders.

"What the hell are you talking about?" I asked.

"Nate, of course!"

I put my mug in the sink. Ellie was obviously spoiling for a fight and this morning, at least, I wasn't inclined to give her one. "You're talking bollocks, Ellie. I don't care about Nate," I said and walked out.

She followed. "Stacie, you're just fooling yourself, aren't you? Of *course* you care! A wonderful, successful, intelligent man like Nate decides he likes you, *you*, my dull sister and *you don't care?* I think *you're* the one talking bollocks!"

Her voice had sharpened and I lost patience. I grabbed my car keys and my bag and slammed out of the house. She minced over the gravel in bare feet while I was unlocking the car.

"This must be wonderful, after all these years of playing second fiddle."

"Oh, fuck off!" I slammed the car door, turned on the engine, and then, goaded, I rolled down the window.

"Get over it, Ellie. Whatever he feels about me, he doesn't want *you*. Now just bloody grow up!"

Her mouth opened in an 'O' of surprise. Whatever she might have expected from me, cruel honesty wasn't top of the list. I saw the tears start, but I put the car into gear and drove away.

I was much more cheerful when I drew up at Holly's. I had just signed my lease, and I skipped across the yard. Mary was in the paddock, leading a discontented-looking boy of about eleven on a small pony. I waved a greeting and strolled to the stables to saddle Wellington.

Mary called over to me as I led him from the stall. "Hello, stranger!" I managed a smile and her eyes narrowed. "You're looking bright and breezy?"

I grinned, but she destroyed my mood with her next words. "Ellie okay?"

My mouth twisted. "You know Ellie."

Mary nodded. She'd witnessed Ellie's tantrums endless times. She shook her head, muttered something, and waved a hand in farewell, turning her attention back to the sulky boy.

I set off, deciding to go by the lane before cutting across the fields. Wellington, sensing my mood, became tense and skittish. I pushed Ellie to the back of my mind as I concentrated on keeping him under control. In the end, I pushed him to a gallop, and we both calmed down.

The air was warm and close, clouds scudding across a bright sky. It seemed slightly oppressive.

"Not more bloody storms," I muttered, remembering John Dillington in his cloak. I pulled on the reins and slowed Wellington to a canter, then drew a deep breath, trying to stay relaxed.

I sorted through the past few days in my head. Nate's attention, now I examined it, perhaps was less sexual than I had imagined. Away from the hothouse of home, I could examine it more objectively. It seemed more and more like the early relationship I had had with Seb. Conversation, focused on what I thought and felt, had been the building blocks of that relationship. With Nate, I could see the same hallmarks.

Nate still stood closer to me than I wanted, touched me more than I wanted. But this happened both in and out of sight of Ellie. So he wasn't deliberately stirring things between my sister and me, I realised.

I slowed to a walk, taking a cut across the fields, away from the road. The weather had been so hot this summer, farmers had already cut the wheat and barley fields, the straw in bales waiting for collection.

I thought of Ellie. Spoilt all her life, the pretty, clever sister with grace and charm; rejection would be a novelty for her. I wasn't sure how she'd react.

"The sooner I move out, the better," I said to Wellington, who shook his head in agreement.

My mood lightened as I remembered the house contract and Seb's most recent text, which had arrived overnight.

Fret not, I'll see you soon.

I'd emailed late the night before, telling him about the visions I'd had since I was a child. The words had been difficult to write and, looking back, I wondered if he would still believe me when it was in black and white. My entire body yearned when I thought of him. I wanted to see him again.

Wellington neighed softly. I looked up and Sarah was standing by the hedge.

I pulled up and dismounted, tethering Wellington to a nearby blackthorn tree. Sarah looked different, a little sad, and I searched my brain for the date of her death – not today, but soon.

"Well met, Eustacia."

"Hello." It struck me once more how different her voice sounded and I wondered what my other spirits might have sounded like, had they spoken to me.

"My time is close," she said, getting straight to the point, and I shivered. "While I have travelled my path, you must take care to keep to yours, if you are to be safe and fulfil your true destiny. Beware of false desires, they may have heat for you, but there will be no light."

"I know I am in danger," I said. "John told me."

"If you remember your heart's desire, we can protect you," she said. "But you must stay strong, vigilant, and be true to your heart."

"Well, yes, but I don't know what that means! Can't you tell me?"

"You do not know your own heart?" she asked, her eyebrows lifting above grey eyes.

My mouth opened and then closed. *Did* I know my own heart? What mattered most to me? In a split second, I sorted through everything I valued in my life. Seb was there, Gran, but most surprisingly – my job. Teaching was my passion, I realised. And *that* was what was at risk? I panicked.

"But you *must* help me! I'm jumping at shadows, worried about everything! Should I go away? Hide?"

"You have hidden much in your life, have you not?" she said, her head on one side. I felt my face flush. "You must make your own choices. But mark me well – those choices you make will bend your future, and the futures of many, many others."

Like dominoes, I realised. Whatever I did would impact those around me, whether that was Seb, Ellie, Nate, Gran... the kids I taught. All at once I felt weighed down with responsibility.

Out of my turmoil, a thought struck me. "Why did you refuse confession from John Dillington when he offered it? Why didn't you take his help? Could he not have *saved* you?"

She looked a little surprised and shook her head.

"It was my fate. He could not have saved me, and he had a bigger destiny to fulfil. Just as you do." A pause. "And I do not lie."

"What, *ever*?"

"Ever," she said, turning grey eyes on me.

The wheels went around in my head. "Is *that* why you couldn't take confession? *Because* you would tell the truth and you are *actually* a witch?"

A smile lit her face, changing her into a beautiful young woman. She shrugged, and once more, I saw a strand of her bright red hair escape from the cap. A cloud passed over the sun and she faded before my eyes.

"I can stay no longer. My story is unfinished, but it weaves with yours," she said. "You can help me complete it and in doing so, you will start the path to your own destiny."

A group of crows took off from the tree branches right above my head and my eyes flicked upwards. Sarah had gone when I looked back. I huffed in exasperation.

"After all, what damage would hanging around to properly explain do to the drama here?" I muttered as I untangled Wellington's reins.

I swung myself into the saddle and headed back to the stables.

I spent longer than I needed to at the stables. I needed to talk to Gran, I knew, but I wanted my thoughts straight before I did. So I took more time rubbing Wellington down. Maybe I'd even bring Seb and teach him to ride. If I survived my 'peril' in the next few days.

The drive back was thoughtful and a little uneasy.

My phone, lying on the passenger seat, pinged. It was Gran. *Are you around?*

I pulled the car to one side of the lane and dialled the number.

"Hi, Gran. What's up? I was going to come and see you, I've had another visit from Sarah. Oh, and I've signed a contract on a house."

"Have you? It's all about houses today," she said, and I frowned, not understanding. "That's good news on your lease, though! Where are you?"

I explained.

"Can you detour to see me? You can tell me about Sarah and your new place. But there's something I need to show you about the cottage Nate's buying."

I stared at the documents on the table.

"You're having a laugh, aren't you, Gran? Tell me you are!"

"Of course not. Would I joke about this? You look shell-shocked, let me make you some coffee. I could do with some myself."

While she was in the kitchen, I looked at the photocopied page, entitled The History of Lewsbury. The village had been fiercely Royalist in the English Civil War and, when subdued, Oliver Cromwell had renamed it. Its original name had been Leyton.

"This is the village where Sarah lived, isn't it?" I said through dry lips. Gran thrust coffee into my hands.

"Yes, it seems to be."

"And the house Nate is buying?"

"Appears to be what was the rectory. Where John Dillington lived. You said that the house was ancient."

I nodded.

No wonder I had felt so strange walking into it. And the upstairs bedroom... had Sarah been there? The *bedroom*? I wondered, not for the first time, what had gone on between my distant relative and the reverend.

I took a deep swig of coffee.

"What now?" I said.

"Thursday is the eleventh of August – the day she died," Gran said. "I think you should stay here with me tonight and tomorrow."

Part of me so wanted to agree. "But what about Ellie? If Nate is involved in all this, doesn't she need protecting too? And what about Sarah's story? She told me her story was unfinished and that I could help her complete it."

Gran snorted. "Well, I'd rather it didn't finish with *you*, Stacie! I'm seriously worried about all this and the best thing I can think to do is for you to remain here."

"But, Gran, we're dealing with some weird shit here! I'm not sure I'd avoid this wherever I was, and whatever 'this' is!"

She did the nearest thing I'd ever seen to wringing her hands.

"But—"

"And whatever it is, Gran, I can't drag you into it! You can't walk without crutches, let alone run away!" I forced a smile, gesturing at her crutches. "Sarah told me they would protect me. All I have to do is just stay on my path, she said."

"Which is?"

"No idea. I'm hoping inspiration will strike at the vital moment."

She laughed softly and quiet fell between us. At last, she said, "Very well, then. Tell me all about your house."

I put my nervous energy into digging the garden when I got home. It seemed the most normal thing I could do in this strange time, and I prised out weeds from the hard, dry earth with all the strength I could muster. I'd not seen Ellie since I'd left for Holly's. I was just getting to the pale roots of a dandelion when a shadow fell over me. It was Nate, bearing a mug.

"I wondered if you could do with a drink?"

I sat back on my heels.

"Thanks, that's nice of you."

He handed me the mug and I clambered to my feet and took it, sipping the coffee. I sighed with appreciation. He had noticed I liked it strong.

"What are you doing this evening?" Nate asked.

"Um… why?"

He grimaced. "Look, I'm not going to jump you! I wanted someone to come to the cottage. We're nearly completed on the sale and I wanted to measure up, y'know, curtains and blinds, and… stuff?"

He looked so out of his depth, I smiled. And I remembered his words – this was just normal interaction, not a come-on.

"Soft furnishings not your thing?"

He burst out laughing. "Nope. Definitely not."

I looked down at my filthy hands, dirt under the nails. I had no idea if I could even get over the threshold to the cottage, given my reaction last time. And in any case, wasn't it completely foolhardy to put myself near a place that obviously held some significance? I bit my lip. Come on, Sarah! Where are you now with the advice? Is this the path?

"Please?" Nate's voice cut into my thoughts. I could find no reason to say no and there was something so flattering about his persistence that he swayed me, despite my misgivings.

"I'll get changed."

*

"Hold it higher," I said, with one end of the tape measure in hand. I focused on the normality of this little domestic scene, keeping my dread tamped down. So far, I'd seen the cottage as it was, rather than how it had been. Sarah had not appeared, nor John. It might be fine.

"Like this?"

"Yes. Okay, that's two metres fifty."

I scribbled it down.

"I think that's it. Unless you think I need to change the drapes in the second bedroom?"

"No," I blurted as I pushed the chair back to its original position and sat on it to re-lace my trainers.

"Are you sure? I thought they might look old-fashioned." Nate frowned.

"Well, they are in keeping with the house," I said, with my head still down. Nothing and no one would drag me upstairs.

"You might be right. Thanks for your help, Stacie, I'd never have done this alone!"

I smiled, getting to my feet. "No problem. Shall we get back then?"

"Sure. Can I buy you supper?"

"Um… probably best not to. I've no idea what Ellie was

planning for dinner and she'd be pissed off if we messed up her plans."

He looked at me with his head on one side. "I didn't think you and Ellie were on speaking terms. Will she be cooking you dinner?"

"I don't want to make things any worse than they are," I said finally, after a moment's silence.

"It's just supper. As a thank you. As friends. Or does she dictate your friends as well as your love life?"

"She's hurting. I don't want to add to it."

"Has she always been as considerate of you?"

Never. In a moment, the slights, the insults, the thousand dismissive comments, all flooded through my brain.

"Tell you what, buy me a drink instead," I said. "We can get a quick one on the way back."

He grinned, hugged me, and then released me before I could protest. Then we walked out to the bike.

※

I was laughing when I opened the door to the house, but this died when I caught sight of Ellie's face.

"Hi, Ellie," Nate said easily, coming up behind me.

"Hello. Had a nice time?"

"Just a visit to the pub. Stacie helped me measure up for curtains at the cottage, and I bought her a drink as a thank you."

"Nice."

I edged towards the stairs.

"I wondered about takeout for dinner? I ought to cook, but takeout is probably safer!" Nate continued, ignoring the atmosphere.

"Whatever," Ellie said, her eyes locked on me like a target.

"What would you like?" Nate pressed. Ellie looked at him.

"I'm not hungry."

"No? I was going to ask you to come out with me on the

bike to collect it. I thought the Chinese in the village had a good rep."

"I'm not dressed for that."

He smiled and I saw her soften a fraction.

"Come on, Ellie, come for a spin on the bike." His voice was like caramel. I watched, fascinated, as Ellie's stiff defences crumbled.

"Okay, I'll change." She headed up the stairs, bumping past me.

"Boots and jeans!" Nate called up after her. I relaxed.

"Okay?" he asked me in a low voice. I nodded. "Good. I didn't want her in a filthy mood because you helped me."

He raised his hand to a lock of hair which had fallen across my face and smoothed it behind my ear. The gesture was so intimate, my heart quickened. My lips parted.

His gaze locked on my mouth.

"Stacie," he whispered.

I swayed towards him for a moment, before I turned my head. Keep to the path, keep to the path.

CHAPTER TWENTY-SIX
SARAH

Sarah drew her cloak more closely about her as best she could as they opened the door of the gaol. The light hurt her eyes for a moment before she saw the sky, blue and clear.

"A fine day for a witch-burning," said Sam, gloating. She ignored him, but shivered.

She made the walk from the gaol in unnatural quiet, the people from the village lining the streets. Sarah felt her cheeks heat with shame at the stares of the people, their eyes cold, their faces stern. She looked at no one, but walked steadily, her head high.

The whispers in the crowd reached her ears.

"Shameless! I always knew…"

"She treated my Joseph, you know…"

"Did you hear of the familiar? A two-headed rat, they say…"

"A wanton hussy, in league with the Devil."

The last, of course, was from Mistress Whyte. Sarah, unable to stop herself, looked up and saw the matron, whose small eyes gleamed with malice. Determined to have at least some revenge before the end, Sarah looked her full in the face and smiled. To her satisfaction, she observed Mistress Whyte grow pale, cross herself, and move away.

Buoyed, she walked on. In truth, the distance from the gaol to the village green was short, but it seemed to take hours. Her triumph was short-lived. The pyre when it came into view made her gasp in shock and stumble. Joseph caught her arm and gently pulled her upright. She thanked him under her breath.

The pyre was bigger than she had imagined, with a rough set of steps up to where she would be tied. She shuddered, afraid. Her hands, tied in front of her, began to tremble. The magistrates, dressed all in black, stood by.

Nearby, she also saw Parson Dillington, looking pale and ill. Dark circles ringed his eyes, as though he had not slept. His face looked pinched. Prudence was also there, in the crowd with her maid. As the people came into focus, Sarah looked at many of the children who had been in her care at one time or another. She didn't recognise their faces, so hard were they.

Joseph untied her hands, and she rubbed her wrists.

"Sarah Bartlett, you have been accused of witchcraft and therefore are condemned to burn at the stake!" said Justice Darcy. "Our worthy Parson Dillington is offering you salvation through confession. Parson?"

Parson Dillington stepped forward and Sarah thought he moved like an old man. Her heart swelled; she wished she might have spared him this. But his future lay elsewhere, not married to the village healer, but bearing the memory of her with him.

"Mistress Bartlett," he said under his breath. "Will you not confess? I cannot help you if you do not."

She smiled and shook her head.

"I cannot confess. I told you I could not."

"Exorcism would save you!"

"There is nothing to exorcise. I am not evil, I do no harm."

"Then live! A little dissemblance might save your life!"

She frowned.

"Do you not listen, sir? I ask for no forgiveness because I have done nothing wrong. And I cannot lie."

He stared, what appeared to be anger growing in his face. She knew it was terror for what she would face, pain at losing her.

"I cannot lie," she repeated. "It is not in my nature. But you must take heed, sir, the crowd grows curious." Sarah glanced around at the muttering crowd, where a few fingers were pointing. She recognised too the fear in his face, for himself, perhaps even for Prudence.

He shook his head as if in disbelief.

"Sarah Bartlett, you have been condemned as a witch! You have refused confession and I believe you in league with the Devil! May God have mercy on your soul!" he said in an agonised voice which the crowd whistled at. There was a scuffle in the crowd and, to Sarah's dismay, Abigail forced herself through to the front.

"Nay! Nay, sir! Do not forsake her! She is headstrong, not evil!" Abigail cried, falling on to her knees in front of the parson, whose face was now as white as parchment. "A little patience will bring her to womanly submission! But on my life, she is no witch!"

Sarah strode over to her and knelt down.

"Abigail! Be silent, or you will bring the wrath of the magistrates on your head! It is unsafe to protest! And you have your family to care for!" she hissed as Abigail sobbed.

"But you are my friend! I love you!"

"I know! And as your friend, I urge you to silence!" She put her hands around Abigail's face and said softly in her ear. "You need to take care of Rebecca and the child to come!"

Abigail stared.

"How—"

"Hush! Be quiet, sweeting," Sarah warned, grateful for Thomas, who had at last arrived, and hauled Abigail to her feet. He dragged her away. Her fingers could still feel the softness of Abigail's skin as Thomas disappeared into the crowd. She stood and faced Justice Darcy, who sneered at her.

"Your charms seem powerless against our blacksmith. Mayhap he will beat some sense into his disobedient wife."

Even with death at hand, Sarah suppressed a smile. She doubted it. Thomas had never laid a hand on Abigail, who was herself quite handy with a skillet. There would be no beating, but in her mind, she envisioned Abigail sobbing, held safe on his lap, as he stroked her back and whispered nonsense into her ears. The vision brought tears to her eyes, and she blinked. For a moment, all was silent and still.

"Burn the witch!" came the cry, and soon a chant ran through the crowd. Sarah's knees buckled a little. Forcing herself upright, she shook off the meaty hands of Sam and walked on unsteady legs towards the enormous pyre. Her hands were roughly tied behind the stake and she stood as proud as she could as Sam, gloating, put a torch to the wood. She smelled the tar.

The wind blew it out, to the consternation of the crowd.

The justices muttered and conferred, and another torch was found, larger this time. Sarah glanced at the pastor who was tight-lipped. Prudence was standing in front of him, half his height, but she saw that his fingers were gripped around her shoulders, holding her firm.

He's going to make her watch me burn, she thought, and part of her was glad, the other part repelled.

The smoke from the larger torch blew in her face and she coughed. Still the pyre failed to light and Sarah could see the crowd growing restless. She wondered, if they couldn't burn her, would they hang her? Would that be preferable?

Sarah smiled wryly as she debated the pros and cons of hanging or burning, and Mistress Whyte screamed, "Look! Look! She smirks! The witch is laughing at us!"

In alarm, Sarah watched the fury of the crowd, their faces distorted with hatred. The crowd seemed to press forward. In haste, Sam took another torch and this time, the wood caught.

The crowd cheered and clapped, and Sarah noticed the child Robert, jumping around with the rest of the boys on his lame leg. Her gorge rose in her throat.

The crackling of the wood filled her ears, and the smoke made her eyes sting and water. She began to cough. Dragging breath through her lungs she saw the parson, his eyes fixed on her, his face a white mask of pain and misery. His lips were moving, but she couldn't tell what he was saying.

The heat around her legs built, tearing at her skin, her skirts beginning to smoulder. Her head swam, and through the noise and the smoke, she heard Abigail's voice crying her name. Sarah looked up and above the crowd, catching Thomas's eye as he held his near-hysterical wife. She smiled and shook her head. Thomas, looking startled, stared at her before he nodded slowly and led Abigail away into the smithy.

It would soon be time. She closed her eyes and tipped her head back. The cap which had given her so much trouble fell away from her head, and her hair, bright as the flames that licked around her skirts, tumbled to her shoulders and hung at her waist. There was a cry and she glanced at the parson who had fallen to his knees, praying. He rocked backwards and forwards, barely able to contain his sorrow, but maintaining a face of stone. Prudence stood immobile, her eyes wide and fixed, a dawning expression of horror on her face.

Thinking hard, Sarah saw Dorothy with her kinfolk many miles away, sipping ale and laughing over a family memory. Sarah reached out and stroked her mind, and Dorothy paused, startled for a moment, before closing her eyes. Sarah saw a tear fall on Dorothy's cheek, sliding down the worn skin before she shook her head and clasped the hand of her concerned nephew, forcing a smile.

Farewell, Dorothy, she said in her mind, Remember me kindly. In Chichester, Dorothy nodded, her mouth twisted in grief.

She hissed in pain as the flames leapt and burnt her thigh. The smoke, black and acrid, clogged her throat, making it hard to breathe. She concentrated harder, bringing to mind the stream in the woods, the glades, and green, dappled light. She focused on the call of the birds and the rustle of wheat fields in the wind, the air lifting her hair and the cry of the curlews settling around her. In her mind, the owls swooped in joy and the bats danced in front of her. The light behind her eyes flickered and glinted like sunshine on water. She had said her goodbyes.

"Take care, my love!" she cried in her thoughts, and the parson's head shot up and he jumped to his feet, his mouth open in astonishment. She smiled at him before beginning to choke. She gasped, and she threw back her head, her hair catching light in the dancing flames. Sarah steadied herself and made her mind blank, raising her gaze upward.

The blue of the sky, tinged with wisps of black, curling smoke, was the last thing she knew.

CHAPTER TWENTY-SEVEN
STACIE

"Congratulations, Nate!" smiled Ellie the following day, going across to hug him. He looked wary but accepted the hug, patting her shoulder. I looked on, filled with relief. Ellie's eyes were shining – were those tears?

"This calls for a celebration – your first property in England!"

I watched as she dived into the kitchen and began opening cupboards to find glasses. She pulled out a bottle of champagne from the wine rack and threw it into the top drawer of the freezer.

"Congratulations," I said, wondering if I'd get the same response when I shared the news about my own house. His smile looked pained.

"I bet you can't wait for me to be out of your hair."

I didn't know how to respond and, in the end, settled for, "It will give you your own space, and some peace and quiet."

"Yeah. Thanks."

He sounded heartfelt; there at least, I knew how he felt.

I got up, my movements stiff. I'd been awake for hours, watching the shadows shorten on the walls of my room as the sun rose. The clock ticked away the minutes, and I waited for a sign that Armageddon was at the door. But there had been nothing. No catastrophe, no visitations from Sarah or John Dillington, the house was still standing. The only thing that was happening was the flood of text messages from Gran every forty minutes, asking how I was. I flexed my shoulders.

"No hug of congratulation from you then?" he said, only just audibly, and I froze.

"As I keep telling you, I'm taken."

Ellie came back. Her cheeks were flushed, hectic even in the white oval of her face. Her eyes gleamed and everything in her body looked angular. I tried to calculate how much weight she'd lost.

"So, when do you pick up the keys?" I asked him.

He gave me a steady look but said, "Tomorrow lunchtime. I'll be packing tonight and tomorrow, but it shouldn't take long."

"Have you got a van booked?" I asked. The practicalities of his leaving seemed a nice, safe topic and who knew, I might use his contacts myself.

"No, but Ellie mentioned a place to call."

"I'll drive you there in a bit," Ellie said. "It should be really easy, I'll help."

"You're so sweet." He smiled at her. Again, the flush of her cheeks made me think she might be ill.

"I'll be so sorry to see you go. Stacie's not much of a riveting conversationalist!" she continued, busying herself with glasses for the champagne.

"Love you too, sis," I said with a wry smile.

Nate frowned, but Ellie didn't seem to care.

"I'll cook us something nice tonight unless you were planning to eat out?" She didn't include me in the invitation. I picked up my bag and car keys and walked towards the front door. Doomsday or not, I needed some air.

"That would be nice," Nate said. "Hey, Stacie, will you be able to join us too?" he called, his eyes following me.

THE VISITOR

No, I'm keeping an eye out for the end of the world. "No, I'm afraid not, I'm hoping to see an old colleague." The lie didn't trip easily off my tongue. Jo wasn't back yet, but Ellie didn't know that, and she nodded enthusiastically.

"See you later, then! Oh, and can you bring me some double cream?"

Given my chores, I climbed into my car and relaxed for the first time that day. The good news was that I had completed all my pre-work for the term and all I had to do was finish one of the GCSE set books. The summerhouse looked like it would be my refuge while Nate packed up his stuff and Ellie sobbed her farewells.

I drove with uncommon care to shop in the village and then called Gran. She answered on the first ring.

"Stacie?" Her voice was sharp with alarm.

"Everything's fine, Gran," I soothed. "How are you?"

"Worried sick about you, my girl!" I glanced at my watch. Past one o'clock.

"Look, I've just picked up a couple of chocolate eclairs and I wanted to know if you were offering coffee."

"Don't be daft. The coffee is always on."

"Well, I have news. I'll be with you in ten minutes."

"Drive carefully, please."

༶

"So he's moving out?"

I nodded.

"Completes tomorrow, picks the keys up at lunchtime. Oh, wow, this is sublime," I said, my voice a little indistinct as I sank my teeth into the pastry.

"Thank goodness. What's happened today?"

I focused on the gentle domesticity of the day – shopping, drinking coffee.

"It's been quiet so far, other than Nate's news."

"I wonder if your ghosts will return when he leaves?"

"Certainly hope so. I could do with the company."

"Ellie still unfriendly?"

"We've spoken a dozen words since your birthday. She looks through me most of the time. God alone knows what the folks are going to say when they come back to World War Three."

Gran nibbled her eclair, and I stared when I realised that in one bite, half of mine had disappeared.

I toyed with my coffee cup.

"I'm *so* looking forward to moving out," I said.

She smiled. "I could have helped with the deposit, Stacie."

I shook my head.

"Nope. Under my own steam, or not at all. And I'm thinking of taking a job down the pub to bump up my income."

Gran looked appalled.

"A barmaid? God, your father will hit the roof!"

I shrugged.

"We can't all take home university salaries. But it'll be such a relief to leave. Ellie will drive me mad soon, if she doesn't kill me."

Gran's head came up sharply.

"You said you weren't speaking," she said slowly. "Not that she might do you harm."

I waved my fork around.

"Oh, not *physical* damage! But she seems like she just hates me sometimes! And since I pointed out that for once in her life someone preferred me to her, she's liked me somewhat less than her usual sisterly indifference."

She put down her fork, looking worried.

"You will take care, won't you? *Especially* today."

"You're not suggesting that Ellie would do anything to me, are you?" I stared at her, appalled by the thought.

"No. No, of course not. No. But you *will* take care?"

"Of course I will!" There was a pause as I finished my coffee. "But I can't stay here all day, Ellie's waiting for her cream."

"Are you at home tonight?"

I didn't fancy it much, if I was honest. The thought of witnessing my sister's last attempt to get Nate to notice her made me feel ill. Being away from both of them seemed sensible, and I said so.

"Why not spend the evening here?" Gran said eagerly. "You can be out of the way of Ellie and your unwanted guest, and with me, which will make me feel much better about today."

Arrangements made, I left for home.

❦

The house was quiet when I opened the door, and I paused for a second, listening. There was the clatter of pans from the kitchen.

"Hi, Ellie." I faltered as Ellie spun round, a wicked-looking carving knife in her hand. I stepped backwards, my conversation with Gran flashing through my head.

"What?" Ellie said. She stepped towards me, and I took another step backwards.

She frowned, and then her brow cleared as her eyes flicked to the blade.

"What do you want, Stacie?"

"It would be nice if you put the knife down, for a start."

She waved it in my face instead, and I put my hands up. She laughed and, to my intense relief, tossed the knife onto the counter. I let out a breath I hadn't realised I was holding.

"Your cream?" She took it from me without a word. I hesitated.

"I thought you were going out?" Her voice had hardened.

"I am. Do you need any help?"

Even as I spoke the words, they sounded ridiculous. I could cook, sure, but Ellie had a dozen French cookery courses under her belt.

"I don't think so, do you? Or are you just wanting to get in my way?"

I frowned at her.

"Oh, get over yourself, Ellie. I'm not hanging around to mess up your seduction attempts!" I turned away and then back. "But remember what I said, and try not to make an idiot of yourself, won't you?"

Her fists clenched, and I backed away.

The afternoon wore on. I stayed in my room, pretending to read. Nothing happened, other than some amazing smells wafting up the stairs from the kitchen. I'd been expecting overcast skies, silent birds, a heavy and threatening atmosphere to mark the day that Sarah had died. The sun shone and I could hear the blue tits twittering as they took turns to raid the bird feeder.

A text made my phone vibrate.

Hi Stacie – looking forward to seeing you, but only if you can guarantee ghosts! Oz wasn't so great without you. Seb XX.

I smiled. Cheeky git, I thought. I might try to call him later. I grabbed my bag and headed for an evening of safety, I hoped. Gentle TV and homemade pie at my grandmother's house. There wasn't a lot that could happen, surely?

❦

The sound of laughter as I came through the door later that evening was a surprise. My evening had been completely, almost preternaturally ordinary. No bumps in the night, no loose wiring, no thunderstorms where all the lights went out. So when Gran began to droop with weariness, I'd insisted I came home, despite her concerns I should stay close.

As I'd driven along well-lit roads at a steady thirty miles an hour, I'd wondered if Gran and I were both imagining things and the day would pass without incident.

I hesitated on the threshold and then started tiptoeing up the stairs, hoping to make it to my room without interaction.

"Stacie!" called Nate, appearing in the hall with a bottle of wine. "Don't hide away upstairs, come and join us!"

"I—"

"Oh no, you don't!" he said, grabbing my hand and pulling me towards the sitting room. "We need to celebrate my new house!"

Christ. Drunk academics. That was all I needed.

"Ellie, we need another glass!"

"Oh, do we?"

"Yeah, don't be mean! We've had such a cool time, haven't we?"

She smiled at him, a little bleary.

"Listen, it's fine, I don't want to intrude." I tried to pull away.

"You're not intruding, Stacie, you *live* here!" Nate waved aside my objections and pushed me on to the sofa. "Hell, I'll get the glass!"

While he went to the kitchen, Ellie took another swig of her wine. She swallowed and avoided looking at me.

I caught the faint smell of wine dregs and looked at the bottles collected on the coffee table. They'd certainly been necking the wine since I left. There must be four, shit, no *five* bottles on the table, including the one we were drinking from. Nate returned with a glass and swooped on the latest bottle, pouring a generous glass.

"Cheers! Here's to my new house!"

"Cheers."

I sipped. God, this was the good stuff. Had Ellie raided Dad's cellar? He'd be apoplectic if she'd touched some of his favourite bottles.

"How was your evening?" Nate asked, sinking back into the armchair and fixing hazel eyes on me.

"Oh, nice, thanks."

"How was Jo?" Ellie said.

"Jo's like Jo," I said, keeping my eyes on my wine. Which was true, I thought to myself.

"She's been away, hasn't she?" Ellie persisted.

"For weeks. But she had to come back sometime – if she

wanted to keep her job, at any rate." Also true. "How was the meal? Smelt wonderful," I said, moving the conversation on.

"It was truly delicious!" Nate enthused while Ellie did her best to look modest. "Sole meunière and the most glorious dessert! You should have re-arranged your friend, you missed such a treat!"

"Jo's a bit of a force of nature," I said, again with perfect truth. And then, some devil prompted me to add, "And Ellie had shopped for two, not three."

Ellie glared at me and I smiled back. An awkward silence fell, and I put down my wine glass.

"Thanks for the drink. I'm sorry to duck out, but I need to make a call."

"At this hour?" Nate glanced at his watch.

"It's to Seb," I said deliberately. His eyes flew to my face.

"Oh, lover boy has reappeared, has he?" Ellie giggled.

"You know, in every way but one, he never went away," I said, standing. A light in Nate's eyes seemed to flare, and a thick silence descended. Ellie's gaze switched between the two of us. I wished them goodnight and walked out of the room.

§

I couldn't get through to Seb. I tried a number of times and just got his voicemail. It was five to midnight when I gave up, frustrated that I hadn't been able to speak to him.

I threw the phone on the bed and looked out of the window at the velvet sky. As I calmed down, it occurred to me that there was silence downstairs. Had the party finished?

"Well, thanks for clearing up, chaps!" I thought as I looked at the mess in the kitchen. I thought briefly about washing up and then decided I would be an idiot to do that. But my palms itched. I couldn't bear the chaos and I emptied the sink, heaping dishes and cutlery on one side. I wiped surfaces and reached for the coffee.

The sitting room still had the glasses and bottles on the low table and, tutting, I collected them and rinsed them. It was while I was thumping the cushions that I heard the cry from upstairs. I paused and listened.

I walked to the bottom of the stairs and held my breath. The next cry had me running up the stairs.

"Ellie!" I said under my breath. I opened the door to her room. The rumpled bed was empty and I stopped dead, shying away from the implications. In slow motion, I walked along the corridor to the guest suite and pushed at the open door.

In the dim light, Ellie was straddling Nate. She was moaning as she moved, his hands controlling her hips, Nate's face was creased in concentration, his eyes closed as if he was hanging on to his control. My mouth fell open as a wave of feelings washed over me – repulsion, surprise and finally, something I recognised as intense, white-hot jealousy.

I backed out of the room and Nate looked at me, his eyes widening. He opened his mouth, and I shook my head violently, and quietly shut the door.

Ellie's cry of ecstasy followed me down the hall.

As I closed the curtains in my room, I caught sight of a figure on the lawn, his black cloak fluttering in the light breeze. I locked the door and drew the covers over my head, praying for the morning.

CHAPTER TWENTY-EIGHT
STACIE

I was up early, clattering pans. I turned the radio up loud as an act of defiance as I cleaned the kitchen, the rock music bouncing around the walls. My eyes felt gritty with lack of sleep, and my mouth was sour, but my mind was a careful blank as I concentrated on setting the house to rights.

On a more positive note, at least I'd survived yesterday, I congratulated myself as I rinsed the last plate. I'd sent a text to Gran to say so. I was puzzled too. Yesterday, except for that last scene with Nate, of course, had been so ordinary, so lacking in any kind of threat, Sarah's warnings seemed like a dream.

I looked around at the now gleaming kitchen and plugged in the coffee machine. I emptied the last of the ground coffee into it. My lips tightened as I watched the water drip through the filter, hitting the base of the jug with a hiss.

You didn't want him, Stacie. You *still* don't want him, so why all the drama? I mused. The image of my sister and our visitor popped into my head again and I wiped it clean with an effort. Ellie should be in a better mood, at least.

I walked to the patio to sit with my coffee in the early morning sunshine. The heat was building, a haze in the sky.

Snippets from the morning news spoke of the highest temperatures and lowest rainfall in decades. Looking at the lawn, brown and burnt again after the downpour a week ago, I could believe it.

I sat quietly for about half an hour before Ellie poked her head onto the patio. She looked cross and tired.

"Why the hell is the radio on so loud? You're so fucking inconsiderate!"

I raised my eyebrows.

"Inconsiderate? Talk to me about inconsiderate when you bloody clean up after yourself," I retorted. "And I'm wondering what Dad will say when he sees you've been drinking his best wine."

She shrugged and disappeared, only to appear again a couple of minutes later.

"There's no coffee!"

"No." I sipped my drink and smiled sunnily at her. "There's instant if you're desperate."

She clenched her fists before huffing back indoors. I registered that my heart was beating rather fast, and I focused on my breathing. A large bird flew overhead. An owl, I decided. Weren't they supposed to be nocturnal?

I decided to take myself to Holly's and go out with Wellington. It would be good to get out of the house before Nate was up. Perhaps I could be out all day, see Gran afterwards, that would be ideal.

Afterwards, I wondered if I'd subconsciously wanted the confrontation with Nate. If I'd really wanted to avoid him, I would have got up, dressed and just left, rather than bothering with clearing up, having coffee and sniping with Ellie.

"Stacie," he said, running down the stairs as I was collecting my keys from the hall. My breath caught as I turned to face him. He looked pale and hungover, but despite that, very handsome. I gathered my composure.

"Good morning," I said.

He grimaced, running a hand through his hair. "You Brits

sure are focused on the social niceties! I wanted to talk to you—"

"But we have nothing to say to one another."

He stared at me. "I know how it looked."

"Yep, I'm sure you do, but don't explain, please. It's none of my business."

"Let me explain."

"Just leave it, please, Nate. I don't need or want an explanation, although I'm pretty sure my mother would freak out about last night."

"Will you tell them?"

"What *do* you take me for?" I opened the front door, but his hand came out and slammed it shut. I breathed deeply.

"This is ridiculous," I said. "You have packing to do; I have a horse to ride. Can we dispense with the histrionics?"

"Nate?" Ellie's voice floated down the stairs, thin and uncertain. I glanced up, seeing her wrapped in a bath towel.

"What's going on?" she said to Nate. "Weren't you getting some breakfast?"

"Yeah, I am. Just wanted a word with Stacie."

"And now we've spoken and I'm off," I said, looking hard at him. "I'll see you later."

I escaped to Holly's and the uncomplicated company of Wellington.

My ride was uneventful, although Wellington seemed on edge. Sarah was nowhere to be seen. I didn't know what to think. Was she *really* dead? Even as a ghost? I shook my head as ridiculous thought after ridiculous thought chased around my head. At the end of the ride, with Sarah nowhere in sight, although I saw a ghostly tramp, I was no wiser.

After stabling Wellington and promising I'd see him again soon, I tried to text Gran. I frowned as I realised the signal from my phone was barely operational. I did the usual thing of turning it off and on with no better result.

I couldn't find Mary and decided she was out with a riding group and reluctantly, I climbed back in the car. I tutted to myself, irritated at my self-imposed exile and drove home almost defiantly.

The small van Nate had hired for the removal was parked near the front door, its back doors open. It held a few boxes, but I could tell that the packing was not going as well as I had hoped.

"Christ, I hope they're not shagging again," I muttered as I locked the car.

There were a few half-empty boxes in the hall and noises from upstairs. There were no voices.

"Hello?" I called.

I heard a voice call back. Nate. Then he was standing at the top of the stairs, his arms full of books.

"Hey."

"Hey. How's it going?"

"Slow."

I paused, looking around the hall and into the sitting room.

"Where's Ellie?"

"She left."

I looked up at that. "Oh?"

He came slowly down the stairs and put the books in his hand into the box.

"How long has she been gone?" I asked.

"She went out not long after you."

That sounded like trouble. "Right. So she's not helping you?"

"As you see."

I put my hands on my hips. "What happened?"

He looked at me without expression. "Why would you want to know? I thought you said it was none of your business."

"You had a row?" I was guessing.

He shrugged. "I tried to tell her that I wasn't great at relationships. She wasn't happy."

"No shit."

He threw me a haughty glare and headed back up the stairs. I followed him, anger mounting with every step.

"You *knew* she was in love with you! And that you were bound to hurt her! And yet you couldn't bloody resist, could you?"

He spun round, snarling at me. "Don't fucking lay this all on me! She came to my room and climbed all over me! At first, I thought it was you!"

"*Me?*"

"Yes, God help me, *you*! She was wearing your perfume and your nightdress!"

"Hasn't this been done before by Shakespeare?"

He grabbed me and shook me hard. "Don't fucking do that! Don't take the piss! You have no idea how I felt when I realised it wasn't you!"

He released me and, my breath coming in gasps, I said nothing. He knocked his head gently against the wall and turned to stare at me, his hazel eyes serious.

"I swear to you on my life, I didn't know last night until you walked in while she was on top of me – and then I'm afraid physiology took over." He looked at his hands. "I'm not proud of what happened, but I'm not accepting complete responsibility here. I think your sister needs some help."

I agreed with him. I wondered briefly what her state of mind was and shrank from thinking too deeply about it. Looked like I *wasn't* the only one in the family who might be admitted for mental health treatment.

Nate exhaled. "Look, normally Ellie would be absolutely the kind of girl I'd date. But there's no spark for me. If I'd realised sooner last night that it wasn't you, I wouldn't have slept with her."

It was my turn to sigh. "I take it she didn't say when she was coming back?"

THE VISITOR

He laughed sourly. "She was barely speaking to me at all."

That was Ellie's style. Time to be practical.

"Look, you need to be picking up your keys shortly. Do you need some help with the rest of the packing?"

"I'm nearly done, but yes, that would be great. Thank you."

His room was a tip, with books and clothes everywhere, but tossed on a chair was a nightdress. It was indeed mine and drenched in my perfume.

I picked it up and threw it in the washing basket, grimacing. I began packing books and by silent consent, Nate focused on packing his clothes. To my surprise, I put my hand on a Bible, a handsome book with beautiful gold leaf on the front of it's dark blue leather binding. I stopped, examining it, but the leather was so smooth it slipped from my hand and landed open on the floor. With an exclamation, I picked it up.

The book had opened at the First Epistle of John. I was no believer, but it was a lovely object and the font was so gorgeous, I ran my finger down the page. *There is no fear in love; but perfect love casteth out fear: because fear hath torment. He that feareth is not made perfect in love.*

The words made me pause for a reason I couldn't explain, like a crossword clue I couldn't solve. When Nate came back into the room, I hastily closed the Bible, putting it into the box.

We worked well together and in a scant hour, the job was complete. While he carried the last of the boxes to the van, I stripped his bed, almost holding my breath so as not to smell the combination of my perfume, his scent, and sex. By the time I was rolling the sheets into a ball and Nate returned, I was almost gagging.

"All done?" I asked, forcing myself to speak. He stood silently and nodded.

"Good. Well, good luck with the house. And the future."

I stood awkwardly, not knowing what else to say.

"Isn't there any hope for us, Stacie?"

I shook my head, feeling my eyes grow moist.

Inexplicably, I was crying properly when the van disappeared down the drive.

§⁂

I finished a sandwich I didn't really want and swallowed the last of my coffee. The text I'd composed to Gran, saying that Nate had gone, was still sending from my phone and I tutted at the poor signal. I threw it onto the kitchen counter in frustration. My eyes were pink, but I felt slightly better now the tears had stopped. I hadn't known what I was crying over, other than the sense of something lost.

I looked over the garden, bathing in the afternoon heat. The summerhouse was calling me, waiting to soothe my battered nerves. I collected the book I needed to read, and a bottle of water.

It was blessedly cool in the summerhouse and since I'd given it a much needed clean, the space was comforting. I wondered idly why it was I had never seen my grandfather there, given the times we had spent playing silly games and hiding from the rest of the family when he was alive.

I'd considered calling Ellie and decided that it was politic to leave her to lick her wounds and come back in her own time. I tried to put myself into her place and winced.

It was now crucial to move out as soon as possible, and I toyed with the idea of calling the property agent and asking how flexible the date of my moving in was. I couldn't imagine what our relationship was going to be when she finally came back – even though none of it was my fault. Perhaps that was my peril?

I wasn't that worried that I didn't know where she was. I felt sure she would have gone to Holly's. Despite our differences, we were very similar in some respects, and like me, she relaxed when riding. She'd do her thinking there. With any luck, she'd come to the conclusion that Nate Williams was too old for her.

I sighed. Yeah, right.

And there was Nate himself. What happened now? Dad would be confused and hurt if, having given this visitor the free run of his home, Nate simply disappeared. The strands of their lives were too closely interwoven – if not of friendship, then of professionalism. They might work together; they were part of the same faculty. They might even collaborate. Hopefully.

Nate's grim face came into my mind and with determination, I picked up the part-finished novel to think about something else. I just needed to complete this novel and then I would be ready for the new term. It was nice to come back to something so normal and ordinary, away from the tangled lives of Sarah and John and even Nate and Ellie.

I was excited about the preparation for my new role and eager to finish the book, but the prose of the nineteenth-century book seemed syrupy and difficult to understand. I kept flipping backwards and forwards to remind myself of the plot which seemed pointlessly complicated with endless characters.

A bee buzzed and bumped against the window, breaking my concentration. I put the novel down and took a swig of water. God, I was tired. My very bones ached.

I'd barely slept, what with Nate and Ellie, and John Dillington floating around the lawn at one in the morning. When the sun had slipped through the open curtains, disturbing my uneasy sleep, I'd awoken feeling bone-weary and anxious.

I got up and walked to the door. The garden was still and there were few birds. I imagined they were sheltering from the heat. There was a slight shimmer on the flowerbeds and my gaze sharpened, hoping to see the child with the golden curls. I stared intently. Nothing. I hoped my sightings would return when Nate had really gone, settled into John Dillington's cottage and withdrawn a little from our lives. Or perhaps they would move with me?

There was a thought. I laughed softly, wondering what their

opinion would be of the little terraced house on the edges of the town, with the tiny garden and white front steps outside a battered sky-blue door.

I stretched my arms up, my mood lifting with the idea of finding a space for the cat and the governess in my new home. I wondered about going back to the house for a coffee but picked up the book instead. About twenty pages to go.

"Oh, come on! Just finish it!" I settled down again, determined to focus, and for a while, the words on the pages seemed to come together, making sense, weaving together to tell the story written more than two hundred years ago. An owl hooted, and I frowned. I must check if they were completely nocturnal.

I started to read again. The quiet flowed around me, the sun was hot and soothing. The words began to blur, and my eyelids began to droop. I don't recall when I fell asleep.

CHAPTER TWENTY-NINE
STACIE

John Dillington was galloping towards me on Wellington, his black cloak flying behind him. His face was white, as white as his blond hair, and his eyes were green, bright green. I tried to move towards him, but I wasn't able to move and when I looked down, I found myself tied to a pole so high that the ground fell far, far below me. I struggled, but the cords binding my wrists were tight. I looked at him in panic.

"Mistress! You must rise! I cannot help you if you do not. Sarah! Quickly!" he said urgently, his glorious voice vibrating with tension. He jumped down from Wellington and stretched out his hands to me, looking anguished.

"I can't!" I gasped. "Help me!"

His voice rose. "I will not be silent this time! I will save you! Sarah, sweeting, bestir yourself! You are in grave peril!"

I looked around and far below me, someone moved towards the pole, carrying a lighted torch. I thought it was Ellie, but the figure wore a grey cloak, the hood up. I twisted my head, trying to see who it was, but their face remained in shadow.

"Ellie! Is that you? Help me!"

The figure didn't look up but moved around the pole, setting light to the brushwood stacked at the base. Flames jumped and danced in front of my face and I began to struggle in earnest.

"Rise and live!" John Dillington called loudly.

I gasped and started awake, my heart thumping and tears wet on my cheeks. When I realised I had been dreaming, I blew out a slow breath and closed my eyes, waiting for my pulse to slow down. Just a dream, it was just a dream.

A few minutes later, I opened my eyes. The book was on the floor, where it had slipped from my hands, the bottle of water unfinished by my side. It seemed darker in the summerhouse, and I glanced at my watch. I had slept for about an hour. But it shouldn't be dusk yet.

I saw what had happened. The door had swung closed and, sighing, I struggled out of the squishy chair and collected my book and water. I pushed at the door. It didn't move.

Need to shave a bit off the bottom. God, that'll be a long job, what with taking off the door, smoothing it down and then re-hanging it, I thought.

I pushed again, harder this time. It didn't budge. Peering through the window above the door handle, I saw the padlock on the outside. I frowned. It was closed fast.

How had that happened?

I turned to the chair I had been sitting in. Was the chair visible from the door? I squinted. Hmm. So unless the person was very careless or remarkably unobservant, anyone should be able to notice me sitting there from the door before they locked it.

All this detective work was keeping me calm. But as I reached the end of the deductions, my thoughts leapt to Ellie as the cause of my situation.

"Christ, what a bitch," I muttered, rattling the door with little hope of it moving. I had bought the padlock myself and remembered how chunky it was.

Well, I'd ring… I paused. Who would I call? Gran, I thought finally, given my parents were in Italy, Seb was in Australia, Jo was visiting family, and Ellie probably wouldn't pick up the call, if indeed it was Ellie who had locked me in. Gran would get a cab, she wouldn't be able to drive with her leg still in plaster.

And then it hit me. I didn't have my phone; it was still on the kitchen counter.

Shit.

I considered my options. I could sit quietly, finish the book and wait for Ellie to grow bored and eventually unlock the door. Or I might see if there was another way out.

I paced the windows, seeing again as I did that they were all painted shut and cursing my mother's choice of cheap decorator. I searched vainly for something sharp, knowing with a sinking heart that when I'd cleaned the place, I'd taken all the gardening tools back to the shed. I wondered if I should break a window, although when I looked at the size of the panes, I wasn't sure of the point; they were far too small for me to get anything but my arm through.

I closed my eyes in frustration and then tried to calm down. Get a grip. I was safe, I wasn't hungry – yet – and I had water for the moment. I even had electricity if it grew dark, which meant that someone would notice the lights from the house. I sat down again and picked up the book.

After five minutes of reading the same page, I threw it aside and paced the summerhouse, growing angrier by the minute. I threw my head back and stared at the roof, wondering if escaping that way was an option. I dragged a chair over to climb on and pressed against the roof with my hands. It was pretty solid, and I didn't fancy trying to break through it, even if I had any tools, which I didn't. I jumped down.

When I got hold of Ellie, I'd bloody smack her, I thought, clenching my fists.

It was growing warm with the door and windows shut, and I wiped my forehead, now beaded with sweat. My top had clung to my body, and I tweaked it at the shoulders to get some air to my heated skin.

"Chill. You need to chill," I muttered, once again sitting down.

It was ten minutes later that I smelt burning.

※

I sniffed and rose slowly to my feet. What was burning? Where was the smell of smoke coming from?

I peered through the windows one by one, trying to see if the fire was indeed close by. I was just reassuring myself that it didn't seem to be near the summerhouse when a wisp of smoke licked the side of the door. I walked around slowly and then with increasing panic, pulling furniture back from the walls, knowing that it was ancient and bone dry. And probably with stuffing that would catch fire quickly if it came to it.

Quickly, I pulled all the cushions from the big sofa and threw them to the other side of the room. The sofa was old, huge and heavy, and I had to put my shoulder to it to move it away from the door. I finally pushed it into the centre of the room and started on the bookshelf on the other side of the door, piling books on top of the sofa and dragging the bookshelf away from the walls. Then the cushions went on top of the books.

I had a clear view of the wall now and saw the smoke was starting to curl upwards and my heart beat faster. I grabbed the rug on the floor and pulled it away too so that it wouldn't catch alight. A cough caught in my throat.

"Fuck."

I grabbed a side table and smashed it on the wooden floor as hard as I could. Solid oak, it buckled a bit but stayed in one piece, and I tried again. This time, a leg broke off, and I pulled and twisted until it came away from the table. Wielding it like a club, I began to smash the windows one by one on the other side of the summerhouse. I pushed my face to the broken glass and breathed deeply, the fresh air filling my lungs.

Think, Stacie, think. What can you do?

I looked at the window frames. They were ancient, made of metal, rather than wood and thanks to the last decorator, painted shut. Perhaps if I swung at them with the table leg, they might buckle, and I could climb out of the window.

I turned back to the centre of the room and, with a struggle, I dragged the rug from the floor. It might protect me from the shards of broken glass, I reasoned. But only if I smashed big enough holes in the glass to be able to crawl through.

I grabbed the table leg and for the next few agonising minutes, I hit the window frame with it. I managed a dent in one of the struts, but nothing else. In despair, I threw away the leg. I pulled up a chair and braced my back on it, putting my feet on the frame and pushing with all my strength. It moved a little and I rejoiced, but re-doubling my efforts gave me no more success.

I doubled over, breathless, my legs aching. Something wet was on my hands and saw a splinter dug into my palm, a trickle of blood running down my wrist. I swore and wiped it down my jeans. I would probably need to try with all the windows. I looked around. Six windows in all.

I dragged the heavy chair to each window in turn, smashing all the glass and pushing hard against the frames with my feet. I had limited success at bending the frames, although tantalisingly, they all bent a little before they remained stubbornly rigid. They knew how to build in the forties.

The smoke around the door was building and I was finding it more and more difficult to breathe. I drank some water and whipped off my tee shirt and wrapped it round my face, pouring water on the fabric to create a bit of a barrier. I did not know if it would work, but I was running out of inspiration.

As I backed away from the door and the smoke, my mind was whirring. *Surely* Ellie hadn't done this? I knew she thought herself in love; I knew she'd been hurt, but to do this? My heart was breaking.

A flicker by the door focused my attention. The door had caught alight, and the flames were licking and curling around the bottom of the wood.

I flew to the broken window and screamed for help, my voice sounding weak as the smoke filled my throat. I coughed, as the heat built on my bare back. Choking as the smoke penetrated the damp tee shirt, I felt dizzy and faint.

One of the big, squishy chairs was on casters. I would need to wait until the flames had burnt some of the door away, and maybe the chair would serve as a battering ram when the fire had weakened it further.

But that would mean I'd have to stand and wait while the fire grew in strength. If I didn't break the door down... I dragged my thoughts away from the inevitable conclusion. I tried to steady my breathing so I didn't cough, and fixed my eyes on the door as the fire took hold. It might have been hours, it might have been minutes, but when the summerhouse began to fill with smoke, I knew I had to act.

I pushed the chair to the far side of the summerhouse to give myself a bit of a run-up then rammed the chair as hard as I could against the door and my arms jarred as if I'd run into a brick wall. Before the chair caught fire, I pushed it back and tried again. Sweat ran into my eyes, making them sting, along with the increasingly foul-smelling smoke.

Then, before I took a run-up at the door, one of the struts from the roof sagged at the back of the summerhouse, crackling and groaning. My mouth opened in shock. God above, was the roof going to fall in? Fear gave me added strength.

I tried again, and to my joy, I heard the wood splinter. But the door still wouldn't open. Despairing, and my energy rapidly fading, I heaved it back again. I paused, eyeing the door, knowing that this would probably be the last attempt I would have strength for.

"Right then, you bastard," I muttered through the cloth. "Here I come!"

I breathed through my nose, trying not to cough, and rammed the chair into the door. I heard a splintering noise, then someone was shouting my name. I fell, exhausted and choking, against the chair arm.

A foot slammed through the bottom of the door panel and I dragged myself to my feet to pull the chair away from the door. Strong hands gripped my arms and hauled me through the smouldering wood.

"Seb…" was my last thought before there was an almighty crash and I blacked out.

※

The earth was hard under my aching body.

"I've called the ambulance," said Gran, as if from a long way away.

"I hope they get here soon. I'm worried about her breathing."

Seb. That was Seb's voice. I tried to draw a breath and ended up coughing. His voice was soft at my ear immediately.

"Stacie? Sweetheart, don't try to speak, the ambulance is coming, and we'll get you to hospital as soon as we can."

"Seb?" my voice sounded burned, a cracked whisper of noise. I opened my eyes to see his smoke-blackened face, serious and red-eyed above me.

"Shh. Yes, I'm here. Frankly, this was not the surprise I had in mind when I stepped off the plane this morning."

My lips twitched, and my parched skin stretched and cracked. "How—"

He shushed me.

"There'll be time to talk when you're feeling a bit better. Just lie quiet. You've inhaled a lot of smoke."

I made out Gran's voice, saying something about calling my

parents. I thought I heard Ellie sobbing, but the noise was soft. As I lay on the ground, I took careful stock. The birds were singing. There was something soft and smelling of Seb and smoke under my head. My throat ached and stung, and I had a pain in my hand. I raised it to look and saw blood running down my wrist. I drifted off.

    I don't know how long I lay there, but I was beginning to feel cold and shaky when the ambulance men put an oxygen mask over my nose and mouth and lifted me. As they put me into the ambulance, Seb held my hand. We bumped along for a bit, and the wail of the sirens rang through my head as we picked up speed. Someone put a hand on my forehead and said something low and reassuring. Then there was a prick in my arm and it all went black again.

CHAPTER THIRTY
STACIE

A gentle snore woke me. I tuned in to the persistent bleep of the monitor and felt the oxygen mask still on my face. I had a drip, and the needle pinched my flesh. I drew a deep breath and the pain in my throat surprised me. I groaned and opened my eyes.

Seb was sitting in a chair at one side of the bed, fast asleep. His face looked relaxed under his tousled hair, although I could still see smears of soot on his ears and neck. His clothes were filthy. He looked young and defenceless. I drank in the sight of him, and to my surprise, the tears fell down my cheek. I had wondered if I would see him again. And here we were.

I lay, my mind digesting all I knew about the fire, Sarah, her story. Was it over? Was that it? God, I hoped so. A shadow by the wall drew my attention and Sarah stepped forward. I glanced at Seb. He slept on, oblivious.

I struggled up onto my elbows and tried to speak, but nothing much came out of my throat. Sarah smiled and put her finger to her lips.

"God bless you, Eustacia. You have helped me complete my story, and I am grateful." She faded into the pale jade walls.

Finished? How? Because I'd been almost roasted alive by someone, possibly my younger sister? What the actual fuck? Then I realised: death by burning. But I had survived.

While my mind danced around the thoughts, a nurse came in and Seb jerked awake.

"Stacie! How are you?" He stood up and bent over me, kissing my forehead.

"Can't speak much," I croaked.

"No, and you shouldn't try to," said the nurse. "Just concentrate on breathing the oxygen. In a bit, the doctor will come round and he's going to put a tube down your nose to check the damage to the airways."

I must have looked alarmed.

"It's fine, we'll give you a mild sedative and you won't feel a thing."

Let me be the judge of that, I thought.

Seb stroked my hand and laughed softly. "I'll be right here, if the doctors allow it."

The nurse bustled off and my eyes searched Seb's face, rediscovering its angles and planes, seeming so new, yet so familiar. He perched on the bed and took my hand in both of his. He looked serious, and I frowned.

"Thank God I came," he said in a low voice. "The moment I pulled you clear, the roof collapsed."

I re-lived my moment of terror at the memory of how the strut at the back of the summerhouse had cracked and buckled. And then, as Seb pulled me through the burning door, that groaning, dull explosion. He gripped my hand, and tears gathered in my eyes. I nodded.

There was a tentative knock on the door. Gran poked her head into the room. She looked older than I remembered.

"Can I come in?"

"Of course!" Seb stood up, making room as she manoeuvred her way in on her crutches. "I was about to get us some coffee, although I can't vouch for its quality." He gave me a quick grin and disappeared. Gran sat down and patted my hand.

"Thank God you're all right. But I imagine you've been told not to talk?" I nodded. "Righty-ho. Your mother and dad should be back tonight and I'll try to put them off coming to see you this evening. I imagine you need some more time to recover, and also, to be with Seb?"

I nodded and grasped her hand. She patted my shoulder and reached into the bag slung across her shoulders.

"I brought you some of Francine's lemon drizzle cake. I doubt the cooking here is much to write home about, so you might need something tasty."

I grinned inside the oxygen mask. The man in the stovepipe hat appeared at the bottom of the bed. My eyes widened, and I started, and Gran looked around.

"What?" Her eyes narrowed. "Or… are you receiving visitors again?"

No fool, my wonderful gran. I nodded. She smiled, the first full smile since she had arrived.

"Excellent. I hope they don't mind me being here?" The man in the hat shook his head, and I shook mine in turn. "Well, I'm not staying long, only checking you have something decent to eat. I've got a delivery tomorrow from the supermarket and I'll bring some more goodies in."

I gave a little cough and pulled the mask away from my face. She leaned forward.

"I'm okay, Gran," I whispered.

She said nothing, and I was surprised and appalled to see tears. I squeezed her hand.

"Yes, it's a good thing that Seb arrived when he did. But enough of that. You need to rest." She sat back and pulled out a newspaper. "I've brought you the crossword for when you're stronger."

I looked sideways at her and wondered what she wasn't telling me. Seb returned with the coffee which, as predicted, was diabolical, and they kept me amused until the nurse shooed them away.

༄

The following afternoon, my mother swept in with arms full of flowers, Italian chocolate and books. My father came with a fresh nightgown and my slippers. They both looked brown and well, if anxious.

Seb went away to find chairs for everyone, and when we had exchanged kisses, there was an awkward pause.

"Well," said my father, starting the conversation. "How are you feeling?"

I took the oxygen mask away and croaked that I was okay.

"We've not gotten to the bottom of *why* Eleanor pulled this childish prank of locking you in the summerhouse, but the fire service told us how the fire started early this morning," my mother said, smoothing down her skirts. I reflected that the dress, beautifully cut and elegant, was new and screamed Italian tailoring. I looked up, my attention caught.

"Apparently, there was a wineglass by the door, and it acted as a magnifying glass for the sun, and that's how the grass caught alight," said Dad. "Because it's been so dry, the fire spread very quickly."

I said nothing. That didn't explain the wine glass. And Ellie had set light to the pyre in my dream.

Seb returned with chairs and with one look at my face, turned the conversation to their time in Italy. Eventually, we got round to our erstwhile guest.

"I see Nate has bought a house in record time. He sent a note thanking us for our hospitality," Mother said.

"He's invited us all to his housewarming, but I'm not sure if you'll be able to make it," Dad said. "It's next Saturday."

I glanced at Seb in mild panic.

"Probably best that Stacie gets some rest, she'll want to be fit enough for work at the end of the month," put in Seb. I nodded enthusiastically.

"Probably best," I echoed in a whisper.

"Ellie's not sure either," said Mother. "She's quite shaken up by your accident. I'm not sure she'll be strong enough at the moment."

Seb stared in astonishment, opened his mouth to say something, and when I shook my head, shut up. I imagined that Ellie, despite her confidence, wouldn't be able to look Nate in the face after the stunt with my nightdress and perfume.

"Where is Ellie?" Seb's voice was hard, and my father looked at him nervously.

"She's in bed; the doctor gave her a mild sedative. She's appalled at the trouble she's caused," Mother replied.

A few more minutes and the torture, for all of us, was over. Mother kissed the top of my head, Dad hugged me gingerly and asked me to take good care of myself and ring if I needed anything, and they left. Seb exploded when he was sure they were out of earshot.

"*Ellie* is quite shaken up? For fuck's sake! Do they realise that her spiteful, thoughtless prank nearly got you bloody *killed*?"

"I take it my idiot daughter and her hopeless husband have been to visit," said my grandmother, pushing open the door with her crutch. Seb dived to pull open the door. I smiled to myself. Ellie was always going to be the true centre of their universe, I was a distant planet, circling the sun.

When Gran settled in her chair, she looked at me carefully. I'd slept, despite the hustle of the hospital and nurses coming in at some godforsaken hour to take my blood pressure. My throat was still very sore, but I could probably manage five minutes' conversation with Gran.

"You look brighter," she said.

"I'm getting stronger," I croaked.

The door opened, and a policewoman poked her head through the door.

"Are you Eustacia Hayward?" she asked in firm tones. I nodded, startled at the sight of the uniform, and Seb stiffened, as though protecting me. I squeezed his hand in warning.

"I'm Detective Chief Inspector Anderson," she continued. "We want to talk to you about the fire you were involved in. Can you speak to us now?"

"I don't have much of a voice," I squeaked. She nodded but didn't make a move to leave. Another police officer, a huge bear of a man with an impressive beard, filled the doorway behind her.

"We're investigating the fire, which appears to be accidental. However, it was your sister Ellie who locked you in there, wasn't it?"

I glanced at Seb, not sure what to do.

"You're not being accused of anything, Miss Hayward," the policewoman said.

"But Ellie is, isn't she?" Gran put in, looking upset.

"We're deciding whether to press charges, but before that, we need to know whether you intend to, Miss Hayward," said DCI Anderson, pursing her lips. "There's a case for false imprisonment. And, if help had not arrived in time, we might be questioning her for manslaughter."

࿎

The police left after an hour, promising to return the following day. I sagged with weariness, despite Seb's support, and Gran had grown shocked and increasingly distressed.

The conversation with Ellie that evening was also hard, even with Gran's support. Ellie looked scared, and despite my tiredness, I intended to make sure this was a conversation she wouldn't forget in a hurry.

"I'm sorry I locked you in," she said, biting her lip.

"Yes, it was a lucky escape for me. I'm still not sure why, though. What on earth were you doing?"

"I don't know! I just wanted to punish you." She almost wrung her hands.

"Did you set the fire too?"

"Of course not!"

"How did the wine glass get there?" I wanted to know.

She looked at me earnestly. "I'd been drinking. I was upset after… after Nate left. When I saw you asleep in the chair, I put down my glass to close the padlock. After I locked you in, I panicked and ran away and forgot to pick it up! I didn't mean for the fire to happen, I promise you!"

"So you locked me in the summerhouse because someone you fancied preferred me to you? Sounds a bit unhinged to me."

Ellie was silent.

"Well, what would you call it, Ellie?"

She mumbled something, and I caught the tears in her voice.

"Did you even think about me?" I pressed. "That being locked in might have frightened me? That I might be thirsty? That I might even want to pee? Do you care about me *at all*?"

"Of course I do! You're my sister!"

Silence fell, and she sniffed.

"I know the police have spoken to you, and they've spoken to me as well, asking if I want to press charges," I added, determined to make the point.

Ellie stared at me, all colour drained from her face. Gran made to speak, and I shook my head and she subsided.

"It was an accident! Are you going to press charges?" Her voice wavered.

"That depends on you," I responded, my head on one side. The man in the stovepipe hat nodded from the corner.

"H-how?"

"The police have suggested you should go to a psychiatrist and I agree," I said, and she jumped to her feet.

"A shrink? Why?"

"Why, Ellie? How about that you can't *bear* to lose. You

should talk to the shrink about that! Before you actually hurt someone!"

She burst into tears, putting her face in her hands.

"I'm sorry!" she sobbed. "I couldn't think of anything but Nate! He was in my mind, all the time, and you were in my way! I tricked him into sleeping with me, and I thought it would change everything between us. But it *didn't!* And I was going crazy trying to work out what to do! I'm so, so sorry! When I saw the flames..." she shuddered and took the tissue that Gran held out to wipe her eyes and blow her nose.

My younger sister seemed to be recognisable again. The cold, focused stranger who had inhabited our house for the past few months had cracked to reveal Ellie, my sister, again.

"Will you have counselling?" I asked quietly. She nodded, taking another tissue from Gran. After a few minutes, she grew calm and looked at me from reddened eyes.

"Are... are we okay?" she asked through a rough throat. I regarded her. *Were* we okay? I didn't know, truly.

"We'll be fine, I hope," I said at last. "I'm moving out soon, so a bit of distance should help."

"You're moving out?"

I nodded.

She mumbled something, and I leaned forward to catch what she said.

"I love you," she whispered. "I would never have forgiven myself if anything had happened to you."

I smiled faintly.

"I'm tougher than I look."

She kissed me awkwardly on the cheek and fled.

When Seb came through the door, he stiffened, like an animal sensing danger.

"Come in and cheer me up!" I said, trying not to cough.

"Cheer you up? Ellie's been in, I take it."

Even Gran laughed.

"I still don't understand why you came back from Australia

early," she said. He shot me a glance, and I realised I didn't know the full story.

"I told him about my ghosts, Gran," I said. Seb closed the door to my room.

"And they led me to you, Stacie," he said in a low voice, perching on the bed.

"What?" I croaked, surprised.

"Don't forget, you didn't have your phone with you. When I got off the flight, I tried your mobile and couldn't get a response, nor from the landline. When I went to Greenfields, the place was deserted, but when I rang your phone, I heard it in the kitchen," Seb explained. "I was about to leave when this ginger cat materialised out of the walls and just stared at me."

"My cat?" I gasped. "You saw my cat??"

Seb grinned.

"Well, yes! I recognised it from your email, and then this really stern-looking woman in a blue dress also arrived and waved at me. I tell you, Stacie, even though you'd told me about them, I was *seriously* freaked out!"

I laughed. "Oh my God, you met the governess! And then what happened?"

"She led me around the side of the house, and I saw the patio doors were open. So I knew someone must be around, you'd hardly leave the place unlocked. And I was looking around when this very pale guy with white hair in a black cloak appeared out of nowhere—"

"John Dillington?" said Gran, amazed.

"Dunno, the guy didn't introduce himself!"

"Weren't you scared?" I asked, and he went a bit red.

"Fucking terrified, but he kept gesturing and floating away and coming back and waving at me, so I followed him. And he led me to the bottom of the garden and then I saw the smoke around the summerhouse."

He drew a breath.

"I called 999 and while I was on the phone, I saw you put a window through. It was then I realised you were stuck inside."

"Where was Ellie?" I had to ask.

"She came out into the garden just as I started to run towards the summerhouse. She had hysterics when she saw it was on fire. Your Gran arrived as I pulled you out." He stopped and grabbed my hand. "Christ, if I hadn't been in time."

"I'm hard to get rid of!" I smiled and kissed him. He cupped my cheek, and his serious gaze searched my face. "No, I'm fine," I added, softly. I turned to Gran. "But why were *you* at the house?"

"Ah," she said with the air of someone adding a vital ingredient to the story. "I'd been awake since the early hours. I couldn't believe that the date Sarah died passed us by without a hitch. So I had another look. It wasn't until I'd trawled through all the documents that I realised that I'd got it wrong; they sentenced her on the eleventh, but she didn't *die* until early the following day. So when you didn't answer your phone, I came round in a bit of a panic, I'm afraid."

I let out a long breath.

"That explains a lot. And I haven't told you about the dream I had." I was editing as I was speaking. I decided that things between Ellie and I had been bad enough, so I didn't mention her setting light to the pyre. Just that John woke me up, believing I was Sarah.

After I'd finished, we all looked at one another.

"He still thought you were Sarah? So he was determined to save her this time," mused Gran.

"Yes, I think so. So, thank you, Sarah and John," I said quietly. I hope you're together, I thought.

"Amen to that," said Sarah's voice by my ear, and I jumped a little. Seb frowned, and I reassured him with a smile. Time enough for explanations.

CHAPTER THIRTY-ONE
SARAH AND STACIE

In the half-light, the parson stood motionless at the grave, unmarked and roughly dug. They had bundled her body into a winding sheet, thrown it onto the back of a cart, and trundled out of the village.

That had been days ago. He forgot what day it was. His heart felt wrenched out of his body, and in his chest instead was a gap so fathomless it was beyond his imagining. The owls hooted softly, almost as though they sympathised with his mourning.

It looked so desolate, the mound of earth. He wanted to be angry, but couldn't summon the feeling, and instead, merely looked at the grave. A chasm was between him and the world – unable to be breached, blanketed in muffled noise, muffled feelings.

He knew someone watched him from near the oak tree, but he cared not. His mind was a blank of white, caring for naught and no one. They could rob and beat him, and he'd let them. Death, once a door to the glory of the afterlife, now seemed only an end to his pain.

The figure moved.

"Sir," a soft voice said. Abigail Lester bobbed a curtsey. Her face was white and her eyes red with weeping. She clutched a bouquet of rue and buttercups.

"Well met, Mistress Lester," he said, his voice rusty from lack of use and sorrow.

"I came to place flowers. She was a good soul, sir."

"So you say. But have a care," he replied. "She was adjudged a witch, capable of calling on the Devil. To mourn her shows sympathy and the villagers are not forgiving."

"She was my friend, she loved me and my kin. And I loved her."

She spoke with such quiet dignity, he felt ashamed. He moved aside, and she bent to lay the little bouquet carefully on the surface of the earth. He saw her wipe away a tear before she stepped back and drew a deep breath.

They stood staring at the golden flowers, aglow with the last of the day's light. Then Abigail turned to him.

"But what do you here, sir?"

He was silent. She let the silence drift, determined to have her answer.

"She was not evil, she did much good," he said, so low she had to listen hard.

"And did you love her, sir?"

The question shocked him to the core, and he looked at her, his face angry. Abigail was calm, unmoving. If he made to strike her, she would not dodge the blow. Wildly, he stared at her and then his shoulders slumped.

"Aye. With all my cowardly heart."

A tear ran down his face and Abigail took him by the arm and led him to a nearby tree stump. He laid his head in her lap and sobbed. She patted his shaking shoulders and hushed him like a child.

Eventually, he recovered his manhood, and the sobs subsided. He sat up straight and taking a snowy handkerchief from a pocket he blew his nose and wiped his cheeks. He shook his head as though not knowing how his emotions had overcome him.

Abigail watched him gravely.

"It would please her you had visited, sir. I believe she held you close to her heart."

He shook his head again and fought for control.

"I would that I had been able to save her. Wilful child, stubborn—"

"Sarah was always her own woman; she would have had good reason to do as she did. And honest as the day is long. I believe her when she said she had never told an untruth."

John Dillington nodded in agreement. She had clung to the truth so firmly, he could not seduce her into lying even to save her own skin. He drew a shaky breath and Abigail stood up.

"I must go before my husband fears for me. I have been absent this last hour."

"You must. God bless you, Mistress Lester."

"And you, sir."

Abigail seemed to melt away into the gathering darkness, and he turned once more to the mound of earth. His mind flicked over the memories of that obscenely unfair trial. The complaints, unsubstantiated and prompted by ignorance, fear and jealousy. The baying crowd easily swayed, lacking reason and any sense of God's mercy. He would do more next time. More to question, more to demand truth and proof, rather than hearsay.

On impulse, he strode to a nearby bank and plucked some campion and wild poppies, adding them to the flowers Abigail had laid.

"Thank you, sir," a soft voice said into his ear, and he froze, his breath coming in quick gasps. Slowly, he turned, but there was no one there. Stiffening his limbs, he stumbled over the tree stump and sat with a thump on it.

"Sarah?" he whispered. "Are you an angel or a Devil? Even though you be a Devil, if you can, speak to me again."

"And what would I say?" He stiffened as the voice, sounding amused, came again.

"That you forgive me?" His voice was rusty with grief.

"There is nothing to forgive, this was my fate. And it was my choice."

"But what of mine? What of *our* fate?" He sounded tortured.

"You have another path. You were put on God's earth to be more than a poor woman's husband. Your place is to strive for justice for those such as I."

"But I loved you! We could have been together!"

There was a long silence, and he strained his ears but heard nothing but the breeze rustling the leaves above him. I am losing my wits! he thought. This is naught but grief, conjuring up my desire.

"Not yet. But someday. Before that, you must protect others and fulfil your calling for mercy and truth. We will meet again, I swear. Fare well, my love."

The voice drifted away and once again, he found himself in tears.

At the alehouse that night, there was talk of the parson sitting weeping outside the village boundary, talking to himself. All agreed that he might still be bewitched, and they crossed themselves as protection against the Devil.

"Have you got it?" I said, alarmed, as the overstuffed box seemed to tilt. Seb's voice sounded muffled beneath the weight of it.

"Just about. Good God, couldn't you put less in?" He stood up, hefting the box more securely into his arms, and gingerly walked down the stairs one by one.

"Sebastian, please watch the wall! That's a limited-edition print!" Mother's voice was sharp, and I glanced back into the upstairs hall at the remaining boxes. Nearly done. We'd be out of here soon.

Ellie was in Oxford and, with her absence, I could breathe. My parents had been a mixture of hurt indignation and secret relief that I was moving out. Once they got used to the idea, my mother had done some indelicate digging to find out more about my new place and my new boyfriend. Seb had smiled and remained elusive. My mother and father knew nothing about his money, his knack of making more on the stock exchange, and I wasn't about to enlighten them.

The ginger cat curled its tail around the door and sat in the doorway, blocking my way.

"What?" I asked it.

"What?" called my mother, who has keen hearing.

"Oh, nothing, just looking at what's left to load!" I responded. The cat twitched its ears and faded into a patch of September sunlight. I wondered if the ghosts would travel to my new house. Not having them with me would make my life less full, less vibrant.

I shifted more boxes of varying weights and felt comforted, even cosseted, when Seb only allowed me to carry the light ones. Seb took those filled with books and papers, bits of IT and cables. I took photo frames, costume jewellery and cosmetics. And then it was all done.

I looked around my bedroom, made stark and unfamiliar by the removal of the clothes, postcards and knick-knacks that had made it mine. It now looked as characterful as a hospital room; it was just a place I used to sleep.

The remains of the summerhouse stood, still black and rather frightening. Nothing had happened since the fire brigade had hosed the fire out, much to my annoyance – no repairs, not even pulling it down. Dad had talked of claiming on the insurance. God knew how he'd explain every single window being broken, but that wasn't my problem.

One last glance around and I picked up my rucksack and

closed the door. I had a sense of a new beginning. I had chosen my path.

To my surprise, Mother looked a little tearful as I reached the bottom of the stairs. I tensed. I knew my parents loved me, well, they sort of loved me, but they had also been bewildered by me, confused by me, as if they'd brought the wrong baby home from the hospital. Sometimes I wondered if they had too.

"Right," I said. "I think that's everything. I'll be off then."

"Right. Well, obviously, you'll be round, won't you? Henry! Eustacia's going!"

My father came from his study at a run.

"Really? God, that was quick! Have you left half your stuff here?"

"No, Dad, it's all in the van."

"Goodness. I thought you'd got much more paraphernalia in your room!"

Everyone paused, not knowing what to say next.

"Well..." I said.

"Ready, Stacie?" Seb's calm voice interrupted my awkwardness, and I spun around gratefully.

"See you soon!" I hugged Dad and kissed my mother on the cheek. "I'll invite you round when I'm straight."

"Perhaps you'd like to come to lunch at my place on Sunday?" Seb said unexpectedly to my parents. I kept my face neutral with an effort. *They'll say they're busy.*

"I don't think we're doing anything, are we, Julia?" Dad said. My mouth dropped open, and I shut it with a bit of a snap. My mother nodded enthusiastically.

"Shall we ask Ellie?" Dad asked, his gaze flicking between Seb and me. I stiffened and Seb hugged my shoulders, loosening me up a little. "Sure, if she's free, let me know by Friday so I can plan the food."

I smiled and pulled Seb towards the front door where the governess was waiting for me. I tried a smile, and the lady nodded regally. My smile broadened even further.

"Okay?" Seb said as he put the car into gear. I sagged with relief.

"Yup. Just get me out of here."

"Wave to your folks," he instructed, and obediently, I did so. As he stopped at the end of the road to check the traffic, the ginger cat appeared on the bonnet and I gasped.

"What?" Seb asked, alarmed.

"Just, the cat appeared. I'm sorry, I didn't mean to make you jump."

He peered through the window. "Is it still there?"

The cat stared at me, and then vanished, with what looked like a grin on its face. I sighed.

"No, it's gone now."

We joined the road and drove in silence for a few minutes.

"Do you think you'll see them again, your ghosts?"

"I don't know. I hope so."

"Are you going to be okay without them?"

An interesting question.

"I don't know. Perhaps there'll be new spirits for me to see."

Seb looked a little worried. "What? Will they be in my house too?"

"Why not? DH Lawrence wrote somewhere that the dead are always with us."

"Somehow, I'm not comforted by that."

I laughed, and Seb grinned. "Nice."

"What?" I asked, confused.

"You laughing. I haven't heard it for a while."

"No. Time for you to help me rediscover my lighter side!" He put his hand on my leg and I was moved by the sense of belonging it brought me. I put my hand over his.

"Seb?"

"Yes?"

"I don't think I ever said thank you for saving my life. Bit of an oversight."

He smiled again. "I was just on hand. Mind you, I'd just

flown all the way from bloody Australia; there was no way we weren't going to have a conversation!"

"Don't make a joke of it -"

"Oh, be quiet," he said easily. "I love you. What else was I going to do but save you? By the way, while I was in the hotel at the airport, I took out the Bible in the bedside drawer."

"I didn't know you were religious. Or were you were that bored?"

"Heathen," he said lovingly. "I wondered if it might explain any of this, about loving someone and needing to be brave to show it."

"Does it?" I asked, slightly shamed at my complete lack of biblical knowledge.

"Well, I found something, which says something like, 'There is no fear in love, he that fears is not made perfect in love.'"

I gasped.

"The First Epistle of John," I murmured and he looked surprised.

"That's – that's right. Are *you* religious?"

"Not at all. But I saw it in a Bible when I was helping Nate to pack."

"Coincidence?"

I rolled my eyes at Seb. "What do you think, given my history and the events of the past few months?"

"Fair point." He concentrated on the road.

I was silent, my thoughts whirring. "I wonder if that's it," I murmured.

Seb frowned as he drove. "What? I haven't worked it out yet."

"Might it be that Sarah and John couldn't be together because he wasn't perfect in love?"

"Wasn't he?"

"They hardly lived happily ever after, did they?" I said, my eyebrows raised. "I wouldn't call being burnt at the stake the best start to a wonderful relationship."

"So he had to prove himself to be without fear to be perfect in love?"

"Yes. That would fit…"

"Sounds a bit Buddhist to me," Seb said doubtfully. "Do you think what you went through helped? Where are they both now?"

"I have no idea," I said, but the memory of Sarah's voice at the hospital – 'Amen to that' – gave me hope they had, at last, both found peace and that we had averted the repeat of a tragedy long ago. I realised Sarah had made many sacrifices, all with an impact on people she couldn't know – John, the women he had saved. Even me. Appearing to me to warn me to follow my passion in teaching, and to steer clear of Nate.

We drove for a few moments in silence until Seb turned into a neat, tree-lined street.

"Your new home, milady," said Seb. I smiled, and he opened the door of the van and jumped out.

A mere three hours later, Seb was ordering a Chinese takeaway, and I'd at least made the bed to fall into later. I wasn't sure if Seb would stay – I imagined that neither of us wanted to make any assumptions about the relationship. There was no need to rush it, I decided.

I looked out of the window at the garden, which was the usual rectangular lawn with a few shrubs. I'd go shopping for bulbs at the local garden centre soon, to make sure the spring would not be barren.

"And we can't have that!" I said to myself, with my forehead pressed against the window. As I stared, the shadows seemed to swirl and gather, and then I was looking at two figures standing face to face: John Dillington, complete with cloak, and Sarah, her hair hanging loosely down her back. I drew in a sharp breath and slowly they both turned to me. They were holding hands and smiling at me.

A wave of emotion swelled and clogged my throat. Dimly, I heard Seb come into the room. A few moments later his voice came hesitantly.

"Stacie? Are you okay?"

I turned, smiling through wet eyes.

"I'm very okay."

He came to me and pulled me into a hug.

"It'll be fine," he said.

The ginger cat materialised out of the newly painted wall and strolled to the middle of the floor where it began to wash. I looked around for the lady in blue, my governess, but she wasn't there. I breathed, realising that there was lots of time, swirling forward in patterns and threads, waiting for me to choose my route through it.

I beamed at Seb, nestling into his tall frame. "I know it will."

AFTERWORD

Thank you for reading the first novel in my new Duality series! All the books in this series will contain two stories – just like I've told with Stacie and Sarah in this book.

If you liked The Visitor, *please leave me a review*. It's an enormous help to indie authors like me with no advertising budget! And if you'd like to know when I'm releasing the next book in the series, sign up to my mailing list on my website:
    https://www.sarasartagne.com/keep-in-touch.

I don't send endless emails, just enough to say hello, tell you news and offer some freebies.

Talking of which, if you sign up to the mailing list, I'll send you a free novella called *A Bouquet of White Roses*. This is a prequel to my contemporary romance novel, **The Garden Plot**, which is book 1 of the English Garden Romance series.

Or, if you'd like to connect on Twitter, say hello to me at:
    http://www.twitter.com/SSartagnewriter.

AUTHOR BIO

Having wanted to be a journalist when she was a teenager, Sara actually ended up on the dark side, in PR. From there, it was a short skip to writing for pleasure, and from there to drafting her first book, The Garden Plot. This is the first novel in a romance series where gardens feature in a BIG way - she inherited green fingers from her wonderful grandmother and gardening is a passion.

Sara recently moved from London to York and is loving the open skies and the green fields. And a HUGE garden! Although not a country girl, she's discovered the joys of no streetlights, septic tanks and ordering logs. Going from an underground tube or bus every three minutes, bus timetables in a small Yorkshire town have been a bit of a shock.

Sara loves being a writer although it's not her only job - yet. She's keeping her fingers firmly crossed. The second book in the English Garden Romance series - Love in a Mist - was released in October 2020. Book 3 in the series is out in Spring 2021 and The Visitor is the first novel in the Duality series - where there are always TWO stories, somehow connected.

She loves hearing from readers who have thoughts about her books and characters - and even about gardening! - so please visit http://www.sarasartagne.com (good for news and freebies!) or make contact on Twitter.

twitter.com/Sarasartagneauthor

A Bouquet of White Roses
English Garden Romance novella

Local businessman Sam Winterson thinks that Dawn Andrews is the most beautiful women he's ever seen and he's instantly drawn to her. There's just one problem. She's the florist for his *wedding*.

Dawn Andrews is no marriage-breaker. Trying to deny the fizz of feelings that happen when they meet is the best option, given the handsome young landscape gardener is literally engaged elsewhere. But when Sam rescues her from an assault outside a nightclub, despite her best intentions, Dawn's feelings begin to change.

It's a complete mess. With the wedding only five months away, can they ignore the mutual attraction, turn their backs on each other and carry on as if they'd never met?

A Bouquet of White Roses is a prequel novella to *The Garden Plot*, Book One in Sara Sartagne's English Garden Romance Series. *You can get it for FREE if you visit my website and sign up to my mailing list!*

The Garden Plot
English Garden Romance 1

Sometimes love needs a plan...

Desperate to keep her company afloat, designer Sam Winterson doesn't need a relationship, she needs business! All that stands between her and the commission that might save her company is a mystery businessman. But when a proposed housing development threatens the tranquillity and beauty of her village, Sam's determined to stop it.

Reclusive widower Jonas Keane is not interested in the kind of woman who puts her career before her home and family. Been there, done that. Ordered to stay home to recuperate from illness is as frustrating as hell – but it allows him to oversee the renovation of his own garden while staying a silent partner in a housing development. What he doesn't expect is to run headlong into a budding romance with a blonde, pixie-faced gardener intent on upending his plans.

But Magda, Jonas' daughter is tired of her work-obsessed dad and his picture-perfect girlfriends. She has a plot of her own. When she plants the seeds of romance, can love blossom between a ruthless businessman and an outspoken gardener with a green conscience?

Fans of Jill Mansell and Katie Fforde will enjoy Sara Sartagne's debut novel, a sweet romance with a hint of spice and a HEA!

Love in A Mist
English Garden Romance 2

An aristocratic Englishwoman. A fiery Irishman. Two secrets they'd rather not share.

Ella Sanderson manages the farms and estate at Ashton Manor. She's an old-fashioned girl who knows what she likes. And she doesn't like the ultra-modern garden designed for the ancient house by horticulture's bad boy, Connor McPherson.

Connor is just the type of man she's learned to mistrust. Bright blue eyes and Irish charm may have captivated her employer Lady Susan—but not her! With all her protective instincts on high alert, Ella can't disobey Lady Susan's wishes for the garden, but she can just… not help.

Connor McPherson didn't want the commission, but as the garden will host his best friend's wedding, he couldn't refuse it. If the wettest English weather on record hasn't completely blown his chances of getting the build completed for the big day, he's also battling the snooty estate manager who couldn't be less enthusiastic.

The stage is set for fireworks between the hot-tempered Irishman and the cool, contained estate manager. But when mounting problems force them to work together, Connor realises that beneath her buttoned-up exterior, Ella has a passion equal to his own and a secret she's hidden for years.

As Ella fights to get the garden she hates built in time for the wedding she'd rather not attend and safeguard the manor from unwelcome publicity, she's increasingly drawn to the tempestuous designer. Who, she discovers, has his own secrets to protect…

Meet old friends from *The Garden Plot* in the next in the series of the **English Garden Romance** series.

Printed in Great Britain
by Amazon